SIR RICHARD BURTON

A Plain and Literal Translation of
The Arabian Nights' Entertainments
now intituled

The Book of the
THOUSAND
and
ONE NIGHTS

A Selection by
P. H. NEWBY

Illustrated by
W. M. CUTHILL

D1381722

A PANTHER BOOK

THE BOOK OF THE
THOUSAND AND ONE NIGHTS

A Panther Book

First published in Great Britain by

Arthur Barker Ltd.

PRINTING HISTORY
Arthur Barker Edition published 1950
Second Impression December, 1950
Third Impression January, 1951
Fourth Impression March, 1951
Fifth Impression January, 1952
Sixth Impression July, 1953
Seventh Impression September, 1954
Eighth Impression February, 1956
Panther Edition published September, 1960

Printed in England by Petty & Sons Ltd., Whitehall
Printeries, Leeds, and published by Hamilton & Co.
(Stafford), Ltd. 108, Brompton Road, London, S.W.3

CONTENTS

INTRODUCTION 7

IN THE NAME OF ALLAH, THE COMPASSION-
    ATING, THE COMPASSIONATE! 16

THE TALE OF THE ENSORCELLED PRINCE .. 30

THE BARBER'S TALE OF HIS SECOND BROTHER .. 39

TALE OF GHANIM BIN AYYUB, THE DISTRAUGHT,
    THE THRALL O' LOVE 44

TALE OF THE FIRST EUNUCH, BUKHAYT .. 47

TALE OF THE SECOND EUNUCH, KAFUR 49

THE EBONY HORSE 72

HOW ABU HASAN BRAKE WIND 98

THE LADY AND HER FIVE SUITORS 101

JULNAR THE SEA-BORN AND HER SON KING
    BADR BASIM OF PERSIA 107

THE REEVE'S TALE 142

MA'ARUF THE COBBLER AND HIS WIFE FATIMAH 151

PUBLISHER'S NOTE

Certain of the stories contained in the
original edition have been omitted.

Introduction

IT is little more than two hundred years since the *Arabian Nights* made their first appearance in Europe. The man who let the Jinni out of the bottle was a French scholar, Antoine Galland, who as attaché-secretary to the French Ambassador at the Porte travelled much in the Levant. His *Mille et une Nuits, Contes Arabes traduits en François* was published at intervals between 1704 and 1717, and although fuller and more faithful translations have appeared since that time it was undeniably Galland who captured (and held) the imagination of the west, who introduced Haroun Al-Rashid and Scheherezade to all the drawing-rooms from Moscow to Madrid, and started that delightful oriental strain in European letters which has produced works as various at Voltaire's *Zadig* and Beckford's *Vathek*. For a long time the European mind had been building up fantasies about the classical world of Greece and Rome. Now it launched out into more extravagant fantasy about Baghdad, the Abode of Peace. The mind's eye could see fresh, exciting landscapes where palaces sparkled in the clear air; there was the flash of jewels, the cry of strange birds, flying horses traversed the night sky, spirits arose and revealed the hidden treasures of the earth and with Sinbad the Sailor the common reader could set out on a new Odyssey across blue seas where islands were (in the words of the story-teller) "white like camphor." Galland, however, intended his version of the *Nights* to be popular and this he achieved by emphasising the strange and the miraculous, and ignoring much that was characteristic of the original: the very frank treatment of sex and its perversions, the more savage stories of brutality and corruption, the historical and semi-historical anecdotes. Galland presented a mere fragment of the repertoire to the Western reader, a fragment we should certainly not care to do without, but one that gives no more idea of the original than Lamb's tales do of Shakespeare.

Europe had to wait a long time before a full and faithful translation was attempted. And while it is waiting this would seem a suitable moment to say something of the provenance of the tales; something, but not very much, for this is a subject on which only the word of the most scholarly of Orientalists (I am far from being one!) has any right to be heard—and, even then, such is the merciless ferocity of learned men to one another, he would be cut down almost before he had opened his mouth, so controversial has the matter become. Only one

7

scholar of standing, the celebrated Arabist E. W. Lane, has ever claimed that the work was written by one person or, at the most, two. It is evident that in the book of *The Thousand and One Nights* we have a collection of tales not only from many lands, India, Persia, Greece, Syria and Egypt, but also from different epochs; some of the tales, especially the Beast fables, are very ancient indeed, others have been assigned to dates (these vary with the scholar!) between the tenth and fifteenth centuries A.D. An Index-List of Arabic works (the *Kitab al-Fihrist*) compiled in A.D. 987 tells us that the framework of the book, the story of Scheherazade and the misogynist king, was Persian in origin and that the device was taken over by the Arabs who "polished and embellished" the Persian tales and "wrote others resembling them." Modern scholarship has traced this framework back to Indian folk-lore. In some fairly complete form the *Nights* was well known in Egypt in the twelfth century. The important fact to remember, however, is that no matter what scholars are able to tell us of the origins of these tales they have, in the course of centuries, passed through the hands of many Arab scribes and editors, have been transmuted in the process and so provide us with an infinitely varied and vivid expression of the temperament of medieval Islam. The text upon which most modern translations are based was compiled by some unknown editor in Egypt towards the end of the eighteenth century.

The first attempt to render a complete and faithful translation of the *Nights* into English seems to have been made by Henry Torrens (1838) who had for some years been resident in Bengal, but he died prematurely and only one out of his projected nine or ten volumes was completed. The translation is so painstakingly literal that it makes very tiring reading though, true enough, Torrens (an Irishman to be sure!) could enliven a page by stating that one of the characters who had been miraculously transported from Cairo by a Jinni during the night "awoke sleeping at Damascus." The principal value of E. W. Lane's translation (1839-41) lies in the notes, for his knowledge of Cairo society was encyclopedic; the work was intended for "the drawing-room table" and is, accordingly, a mere castrated selection of the original. The first complete translation was made by John Payne (1882-84) and published by the Villon Society in a limited edition of 500 copies. To these three translations Sir Richard Burton frankly admitted his indebtedness when he came to publish the version (1885-86, in ten volumes, with five supplemental volumes) from which the present selection is made. Burton had been engaged on the translation for many years on and off (he dates his first move in the matter as far back as 1852) for he realised that "while the name of this wondrous treasury of Moslem folk-lore is familiar to almost every English child, no general reader is aware of the valuables it contains, nor indeed will the door open to any but Arabists." This is still largely true even to-day in spite of Payne, Burton and, later, Mardrus the Frenchman; and in this fact lies the excuse for the publication of a selection which will, it is hoped, give the common reader some idea of the range and variety of the *Nights* and, in so doing, rescue them from the nursery where they have lain too long.

Burton's qualifications as a translator of the *Nights* were formidable not only because of his extensive knowledge of Arabic (he was also fluent in Persian and Hindustani, not to mention several lesser Eastern languages and dialects), but because of his extraordinary personality: "Arabia," he said, "is a region so familiar to my mind that even at first sight it seemed a reminiscence of some bygone metempsychic life in the distant past." He was one of that colourful breed of Europeans who are much more at home in the East than their native lands. As a young officer in India he was engaged on intelligence work, passing as a Dervish among the fanatical tribesmen or, in the disguise of a pedlar, penetrating even the mysteries of the harim. While his fellow-officers were taking their afternoon sleep Burton would be hard at work on Gujarati; his native mistress was more to him than the necessary makeshift of Anglo-Indian custom—she was a living dictionary. His physical and mental energy were tireless, and although he managed to win favour under Napier, the conqueror of Sind, he was much too vigorous, independent and unorthodox to receive the official recognition or even the promotion to which he was undeniably entitled.

He first came to public notice because of his successful pilgrimage, disguised as a Pathan, to Mecca and Medina in 1853. His account of the journey is a classic of English travel literature. No enterprise could have borne more powerful testimony to his knowledge of Eastern customs and beliefs, though the expedition he later made to the city of Harar (1854-55) was probably even more hazardous and revealing of his fearlessness and determination. He is in the first rank of English explorers and was the first European, with Speke for company, to reach the Great Lakes of Central Africa. From this time onwards he was a perpetually disappointed man. His unique talents and knowledge were largely wasted in the Consular Service at such unrewarding places as Fernando Po, Santos in Brazil and, for the last years of his life (it was here he did most of the work on the *Nights*) at Trieste. True, there was one Consulate which he held, that of Damascus, which he found very congenial, but he was peremptorily recalled from the post because he (and his wife) had managed to antagonise certain sections of public opinion there. Isabel Burton was, in some ways, as remarkable as her husband. A brave, pathetic, ridiculous woman, she idolised her Richard, intrigued endlessly with Cabinet Ministers for his advancement (and succeeded in landing the K.C.M.G. for him), tried to emulate his talent for disguise by appearing in silk bloomers and a yashmak in the bazars of Damascus, and on his death (she was a devout Roman Catholic and Richard a heretic) she had his heart animated by an electric battery and Extreme Unction administered to what she insisted was a still-living man.

The publication of the *Nights* was an enormous success, it netted Burton a clear profit of £10,000 and he became a celebrity—but a very notorious one, for the great public immediately fastened on to his volumes not so much for their anthropological lore (as had been his intention) but simply because of the eroticism. Krafft-Ebbing and Freud have been at work since Burton died and we find it the more difficult, therefore, to understand the extraordinary impact the volumes, especially the notes and the celebrated Terminal Essay, had upon the Victorian mind. Informed opinion was, however, unanimous in its praise and Burton was well pleased with the result of his labours. It is worth while adding, perhaps, that Isabel virtuously promised not to read the translation, though an emasculated selection of the work was subsequently produced in her name, which *Punch* greeted with the phrase: "Burton—drawn mild!"

Burton's aim was to show what *The Thousand and One Nights* really is, "by writing as the Arab would have written in English. . . Moreover, holding that the translator's glory is to add something to his native tongue, while avoiding the hideous hag-like nakedness of Torrens and the bald literalism of Lane, I have carefully Englished the picturesque turns and novel expressions of the original in all their outlandishness. . . . . Hence peculiar attention has been paid to the tropes and figures which the Arabic language often packs into a single term; and I have never hesitated to coin a word when wanted, such as 'she snorted and snarked,' fully to represent the original." He adds, elsewhere: "I have carefully sought out the English equivalent of every Arabic word, however low it may be or 'shocking' to ears polite; preserving, on the other hand, all possible delicacy where the indecency is not intentional; and, as a friend advises me to state, not exaggerating the vulgarities and the indecencies which, indeed, can hardly be exaggerated.

For the coarseness and the crassness are but the shades of a picture which would otherwise be all lights."

Unlike other translators, Burton attempted to render the balanced sentences, the prose, rhyme and rhythm of certain passages in the original and to which we have nothing quite comparable in English, though he used alliteration to give something of the effect.

So they halted in it other three days, and on the eighth they espied a dust cloud which towered till it walled the whole land; nor was an hour of the day past ere that dust began to drift and was torn to shreds in the lift, and pierced through its shades the starry radiance of lance and the white leven of blades. Presently there appeared beneath it the banners Islamitan and the ensigns Mahometan; the horsemen urged forward, like the letting loose of seas that surged, clad in mail, as they were mackerel-back clouds which the moon enveil; whereupon the two hosts clashed, like two torrents on each other dashed. (King Omar bin al-Nu'uman and his sons).

To the English reader the result may seem artificial and even irritating, but, as Burton pointed out, the effort of rendering the effect of the original was worth making; and if it is remembered that these tales were not meant to be read but heard from the lips of a Rawi, or public reciter, we shall catch some faint echo of his very tones. (The Arabs have a great love of sonorous language and can use it with little self-consciousness. I well remember a man who used to go about the streets of Cairo, his voice raised in measured ecstasy; he was selling bits of wire to clean primus stoves.) "This Saj'a or cadence of the cooing dove," Burton said, "has in Arabic its special duties. It adds sparkle to description and a point to proverb, epigram and dialogue. . . . It defines the boundaries between the classical and the popular styles which jostle each other in the *Nights*."

It must further be said that verse plays an important part in the *Nights*. All the characters, from the Caliph to the humblest peasant, have the most extraordinary capacity not only for quoting the works of their favourite poets but also for extemporising (it was a mark of intelligence) and they do both on even the most improbable occasions, in the jaws of ferocious lions or menaced with imminent death by colossal Jinn. And it is a very poor beauty who does not inspire a dozen couplets of extravagant praise in her honour. Unfortunately, most of this verse has had to be omitted in the present selection, partly because Burton's renderings are not very happy, but mainly because space did not permit. This is the greatest crime I have committed in putting this book together and one Burton would most certainly have frowned upon; as he would have frowned upon my ignoring the division of the tales into nights, for to him this was a feature of considerable importance. I have, however, contrived to include many of his notes for, as he said, much would be otherwise obscure or even incomprehensible without some such aid. The well-known *Ali-Baba and the Forty Thieves* and *Aladdin* are not to be found in any known text of the *Nights* and have therefore been omitted.

The *Nights* give a striking picture of a society outside the Christian and European tradition. They are, accordingly, both a fascination and a challenge to that most powerful of English institutions, the Puritan spirit. The characteristic reaction was that of Richard Lovell Edgeworth (father to Maria) who, while failing to discern any moral purpose in the stories, was nevertheless intelligent enough to read them, in Galland's version, to his children. Romantic love, as we understand it, which was born of the age of chivalry and which we like to think is independent of mere physical charm, has no place in the *Nights;* it is hardly an exaggeration to say that there is no love, only lust, in the whole collection, and where we do seem to come across a tale in the European tradition (*Ghanim, the Thrall of Love*) we are left in little doubt that the theme is no ethereal idealisation of human relationships but a very simple question of sexual attraction. We are also bothered by the fact that luck and chance play a much more important part in an oriental tale than do the merits or demerits of the characters. (This is what disturbed Edgeworth.) Luck, as it happens, is not a cornerstone of our morality. We like our heroes to deserve good fortune as well as win it, they must work hard, they must be brave, they must be strong, they must be good. Our attitude, in its extreme form, was once stated by Maria Edgeworth in a tale she wrote to disprove the existence of such a factor as luck in human affairs. "The lucky man is doubtlessly the prudent man," she said, "the unlucky man is imprudent." An Arab, on the other hand, is much more likely to say that the phenomenally lucky man is the phenomenally good man, for all things are ruled by chance and what is chance but the will of Allah?

It is often said that the oriental temperament is more passive than our own. E. W. Lane, to illustrate the point, told how he was sitting in a Cairo bazar one day when a passer-by asked him why he did not return to his own country. "The true servant of God," Lane replied, "is not elective but passive," and this answer was sufficient to silence all criticism and win great approval. Now the passive temperament is the fatalistic temperament and the obsession of the fatalist is inevitably with destiny. One of the recurring themes of the *Nights* is the impossibility of working against destiny. If it is one's fate to be a beggar then the quicker one gets used to the idea the better for one's peace of mind. Cogia Hassan, the ropemaker, could not make a success of his business in spite of all efforts to help him and his own good management and economy. Success only came when, quite by chance, he caught a fish with a great diamond in its stomach, a diamond of such brilliance that it lit up a dark room. The Arab knows perfectly well what human qualities he most admires—physical beauty, nobility, generosity, ruthlessness—but he is more keenly aware than we are how much all these qualities are at the mercy of circumstance. His mind being set in this way, the stories which he produces are inevitably not so much stories of character as stories of circumstance. A story is born when providence intervenes miraculously, when quite by chance a Jinni is released from a bottle and reveals where wealth is hidden. Or we climb a tree and (Destiny relenting for once) we hear the robber chief say, "Open Sesame!" Or we meet a holy man who is so taken by the beauty of our countenances that he presents us with an ointment which, when placed upon the eyelids, allows us to see through rocks and mountains to the treasures they conceal.

As is to be expected, many of the tales are, as a result, obvious wealth and sex fantasies, and the English mind, which is most self-conscious about sex and is fast becoming self-conscious about money, may be distressed by what it considers an unbecoming naïvety. In reality, these fantasies are not so naïve as they seem, but even if they were it would be hard to remain unresponsive to the gusto with which they stride along and the brilliant invention with which they are tricked out. After the hero has cut off the magician's head and made himself master of the mountain of gold he is entertained for a year and a day by forty beautiful damsels with faces like full moons, with lips of coral and bosoms that are temptation to behold. Then later, perhaps, the Caliph presents him with fifty camel-loads of Egyptian stuffs, he is made chief of the merchants of the city (no doubts here about the dignity of trade!) and when he rides forth forty men march at each stirrup. What could be more satisfying?

The Rawi does not regard his tale as finished when the hero has married the heroine. "The European novelist," said Burton, "marries off his hero and heroine and leaves them to consummate their marriage in privacy; even Tom Jones has the decency to lock the door. But the Eastern story-teller, especially this unknown prose 'Shakespeare,' must usher you with a flourish

13

into the bridal-chamber and narrate to you, with infinite gusto, everything he sees and hears." Not for any prurient reason, but quite simply because the Oriental makes far less mystery about his personal relations than we do and he does not see why, having told three-quarters of the tale, he should not tell the rest. The East conceals far less than the West; Cairo is a less mysterious city than London.

I have said that the fantasy-weaving in the *Nights* is not quite so naïve as it seems; it would be a mistake to imagine that the Oriental is completely unaware of the source of the fascination. Burton, it is true, insisted how completely the Arabs of the desert would surrender to the tales. "The women and children stand motionless as silhouettes outside the ring; and all are breathless with attention; they seem to drink in the words with eyes and mouths as well as with ears. The most fantastic flights of fancy, the wildest improbabilities, the most impossible of impossibilities, appear to them utterly natural, mere matters of everyday occurrence." But these are simple Badawi. The townsman is more sophisticated and for him, I suspect, surrender to the tales will be a form of self-indulgence. It is one of the paradoxes of life in the Near East that an extreme cynicism flourishes side by side with a belief in the most agreeable illusions. "Better good news even if it is untrue than bad news that is the truth," is a common enough sentiment. For this there is no simple explanation, but for the moment it will be enough to say that whereas we are immediately on our dignity when we are being led on by an illusion, the Oriental is prepared to savour it to the full—as the story of the Barmecide feast will show. The more extravagant the fantasy becomes, the more treasure houses, palaces and wives that the hero acquires, the merrier the listener to the tale becomes. But we must not exaggerate. There are many tales in which sex and money fantasies have no part and where the listener has no scope for irony. But the collection as a whole would seem much thinner in substance than it really is if we were to forget the possibility of raillery for it is always present in the oriental mind: and we have only to read such delightful tales as *The Story of Maʾaruf* to discover the raillery rising to the surface.

It may sound odd to recommend *The Thousand and One Nights* as a picture of Arab civilisation. It is hard to see how stories of such exuberant fancy can bear any relation to reality, but of course they have—a very close relation—to the emotional life of the people who created them or coloured them with their imagination; and this emotional life is the distinctive feature of any culture. We find in these pages more than a factual day-to-day account of life in the Arab lands. (Though this is there for the finding; the supernatural plays a much smaller part in the *Nights* than the common reader might suppose.) The kind of life thus recorded has largely passed away, and that within the past hundred years, but the deeper reality of which the tales treat, the temperament of the people, is unchanged and there is no better chart in existence of its deeps and shallows. Pride, shrewdness, a lively sense of humour, a sensibility that is almost feminine and which finds its most characteristic expression in a love of pathos, a piety without great idealism so that disappointment does not (as in Europe) bring despair and recrimination against the idea of God, an uncalculating love of the good things of the world and an indifference to death, a reverence for tradition and an appetite for novelty, a fatalism that is sometimes infuriating and an opportunism that is frequently breath-taking, and above all, that un-analysable human-heartedness which runs from the top to the bottom of society and makes the extreme contrasts of wealth and poverty a little easier to tolerate; all these are the spiritual qualities that stream perpetually to the surface of the chronicles of *The Thousand and One Nights* and break up what would otherwise be the hard glitter of mere inventiveness with the richer colours of the imagination.

P. H. NEWBY

In the Name of Allah, the Compassionating, the Compassionate!

*Praise be to Allah ∽ the Beneficent King ∽ the Creator of the
Universe ∽ Lord of the Three Worlds ∽ Who set up the Firma-
ment without Pillars in its Stead ∽ and Who stretched out the
Earth even as a Bed ∽ and Grace, and Prayer—Blessing be upon
our Lord Mohammed ∽ Lord of Apostolic Men ∽ and upon his
Family and Companion-train ∽ Prayer and Blessings enduring
and Grace which unto the Day of Doom shall remain ∽ Amen! ∽
O thou of the Three Worlds Sovereign!*

AND afterwards. Verily the works and words of those gone
before us have become instances and examples to men of our
modern day, that folk may view what admonishing chances
befell other folk and may therefrom take warning; and that
they may peruse the annals of antique peoples and all that
hath betided them, and be thereby ruled and restrained: Praise,
therefore, be to Him who hath made the histories of the Past
an admonition unto the Present! Now of such instances are
the tales called *A Thousand Nights and a Night*, together with
their far-famed legends and wonders. Therein is related
(but Allah is All-knowing of His hidden things and All-ruling
and All-honoured and All-giving and All-gracious and All-

16

merciful!)[1] that, in tide of yore and in time long gone before, there was a King of the Kings of the Banu Sasan in the Islands of India and China, a Lord of armies and guards and servants and dependents.[2] He left only two sons, one in the prime of manhood and the other yet a youth, while both were Knights and Braves, albeit the elder was a doughtier horseman than the younger. So he succeeded to the empire; when he ruled the land and lorded it over his lieges with justice so exemplary that he was beloved by all the peoples of his capital and of his kingdom. His name was King Shahryar, and he made his younger brother, Shah Zaman hight, King of Samarcand in Barbarian-land. These two ceased not to abide in their several realms and the law was ever carried out in their dominions; and each ruled his own kingdom, with equity and fairdealing to his subjects, in extreme solace and enjoyment; and this condition continually endured for a score of years.

But at the end of the twentieth twelvemonth the elder King yearned for a sight of his younger brother and felt that he must look upon him once more. So he took counsel with his Wazir about visiting him, but the Minister, finding the project unadvisable, recommended that a letter be written and a present be sent under his charge to the younger brother with an invitation to visit the elder. Having accepted this advice the King forthwith bade prepare handsome gifts, such as horses with saddles of gem-encrusted gold; Mamelukes, or white slaves; beautiful handmaids, high-breasted virgins, and splendid stuffs and costly. He then wrote a letter to Shah Zaman expressing his warm love and great wish to see him, ending with these words: "We therefore hope of the favour and affection of the beloved brother that he will condescend to bestir himself and turn his face us-wards. Further-more, we have sent our Wazir to make all ordinance for the march, and our one and only desire is to see thee ere we die; but if thou delay or disappoint us we shall not survive the blow. Wherewith peace be upon thee!" Then King Shahryar, having sealed the missive and given it to the Wazir with the offerings aforementioned, commanded him to shorten his skirts and strain his strength and make all expedition in going and returning. "Harkening and obedience!" quoth the Minister, who fell to making ready without stay and packed up his loads and prepared all his requisites without delay.

---

[1] A deprecatory formula used because the writer is going to indulge in a series of what may possibly be untruths.
[2] The Sons of Sásán are the famous Sassanides whose dynasty ended with the Arabian Conquest (A.D. 641).

This occupied him three days, and on the dawn of the fourth he took leave of his King and marched right away, over desert and hill-way, stony waste and pleasant lea without halting by night or by day. But whenever he entered a realm whose ruler was subject to his Suzerain, where he was greeted with magnificent gifts of gold and silver and all manner of presents fair and rare, he would tarry there three days,[1] the term of the guest-rite; and, when he left on the fourth, he would be honourably escorted for a whole day's march. As soon as the Wazir drew near Shah Zaman's court in Samarcand he despatched to report his arrival one of his high officials, who presented himself before the King; and, kissing the ground between his hands, delivered his message. Hereupon the King commanded sundry of his Grandees and Lords of his realm to fare forth and meet his brother's Wazir at the distance of a full day's journey; which they did, greeting him respectfully and wishing him all prosperity and forming an escort and a procession. When he entered the city he proceeded straightway to the palace, where he presented himself in the royal presence; and, after kissing the ground and praying for the King's health and happiness and for victory over all his enemies, he informed him that his brother was yearning to see him, and prayed for the pleasure of a visit.

He then delivered the letter which Shah Zaman took from his hand and read. It contained sundry hints and allusions which required thought; but, when the King had fully comprehended its import, he said, "I hear and I obey the commands of the beloved brother!" adding to the Wazir, "But we will not march till after the third day's hospitality." He appointed for the Minister fitting quarters of the palace; and, pitching tents for the troops, rationed them with whatever they might require of meat and drink and other necessaries. On the fourth day he made ready for wayfare and got together sumptuous presents befitting his elder brother's majesty, and stablished his chief Wazir viceroy of the land during his absence. Then he caused his tents and camels and mules to be brought forth and encamped, with their bales and loads, attendants and guards, within sight of the city, in readiness to set out next morning for his brother's capital. But when the night was half spent he bethought him that he had forgotten in his palace somewhat which he should have brought with him, so he returned privily and entered his apartments, where he found the Queen, his wife, asleep on his own carpet-bed embracing with both arms

---

[1] This three-days' term (rest-day, chest-day and departure-day) seems to be an instinct-made rule in hospitality. Among Moslems it is a Sunnat or practice of the Prophet.

a black cook of loathsome aspect and foul with kitchen grease and grime.

When he saw this the world waxed black before his sight and he said, "If such case happen while I am yet within sight of the city what will be the doings of this damned whore during my long absence at my brother's court?" So he drew his scymitar and, cutting the two in four pieces with a single blow, left them on the carpet and returned presently to his camp without letting anyone know of what had happened. Then he gave orders for immediate departure and set out at once and began his travel; but he could not help thinking over his wife's treason and he kept ever saying to himself, "How could she do this deed by me? How could she work her own death?" till excessive grief seized him, his colour changed to yellow, his body waxed weak and he was threatened with a dangerous malady, such an one as bringeth men to die. So the Wazir shortened his stages and tarried long at the watering-stations and did his best to solace the King.

Now when Shah Zaman drew near the capital of his brother he despatched vaunt-couriers and messengers of glad tidings to announce his arrival, and Shahryar came forth to meet him with his Wazirs and Emirs and Lords and Grandees of his realm; and saluted him and joyed with exceeding joy and caused the city to be decorated in his honour. When, however, the brothers met, the elder could not but see the change of complexion in the younger and questioned him of his case where he replied, " 'Tis caused by the travails of wayfare and my case needs care, for I have suffered from the change of water and air! but Allah be praised for reuniting me with a brother so dear and so rare!" On this wise he dissembled and kept his secret, adding, "O King of the Time and Caliph of the Tide, only toil and moil have tinged my face yellow with bile and hath made my eyes sink deep in my head." Then the two entered the capital in all honour; and the elder brother lodged the younger in a palace overhanging the pleasure garden; and, after a time, seeing his condition still unchanged, he attributed it to his separation from his country and kingdom. So he let him wend his own ways and asked no questions of him till one day when he again said, "O my brother, I see thou art grown weaker of body and yellower of colour." "O my brother," replied Shah Zaman, "I have an internal wound."[1] Still he would not tell him what he had witnessed in his wife. Thereupon Shahryar summoned doctors and surgeons and bade them treat his brother according to the rules of art, which they did

---

[1] I am sick at heart.

for a whole month; but their sherbets and potions naught availed, for he would dwell upon the deed of his wife, and despondency, instead of diminishing, prevailed, and leachcraft treatment utterly failed. One day his elder brother said to him, "I am going forth to hunt and course and to take my pleasure and pastime; maybe this would lighten thy heart." Shah Zaman, however, refused, saying, "O my brother, my soul yearneth for naught of this sort and I entreat thy favour to suffer me tarry quietly in this place, being wholly taken up with my malady." So King Shah Zaman passed his night in the palace and, next morning, when his brother had fared forth, he removed from his room and sat him down at one of the lattice-windows overlooking the pleasure grounds; and there he abode thinking with saddest thought over his wife's betrayal, and burning sighs issued from his tortured breast.

And as he continued in this case, lo! a postern of the palace, which was carefully kept private, swung open and out of it came twenty slave-girls surrounding his brother's wife who was wondrous fair, a model of beauty and comeliness and symmetry and perfect loveliness and who paced with the grace of a gazelle which panteth for the cooling stream. Thereupon Shah Zaman drew back from the window, but he kept the bevy in sight espying them from a place whence he could not be espied. They walked under the very lattice and advanced a little way into the garden till they came to a jetting fountain amiddlemost a great basin of water; then they stripped off their clothes and behold, ten of them were women, concubines of the King, and the other ten were white slaves. Then they all paired off, each with each: but the Queen, who was left alone, presently cried out in a loud voice, "Here to me, O my lord Saeed!" and then sprang with a drop-leap from one of the trees a big, slobbering, blackamoor, with rolling eyes which showed the whites, a truly hideous sight. He walked boldly up to her and threw his arms round her neck while she embraced him as warmly; then he bussed her and, winding his legs round hers, as a button-loop clasps a button, he threw her and enjoyed her. On like wise did the other slaves with the girls till all had satisfied their passions, and they ceased not from kissing and clipping, coupling and carousing till day began to wane, when the Mamelukes rose from the damsel's bosoms and the blackamoor slave dismounted from the Queen's breast; the men resumed their disguises and all, except the negro who swarmed up the tree, entered the palace and closed the postern-door as before.

Now, when Shah Zaman saw this conduct of his sister-in-law, he said in himself, "By Allah, my calamity is lighter than this! My brother is a greater King among the Kings than I am, yet this infamy goeth on in his very palace, and his wife is in love with that filthiest of filthy slaves. But this only showeth that they all do it and that there is no woman but who cuckoldeth her husband, then the curse of Allah be upon one and all and upon the fools who lean against them for support or who place the reins of conduct in their hands." So he put away his melancholy and despondency, regret and repine, and allayed his sorrow by constantly repeating those words, adding, " 'Tis my conviction that no man in this world is safe from their malice!" When supper-time came they brought him the trays and he ate with voracious appetite, for he had long refrained from meat, feeling unable to touch any dish however dainty. Then he returned grateful thanks to Almighty Allah, praising Him and blessing Him, and he spent a most restful night, it having been long since he had savoured the sweet food of sleep. Next day he broke his fast heartily and began to recover health and strength, and presently regained excellent condition. His brother came back from the chase ten days after, when he rode out to meet him and they saluted each other; and when King Shahryar looked at King Shah Zaman he saw how the hue of health had returned to him, how his face had waxed ruddy and how he ate with an appetite after his late scanty diet. He wondered much and said, "O my brother, I was so anxious that thou wouldst join me in hunting and chasing, and wouldst take thy pleasure and pastime in my dominion!" He thanked him and excused himself; then the two took horse and rode into the city and, when they were seated at their ease in the palace, the food-trays were set before them and they ate their sufficiency. After the meats were removed and they had washed their hands, King Shahryar turned to his brother and said, "My mind is overcome with wonderment at thy condition. I was desirous to carry thee with me to the chase but I saw thee changed in hue, pale and wan to view, and in sore trouble of mind too. But now Alhamdolillah—glory be to God!—I see thy natural colour hath returned to thy face and that thou art again in the best of case. It was my belief that thy sickness came of severance from thy family and friends, and absence from capital and country, so I refrained from troubling thee with further questions. But now I beseech thee to expound to me the cause of thy complaint and thy change of colour, and to explain the reason of thy recovery and the return to the ruddy hue of health which I am wont to view. So speak out and hide naught!"

When Shah Zaman heard this he bowed groundwards awhile his head, then raised it and said, "I will tell thee what caused my complaint and my loss of colour; but excuse my acquainting thee with the cause of its return to me and the reason of my complete recovery; indeed I pray thee not to press me for a reply." Said Shahryar, who was much surprised by these words, "Let me hear first what produced thy pallor and thy poor condition." "Know then, O my brother," rejoined Shah Zaman, "that when thou sentest thy Wazir with the invitation to place myself between thy hands, I made ready and marched out of my city; but presently I minded me having left behind me in the palace a string of jewels intended as a gift to thee. I returned for it alone and found my wife on my carpet-bed and in the arms of a hideous black cook. So I slew the twain and came to thee, yet my thoughts brooded over this business and I lost my bloom and became weak. But excuse me if I still refuse to tell thee what was the reason of my complexion returning." Shahryar shook his head, marvelling with extreme marvel, and with the fire of wrath flaming up from his heart, he cried, "Indeed, the malice of woman is mighty!" Then he took refuge from them with Allah and said, "In very sooth, O my brother, thou hast escaped many an evil by putting thy wife to death, and right excusable were thy wrath and grief for such mishap which never yet befell crowned King like thee. By Allah, had the case been mine, I would not have been satisfied without slaying a thousand women and that way madness lies! But now praise be to Allah who hath tempered to thee thy tribulation, and needs must thou acquaint me with that which so suddenly restored to thee complexion and health, and explain to me what causeth this concealment." "O King of the Age, again I pray thee excuse my so doing." "Nay, but thou must." "I fear, O my brother, lest the recital cause thee more anger and sorrow than afflicted me." "That were but a better reason," quoth Shahryar, "for telling me the whole history, and I conjure thee by Allah not to keep aught back from me."

Thereupon Shah Zaman told him all he had seen, from commencement to conclusion, ending with these words, "When I beheld thy calamity and the treason of thy wife, O my brother, and I reflected that thou art in years my senior and in sovereignty my superior, mine own sorrow was belittled by the comparison, and my mind recovered tone and temper: so throwing off melancholy and despondency, I was able to eat and drink and sleep, and thus I speedily regained health and strength. Such is the truth and the whole truth." When King Shahryar heard this he waxed wroth with exceeding wrath, and rage was like to strangle him; but presently he recovered himself and said, "O my brother, I would not give thee the lie in this matter, but I cannot credit it till I see it with mine own eyes." "An thou wouldst look upon thy calamity," quoth Shah

Zaman, "rise at once and make ready again for hunting and coursing, and then hide thyself with me, so shalt thou witness it and thine eyes shall verify it." "True," quoth the King; whereupon he let make proclamation of his intent to travel, and the troops and tents fared forth without the city, camping within sight, and Shahryar sallied out with them and took seat amidmost his host, bidding the slaves admit no man to him. When night came on he summoned his Wazir and said to him, "Sit thou in my stead and let none wot of my absence till the term of three days." Then the brothers disguised themselves and returned by night with all secrecy to the palace, where they passed the dark hours: and at dawn they seated themselves at the lattice overlooking the pleasure grounds, when presently the Queen and her handmaids came out as before, and passing under the windows made for the fountain. Here they stripped, ten of them being men to ten women, and the King's wife cried out, "Where art thou, O Saeed?" The hideous blackamoor dropped from the tree straightway; and, rushing into her arms without stay or delay, cried out, "I am Sa'ad al-Din Saood!" The lady laughed heartily, and all fell to satisfying their lusts, and remained so occupied for a couple of hours, when the white slaves rose up from the handmaidens' breasts and the blackamoor dismounted from the Queen's bosom: then they went into the basin and, after performing the Ghusl, or complete ablution, donned their dresses and retired as they had done before. When King Shahryar saw this infamy of his wife and concubines he became as one distraught and he cried out, "Only in utter solitude can man be safe from the doings of this vile world! By Allah, life is naught but one great wrong." Presently he added, "Do not thwart me, O my brother, in what I propose"; and the other answered, "I will not." So he said, "Let us up as we are and depart forthright hence, for we have no concern with Kingship, and let us over-wander Allah's earth, worshipping the Almighty till we find someone to whom the like calamity hath happened; and if we find none then will death be more welcome to us than life."

So the two brothers issued from a second private postern of the palace; and they never stinted wayfaring by day and by night until they reached a tree a-middle of a meadow hard by a spring of sweet water on the shore of the salt sea. Both drank of it and sat down to take their rest; and when an hour of the day had gone by, lo! they heard a mighty roar and uproar in the middle of the main as though the heavens were falling upon the earth; and the sea brake with waves before them, and from it towered a black pillar, which grew and grew till it rose skywards and began making for that meadow. Seeing it, they waxed fearful exceedingly and climbed to the top of the tree, which was lofty; whence they gazed to see what might be the matter. And behold, it was a Jinni, huge of height and burly of breast and bulk, broad of brow and black of blee, bearing on his head a coffer of crystal. He strode to land, wading through the deep, and coming to the tree whereupon were the two Kings, seated himself beneath it. He then set down the coffer on its bottom and out of it drew a casket, with seven padlocks of steel, which he unlocked with seven keys of steel

he took from beside his thigh, and out of it a young lady was seen to come, white-skinned and of winsomest mien, of stature fine and thin, and bright as though a moon of the fourteenth night she had been, or the sun raining lively sheen.

The Jinni seated her under the tree by his side and looking at her said, "O choicest love of this heart of mine! O dame of noblest line, whom I snatched away on thy bride night that none might prevent me taking thy maidenhead or tumble thee before I did, and whom none save myself hath loved or hath enjoyed: O my sweetheart! I would lief sleep a little while." He then laid his head upon the lady's thighs; and, stretching out his legs which extended down to the sea, slept and snored and snarked like the roll of thunder. Presently she raised her head towards the tree-top and saw the two Kings perched near the summit; then she softly lifted off her lap the Jinni's pate which she was tired of supporting and placed it upon the ground; then standing upright under the tree signed to the Kings, "Come ye down, ye two, and fear naught from this Ifrit."[1] They were in a terrible fright when they found that she had seen them and answered her in the same manner, "Allah upon thee and by thy modesty, O lady, excuse us from coming down!" But she rejoined by saying, "Allah upon you both that ye come down forthright, and if you come not, I will rouse upon you my husband, this Ifrit, and he shall do you to die by the illest of deaths"; and she continued making signals to them. So, being afraid, they came down to her and she rose before them and said, "Stroke me a strong stroke, without stay or delay, otherwise will I arouse and set upon you this Ifrit who shall slay you straightway." They said to her, "O our lady, we conjure thee by Allah, let us off this work, for we are fugitives from such and in extreme dread and terror of this thy husband. How then can we do it in such a way as thou desirest?" "Leave this talk: it needs must be so"; quoth she, and she swore them by Him[2] who raised the skies on high, without prop or pillar, that, if they worked not her will, she would cause them to be slain and cast into the sea. Whereupon out of fear King Shahryar said to King Shah Zaman, "O my brother, do thou what she biddeth thee do"; but he replied, "I will not do it till thou do it before I do." And they began disputing about futtering her. Then quoth she to the twain, "How is it I see you disputing and demurring; if ye do not come forward like men and do the deed of kind ye two, I will arouse upon you the Ifrit."

At this, by reason of their sore dread of the Jinni, both did by her what she bade them do; and, when they had dismounted from her, she said, "Well done!" She then took from her pocket a purse and drew out a knotted string, whereupon were strung five hundred and seventy seal-rings, and asked. "Know ye what be these?" They answered her saying, "We know not!" Then quoth she, "These be the signets of five hundred and seventy men who have all futtered me upon the horns of

---

[1] This variety of the Jinn is generally, but not always, a malignant being, hostile and injurious to mankind. (Koran xxvii. 39.)

[2] This introduction of the name of Allah into an indecent tale is essentially Egyptian and Cairene.

this foul, this foolish, this filthy Ifrit; so give me also your two seal-rings, ye pair of brothers." When they had drawn their two rings from their hands and given them to her, she said to them, "Of a truth this Ifrit bore me off on my bride night, and put me into a casket and set the casket in a coffer and to the coffer he affixed seven strong padlocks of steel and deposited me on the deep bottom of the sea that raves, dashing and clashing with waves; and guarded me so that I might remain chaste and honest, quotha! that none save himself might have connexion with me. But I have lain under as many of my kind as I please, and this wretched Jinni wotteth not that Destiny may not be averted nor hindered by aught, and that whatso woman willeth the same she fulfilleth however man nilleth."

Hearing these words they marvelled with exceeding marvel, and she went from them to the Ifrit and, taking up his head on her thigh as before, said to them softly, "Now wend your ways and bear yourselves beyond the bounds of his malice." So they fared forth saying either to other, "Allah! Allah!" and, "There be no Majesty and there be no Might save in Allah, the Glorious, the Great; and with Him we seek refuge from women's malice and sleight, for of a truth it hath no mate in might. Consider, O my brother, the ways of this marvellous lady with an Ifrit who is so much more powerful than we are. Now since there hath happened to him a greater mishap than that which befell us and which should bear us abundant consolation, so return we to our countries and capitals, and let us decide never to intermarry with womankind and presently we will show them what will be our action." Thereupon they rode back to the tents of King Shahryar, which they reached on the morning of the third day; and, having mustered the Wazirs and Emirs, the Chamberlains and high officials, he gave a robe of honour to his Viceroy and issued orders for an immediate return to the city. There he sat him upon his throne and sending for the Chief Minister, the father of the two damsels who (Inshallah!) will presently be mentioned, he said, "I command thee to take my wife and smite her to death; for she hath broken her plight and her faith." So he carried her to the place of execution and did her die. Then King Shahryar took brand in hand and repairing to the Serraglio slew all the concubines and their Mamelukes. He also sware himself by a binding oath that whatever wife he married he would abate her maidenhead at night and slay her next morning to make sure of his honour; "For," said he, "there never was nor is there one chaste woman upon the face of earth." Then Shah Zaman prayed for permission to fare homewards; and he went forth equipped and escorted and travelled till he reached his own country.

Meanwhile Shahryar commanded his Wazir to bring him the bride of the night that he might go into her; so he produced a most beautiful girl, the daughter of one of the Emirs, and the King went in unto her at eventide, and when morning dawned he bade his Minister strike off her head; and the Wazir did accordingly for fear of the Sultan. On this wise he continued for the space of three years, marrying a maiden every night and killing her the next morning, till folk raised an outcry against him and cursed him, praying Allah utterly to destroy him and his rule; and women made an uproar and mothers wept and parents fled with their daughters till there remained not in the city a young person fit for carnal copulation.

Presently the King ordered his Chief Wazir, the same who was charged with the executions, to bring him a virgin as was his wont; and the Minister went forth and searched and found none; so he returned home in sorrow and anxiety fearing for his life from the King. Now he had two daughters, Shahrazad and Dunyazad hight, of whom the elder had perused the books, annals and legends of preceding Kings, and the stories, examples and instances of bygone men and things; indeed it was said that she had collected a thousand books of histories relating to antique races and departed rulers. She had perused the works of the poets and knew them by heart; she had studied philosophy and the sciences, arts and accomplishments; and she was pleasant and polite, wise and witty, well read and well bred. Now on that day she said to her father, "Why do I see thee thus changed and laden with cark and care?" When the Wazir heard from his daughter these words he related to her, from first to last all that had happened between him and the King. Whereupon said she, "By Allah, O my father, how long shall this slaughter of women endure? Shall I tell thee what is in my mind in order to save both sides from destruction?" "Say on, O my daughter," quoth he, and quoth she, "I wish thou wouldst give me in marriage to this King Shahryar; either I shall live or I shall be a ransom for the virgin daughters of Moslems and the cause of their deliverance from his hands and thine." "Allah upon thee!" cried he in wrath exceeding that lacked no feeding, "O scanty of wit, expose not thy life to such peril! How durst thou address me in words so wide from wisdom and un-far from foolishness? Know that one who lacketh experience in worldly matters readily falleth into misfortune; and whoso considereth not the end keepeth not the world to friend, and the vulgar say: 'I was lying at mine ease; nought but my officiousness brought me unease'." "Needs must thou," she broke in, "make me a doer of this good deed, and let him kill me an he will: I shall only

27

die a ransom for others." "O my daughter," asked he, "and how shall that profit thee when thou shalt have thrown away thy life?" and she answered, "O my father it must be, come of it what will! Leave such talk and tattle. I will not listen to thy words and, if you deny me, I will marry myself to him despite the nose of thee. And first I will go up to the King myself and alone and I will say to him: I prayed my father to wive me with thee, but he refused, being resolved to disappoint his lord, grudging the like of me to the like of thee." Her father asked, "Must this needs be?" and she answered, "Even so."

Hereupon the Wazir, being weary of lamenting and contending, persuading and dissuading her, all to no purpose, went up to King Shahryar and, after blessing him and kissing the ground before him, told him all about his dispute with his daughter from first to last and how he designed to bring her to him that night. The King wondered with exceeding wonder; for he had made an especial exception of the Wazir's daughter, and said to him, "O most faithful of Counsellors, how is this? Thou wottest that I have sworn by the Raiser of the Heavens that after I have gone into her this night I shall say to thee on the morrow's morning: Take her and slay her! and, if thou slay her not, I will slay thee in her stead without fail." "Allah guide thee to glory and lengthen thy life, O King of the Age," answered the Wazir, "it is she that hath so determined: all this have I told her and more; but she will not hearken to me and she persisteth in passing this coming night with the King's Majesty." So Shahryar rejoiced greatly and said, " 'Tis well; go get her ready and this night bring her to me." The Wazir returned to his daughter and reported to her the command saying, "Allah make not thy father desolate by thy loss!"

But Shahrazad rejoined with exceeding joy and gat ready all she required and said to her youngest sister, Dunyazad, "Note well what directions I entrust to thee! When I have gone into the King I will send for thee and when thou comest to me and seest that he hath had his carnal will of me, do thou say to me: 'O my sister, an thou be not sleepy, relate to me some new story, delectable and delightsome, the better to speed our waking hours'; and I will tell thee a tale which shall be our deliverance, if so Allah please, and which shall turn the King from his blood-thirsty custom." Dunyazad answered, "With love and gladness." So when it was night their father the Wazir carried Shahrazad to the King who was gladdened at the sight and asked, "Hast thou brought me my need?" and he answered, "I have." But when the King took her to his bed and fell to toying with her and wished to go into her she wept; which made him ask, "What aileth thee?" She replied, "O King of the Age, I

28

have a younger sister and lief would I take leave of her this
night before I see the dawn." So he sent at once for Dunyazad
and she came and kissed the ground between his hands, when
he permitted her to take her seat near the foot of the couch.
Then the King arose and did away with his bride's maidenhead and the three fell asleep. But when it was midnight
Shahrazad awoke and signalled to her sister Dunyazad who
sat up and said, "Allah upon thee, O my sister, recite to us
some new story, delightsome and delectable, wherewith to while
away the waking hours of our latter night." "With joy and
goodly gree," answered Shahrazad, "if this pious and auspicious
King permits me." "Tell on," quoth the King, who chanced
to be sleepless and restless and, therefore, was pleased with the
prospect of hearing her story. So Shahrazad rejoiced; and thus,
on the first night of the Thousand Nights and a Night, she
began with

The Tale of the Ensorcelled Prince

KNOW then, O my lord, that whilome my sire was King of this city, and his name was Mahmud, entitled Lord of the Black Islands, and owner of what are now these four mountains. He ruled threescore and ten years, after which he went to the mercy of the Lord and I reigned as Sultan in his stead. I took to wife my cousin, the daughter of my paternal uncle,[1] and she loved me with such abounding love that whenever I was absent she ate not and she drank not until she saw me again. She cohabited with me for five years till a certain day when she went forth to the Hammam bath; and I bade the cook hasten to get ready all requisites for our supper. And I entered this place and lay down on the bed where I was wont to sleep and bade two damsels to fan my face, one sitting by my head and the other at my feet. But I was troubled and made restless by my wife's absence and could not sleep; for although my eyes were closed my mind and thoughts were wide awake. Presently I heard the slave-girl at my head say to her at my feet, "O Mas'udah, how miserable is our master and how wasted in his youth and oh! the pity of his being so betrayed by our mistress, the accursed whore!" The other replied, "Yes, indeed, Allah curse all faithless women and adulterous; but the like of our master with his fair gifts, deserveth something better than this harlot who lieth abroad every night." Then quoth she who sat by my head, "Is our lord dumb or fit only for

---

[1] An Arab holds that he has a right to marry his first cousin, the daughter of his father's brother, and if any win her from him a death and a blood-feud may result.

bubbling that he questioneth her not!" and quoth the other, "Fie on thee! doth our lord know her ways or doth she allow him his choice? Nay, more, doth she not drug every night the cup she giveth him to drink before sleep-time, and put Bhang[1] into it? So he sleepeth and wotteth not whither she goeth, nor what she doeth; but we know that, after giving him the drugged wine, she donneth her richest raiment and perfumeth herself and then she fareth out from him to be away till break of day; then she cometh to him, and burneth a pastile under his nose and he awaketh from his death-like sleep."

When I heard the slave-girls' words, the light became black before my sight and I thought night would never fall. Presently the daughter of my uncle came from the baths; and they set the table for us and we ate and sat together a fair half-hour quaffing our wine as was ever our wont. Then she called for the particular wine I used to drink before sleeping and reached me the cup; but, seeming to drink it according to my wont, I poured the contents into my bosom; and, lying down, let her hear that I was asleep. Then, behold, she cried, "Sleep out the night, and never wake again: by Allah, I loathe thee and I loathe thy whole body, and my soul turneth in disgust from cohabiting with thee; and I see not the moment when Allah shall snatch away thy life!" Then she rose and donned her fairest dress and perfumed her person and slung my sword over her shoulder; and, opening the gates of the palace, went her ill way. I rose and followed her as she left the palace, and she threaded the streets until she came to the city gate, where she spoke words I understood not, and the padlocks dropped of themselves as if broken and the gate-leaves opened. She went forth (and I after her without her noticing aught) till she came at last to the outlying mounds[2] and a reed fence built about a round-roofed hut of mud-bricks. As she entered the door I climbed upon the roof which commanded a view of the interior. And lo! my fair cousin had gone into a hideous negro slave with his upper lip like the cover of a pot, and his lower like an open pot; lips which might sweep up sand from the gravel-floor of the cot. He was to boot a leper and a paralytic, lying upon a strew of sugar-cane trash and wrapped in an old blanket and the foulest rags and tatters. She kissed the earth before him, and he raised his head so as to see her and said, "Woe to thee! what call hadst thou to stay away all this

---

[1] A preparation of hemp.
[2] The rubbish heaps which outlie Eastern cities, some (near Cairo) are over a hundred feet high.

time? Here have been with me sundry of the black brethren, who drank their wine and each had his young lady, and I was not content to drink because of thine absence."

Then she, "O my lord, my heart's love and coolth[1] of my eyes, knowest thou not that I am married to my cousin whose very look I loathe, and hate myself when in his company? And did not I fear for thy sake, I would not let a single sun arise before making his city a ruined heap wherein raven should croak and howlet hoot, and jackal and wolf harbour and loot; nay I had removed its very stones to the back side of Mount Kaf."[2] Rejoined the slave, "Thou liest, damn thee! Now I swear an oath by the valour and honour of blacka-moor men (and deem not our manliness to be the poor manli-ness of white men), from to-day forth if thou stay away till this hour, I will not keep company with thee nor will I glue my body with thy body and strum and belly-pump. Dost play fast and loose with us, thou cracked pot, that we may satisfy thy dirty lusts? stinkard! bitch! vilest of the vile whites!" When I heard his words, and saw with my own eyes what passed between these two wretches, the world waxed dark before my face and my soul knew not in what place it was. But my wife humbly stood up weeping before and wheedling the slave, and saying, "O my beloved, and very fruit of my heart, there is none left to cheer me but thy dear self; and, if thou cast me off who shall take me in, O my beloved, O light of my eyes?" And she ceased not weeping and abasing herself to him until he deigned to be reconciled with her.

Then she was right glad and stood up and doffed her clothes, even to her petticoat-trousers, and said, "O my master what hast thou here for thy handmaiden to eat?" "Uncover the basin," he grumbled, "and thou shalt find at the bottom the broiled bones of some rats we dined on; pick at them, and then go to that slop-pot where thou shalt find some leavings of beer which thou mayest drink." So she ate and drank and washed her hands, and went and lay down by the side of the slave, upon the cane-trash, and, stripping herself stark naked, she crept in with him under his foul coverlet and his rags and tatters.

When I saw my wife, my cousin, the daughter of my uncle, do this deed, I clean lost my wits, and, climbing down from the roof, I entered and took the sword which she had with her and drew it, determined to cut down the twain. I first struck at the slave's neck and thought that the death decree had fallen

---

[1] All coolness is pleasant to dwellers in hot lands.
[2] Popularly rendered Caucasus.

on him for he groaned a loud hissing groan, but I had cut only
the skin and flesh of the gullet and the two arteries! It awoke
the daughter of my uncle, so I sheathed the sword and fared
forth for the city; and, entering the palace, lay upon my bed
and slept till morning when my wife aroused me, and I saw
that she had cut off her hair and had donned mourning garments. Quoth she, "O son of my uncle, blame me not for what
I do; it hath just reached me that my mother is dead, and my
father hath been killed in holy war, and of my brothers one
hath lost his life by a snake-sting and the other by falling down
some precipice; and I can and should do naught save weep and
lament." When I heard her words I refrained from all reproach
and said only, "Do as thou list; I certainly will not thwart
thee." She continued sorrowing, weeping and wailing one
whole year from the beginning of its circle to the end, and
when it was finished she said to me, "I wish to build me in
thy palace a tomb with a cupola, which I will set apart for
my mourning and will name the House of Lamentations."
Quoth I again, "Do as thou list!"

Then she builded for herself a cenotaph wherein to mourn,
and set on its centre a dome under which showed a tomb like
a Santon's sepulchre. Thither she carried the slave and lodged
him; but he was exceeding weak by reason of his wound, and
unable to do her love-service; he could only drink wine and
from the day of his hurt he spake not a word, yet he lived on
because his appointed hour was not come. Every day, morning
and evening, my wife went to him and wept and wailed over
him and gave him wine and strong soups, and left not off
doing after this manner a second year; and I bore with her
patiently and paid no heed to her. One day, however, I went
into her unawares; and I found her weeping and beating her
face and crying, "Why art thou absent from my sight, O my
heart's delight? Speak to me, O my life; talk with me, O my
love!" When she had ended for a time her words and her
weeping I said to her, "O my cousin, let this thy mourning
suffice, for in pouring forth tears there is little profit!" "Thwart
me not," answered she, "in aught I do, or I will lay violent
hands on myself!" So I held my peace and left her to go her
own way; and she ceased not to cry and keen and indulge her
affliction for yet another year. At the end of the third year I
waxed aweary of this longsome mourning, and one day I
happened to enter the cenotaph when vexed and angry with
some matter which had thwarted me, and suddenly I heard her
say, "O my lord, I never hear thee vouchsafe a single word to
me! Why dost thou not answer me, O my master?" and she
began reciting:

B

> O thou tomb! O thou tomb! be his beauty set in shade?
> Hast thou darkened that countenance all-sheeny as the noon?
> O thou tomb! neither earth nor yet heaven art to me
> Then how cometh it in thee are conjoined my sun and moon?

When I heard such verses as these, rage was heaped upon my rage; I cried out, "Well-away! how long is this sorrow to last?" and I began repeating:

> O thou tomb! O thou tomb! be his horrors set in blight?
> Hast thou darkened his countenance that sickeneth the soul?
> O thou tomb! neither cess-pool nor pipkin art to me
> Then how cometh it in thee are conjoined soil and coal?

When she heard my words she sprang to her feet crying, "Fie upon thee, thou cur! all this is of thy doings; thou hast wounded my heart's darling and thereby worked me sore woe and thou has wasted his youth so that these three years he hath lain abed more dead than alive!" In my wrath I cried, "O thou foulest of harlots and filthiest of whores ever futtered by negro slaves who are hired to have at thee![1] Yes, indeed it was I who did this good deed"; and snatching up my sword I drew it and made at her to cut her down. But she laughed my words and mine intent to scorn crying, "To heel, hound that thou art! Alas for the past which shall no more come to pass nor shall any one avail the dead to raise. Allah hath indeed now given unto my hand him who did to me this thing, a deed that hath burned my heart with a fire which died not and a flame which might not be quenched!" Then she stood up; and, pronouncing some words to me unintelligible, she said, "By virtue of my egromancy become thou half stone and half man"; whereupon I became what thou seest, unable to rise or sit, and neither dead nor alive. Moreover, she ensorcelled the city with all its streets and garths, and she turned by her gramarye the four islands into four mountains around the tarn whereof thou questionest me; and the citizens, who were of four different faiths, Moslem, Nazarene, Jew and Magian, she transformed by her enchantments into fishes; the Moslems are the white, the Magians red, the Christians blue and the Jews yellow. And every day she tortureth me and scourgeth me with an hundred stripes, each of which draweth floods of blood and cutteth the skin of my shoulders to strips; and lastly she clotheth my upper half with a haircloth and then throweth over them these robes.

After this the Sultan turned towards the young Prince and said, "O youth, thou hast removed one grief only to add

---

[1] The words are the very lowest and coarsest, but the scene is true to Arab life.

another grief; but now, O my friend, where is she; and where is the mausoleum wherein lieth the wounded slave?" "The slave lieth under yon dome," quoth the young man, "and she sitteth in the chamber fronting yonder door. And every day at sunrise she cometh forth, and first strippeth me, and whippeth me with an hundred strokes of the leathern scourge, and I weep and shriek; but there is no power of motion in my lower limbs to keep her off me. After ending her tormenting she visiteth the slave, bringing him wine and boiled meats. And to-morrow at an early hour she will be here." Quoth the King, "By Allah, O youth, I will assuredly do thee a good deed which the world shall not willingly let die, and an act of derring-do which shall be chronicled long after I am dead and gone by."

Then the King sat him by the side of the young Prince and talked till nightfall, when he lay down and slept; but, as soon as the false dawn showed, he arose and, doffing his outer garments, bared his blade and hastened to the place wherein lay the slave. Then he was ware of lighted candles and lamps, and the perfumes of incenses and unguents; and, directed by these, he made for the slave and struck him one stroke, killing him on the spot: after which he lifted him on his back and threw him into a well that was in the palace. Presently he returned and, donning the slave's gear, lay down at length within the mausoleum with the drawn sword laid close to and along his side. After an hour or so the accursed witch came; and, first going to her husband, she stripped off his clothes and, taking a whip, flogged him cruelly while he cried out, "Ah! enough for me the case I am in! take pity on me, O my cousin!" But she replied, "Didst thou take pity on me and spare the life of my true love on whom I doated?" Then she drew the cilice over his raw and bleeding skin and threw the robe upon all and went down to the slave with a goblet of wine and a bowl of meat-broth in her hands. She entered under the dome weeping and wailing, "Well-away!" and crying, "O my lord! speak a word to me! O my master! talk awhile with me!"

The King lowered his voice and, twisting his tongue, spoke after the fashion of the blackamoors and said, "'lack! 'lack! there be no Ma'esty and there be no Might save in Allaah, the Gloriose, the Great!" Now when she heard these words she shouted for joy, and fell to the ground fainting; and when her senses she returned she asked, "O my lord, can it be true that thou hast power of speech?" and the King, making his voice small and faint, answered, "O my cuss! dost thou deserve that I talk to thee and speak with thee?" "Why and wherefore?" rejoined she; and he replied, "The why is that all the livelong

day thou tormentest thy hubby; and he keeps calling on 'eaven
for aid until sleep is strange to me even from evenin' till
mawnin', and he prays and damns, cussing us two, me and
thee, causing me disquiet and much bother: were this not so,
I should long ago have got my health; and it is this which pre-
vents my answering thee." Quoth she, "With thy leave I will
release him from what spell is on him"; and quoth the King,
"Release him and let's have some rest!" She cried, "To hear is
to obey"; and, going from the cenotaph to the palace, she took
a metal bowl and filled it with water and spake over it certain
words which made the contents bubble and boil as a cauldron
seetheth over the fire. With this she sprinkled her husband,
saying, "By virtue of the dread words I have spoken, if thou
becamest thus by my spells, come forth out of that form into
thine own former form."

And lo and behold! the young man shook and trembled;
then he rose to his feet and, rejoicing at his deliverance, cried
aloud, "I testify that there is no god but *the* God, and in very
truth Mohammed is His Apostle, whom Allah bless and keep!"
Then she screamed these words in his face. "Go forth and
return not hither, for if thou do I will surely slay thee"; So he
went from between her hands; and she returned to the dome
and, going down to the sepulchre, she said, "O my lord, come
forth to me that I may look upon thee and thy goodliness!"
The King replied in faint low words, "What thing hast thou
done? Thou hast rid me of the branch but not of the root."
She asked, "O my darling! O my negroling! what is the
root?" And he answered, "Fie on thee, O my cuss! The people
of this city and of the four islands every night when its half
passed lift their heads from the tank in which thou hast turned
them to fishes and cry to Heaven and call down its anger on
me and thee; and this is the reason why my body's baulked
from health. Go at once and set them free; then come to me
and take my hand, and raise me up, for a little strength is
already back in me."

When she heard the King's words (and she still supposed
him to be the slave) she cried joyously, "O my master, on my
head and on my eyes be thy command, Bismillah!" So she
sprang to her feet and, full of joy and gladness, ran down to
the tarn and took a little of its water in the palm of her hand
and spake over it words not to be understood; the fishes lifted
their heads and stood up on the instant like men, the spell on
the people of the city having been removed. What was the lake
again became a crowded capital; the bazars were thronged
with folk who bought and sold; each citizen was occupied with
his own calling and the four hills became islands as they were

36

whilome. Then the young woman, that wicked sorceress, returned to the King and (still thinking he was the negro) said to him, "O my love! stretch forth thy honoured hand that I may assist thee to rise." "Nearer to me," quoth the King in a faint and feigned tone. She came close as to embrace him when he took up the sword lying hid by his side and smote her across the breast, so that the point showed gleaming behind her back. Then he smote her a second time and cut her in twain and cast her to the ground in two halves. After which he fared forth and found the young man, now freed from the spell, awaiting him and gave him joy of his happy release while the Prince kissed his hand with abundant thanks.

Quoth the King, "Wilt thou abide in this city or go with me to my capital?" Quoth the youth, "O King of the Age, wottest thou not what journey is between thee and thy city?" "Two days and a half," answered he; whereupon said the other, "An thou be sleeping, O King, awake! Between thee and thy city is a year's march for a well-girt walker, and thou haddest not come hither in two days and a half save that the city was under enchantment. And I, O King, will never part from thee; no, not even for the twinkling of an eye." The King rejoiced at his words and said, "Thanks be to Allah who hath bestowed thee upon me! From this hour thou art my son and my only son, for that in all my life I have never been blessed with issue." Thereupon they embraced and joyed with exceeding great joy; and, reaching the palace, the Prince who had been spellbound informed his lords and his grandees that he was about to visit the Holy Places as a pilgrim, and bade them get ready all things necessary for the occasion. The preparations lasted ten days, after which he set out with the Sultan, whose heart burned in yearning for his city whence he had been absent a whole twelvemonth.

They journeyed with an escort of Mamelukes[1] carrying all manner of precious gifts and rarities, nor stinted they wayfaring day and night for a full year until they approached the Sultan's capital, and sent on messengers to announce their coming. Then the Wazir and the whole army came out to meet him in joy and gladness, for they had given up all hope of ever seeing their King; and the troops kissed the ground before him and wished him joy of his safety. He entered and took seat upon his throne and the Minister came before him and, when acquainted with all that had befallen the young Prince, he congratulated him on his narrow escape. When order was restored throughout the land the King gave largesse to many

---

[1] White slaves trained to arms.

of his people, and said to the Wazir, "Hither the Fisherman who brought us the fishes!" So he sent for the man who had been the first cause of the city and the citizens being delivered from enchantment and, when he came into the presence, the Sultan bestowed upon him a dress of honour, and questioned him of his condition and whether he had children. The Fisherman gave him to know that he had two daughters and a son, so the King sent for them and, taking one daughter to wife, gave the other to the young Prince and made the son his head treasurer. Furthermore, he invested his Wazir with the Sultanate of the City in the Black Islands whilome belonging to the young Prince, and dispatched with him an escort of fifty armed slaves together with dresses of honour for all the Emirs and Grandees. The Wazir kissed hands and fared forth on his way; while the Sultan and the Prince abode at home in all the solace and the delight of life; and the Fisherman became the richest man of his age, and his daughters wived with the Kings, until death came to them.

The Barber's Tale of his Second Brother

KNOW, O Commander of the Faithful, that my second brother's name was Al-Haddar, that is, the Babbler, and he was the paralytic. Now it happened to him one day, as he was going about his business, that an old woman accosted him and said, "Stop a little, my good man, that I may tell thee of somewhat which, if it be to thy liking, thou shalt do for me, and I will pray Allah to give thee good of it!" My brother stopped and she went on, "I will put thee in the way of a certain thing, so thou not be prodigal of speech." "On with thy talk," quoth he; and she, "What sayest thou to handsome quarters and a fair garden with flowing waters, flowers blooming, and fruit growing, and old wine going and a pretty young face whose owner thou mayest embrace from dark till dawn? If thou do whatso I bid thee thou shalt see something greatly to thy advantage."

"And is all this in the world?" asked my brother; and she answered, "Yes, and it shall be thine, so thou be reasonable and leave idle curiosity and many words, and do my bidding." "I will indeed, O my lady," said he. "How is it thou hast preferred me in this matter before all men and what is it that so much pleaseth thee in me?" Quoth she, "Did I not bid thee be spare of speech? Hold thy peace and follow me. Know, that the young lady, to whom I shall carry thee, loveth to have her own way and hateth being thwarted and all who gainsay; so,

39

if thou humour her, thou shalt come to thy desire of her."
And my brother said, "I will not cross her in anything." Then
she went on and my brother followed her, an-hungering after
what she described to him, till they entered a fine large house,
handsome and choicely furnished, full of eunuchs and
servants and showing signs of prosperity from top to bottom.
And she was carrying him to the upper story when the people
of the house said to him, "What dost thou here?" But the old
woman answered them, "Hold your peace and trouble him
not: he is a workman and we have occasion for him."

Then she brought him into a fine great pavilion, with a
garden in its midst, never eyes saw a fairer, and made him sit
upon a handsome couch. He had not sat long, before he heard
a loud noise and in came a troop of slave-girls surrounding a
lady like the moon on the night of its fullest. When he saw her,
he rose up and made an obeisance to her, whereupon she welcomed him and bade him be seated. So he sat down and she
said to him, "Allah advance thee to honour! Is all well with
thee?" "O my lady," he answered, "all with me is right well."
Then she bade bring in food, and they set before her delicate
viands; so she sat down to eat, making a show of affection to
my brother and jesting with him, though all the while she
could not refrain from laughing; but as often as he looked at
her, she signed towards her handmaidens as though she were
laughing at them. My brother (the ass!) understood nothing;
but, in the excess of his ridiculous passion, he fancied that the
lady was in love with him and that she would soon grant him
his desire.

When they had done eating, they set on the wine and there
came in ten maidens like moons, with lutes ready strung in
their hands, and fell to singing with full voices, sweet and sad,
whereupon delight gat hold upon him and he took the cup
from the lady's hands and drank it standing. Then she drank
a cup of wine and my brother (still standing) said to her,
"Health," and bowed to her. She handed him another cup and
he drank it off, when she slapped him hard on the nape of his
neck. Upon this my brother would have gone out of the house
in anger; but the old woman followed him and winked to him
to return. So he came back and the lady bade him sit, and he
sat down without a word. Then she again slapped him on the
nape of his neck; and the second slapping did not suffice her,
she must needs make all her handmaidens also slap and cuff
him, while he kept saying to the old woman, "I never saw
aught nicer than this." She on her side ceased not exclaiming,
"Enough, enough, I conjure thee, O my mistress!"; but the
women slapped him till he wellnigh swooned away. Presently

my brother rose and went out to obey a call of nature, but the old woman overtook him, and said, "Be patient a little and thou shalt win to thy wish." "How much longer have I to wait?" my brother replied, "this slapping hath made me feel faint." "As soon as she is warm with wine," answered she, "thou shalt have thy desire."

So he returned to his place and sat down, whereupon all the handmaidens stood up and the lady bade them perfume him with pastiles and besprinkle his face with rose-water. Then said she to him, "Allah advance thee to honour! Thou hast entered my house and hast borne with my conditions, for whoso thwarteth me I turn him away, and whoso is patient hath his desire." "O mistress mine," said he, "I am thy slave and in the hollow of thine hand!" "Know then," continued she, "that Allah hath made me passionately fond of frolic; and whoso falleth in with my humour cometh by whatso he wisheth." Then she ordered her maidens to sing with loud voices till the whole company was delighted; after which she said to one of them, "Take thy lord, and do what is needful for him, and bring him back to me forthright." So the damsel took my brother (and he not knowing what she would do with him); but the old woman overtook him and said, "Be patient; there remaineth but little to do." At this his face brightened and he stood up before the lady while the old woman kept saying, "Be patient; thou wilt now at once win to thy wish!"; till he said, "Tell me, what she would have the maiden do with me?" "Nothing but good," replied she, "as I am thy sacrifice! She wisheth only to dye thy eyebrows and pluck out thy mustachios." Quoth he, "As for the dyeing of my eyebrows, that will come off with washing, but for the plucking of my mustachios that indeed is a somewhat painful process." "Be cautious how thou cross her," cried the old woman "for she hath set her heart on thee."

So my brother patiently suffered her to dye his eyebrows and pluck out his mustachios; after which the maiden returned to her mistress and told her. Quoth she, "Remaineth now only one other thing to be done; thou must shave his beard and make him a smooth o' face." So the maiden went back and told him what her mistress had bidden her do; and my brother (the blockhead!) said to her, "How shall I do what will disgrace me before the folk?" But the old woman said, "She would do on this wise only that thou mayst be as a beardless youth and that no hair be left on thy face to scratch and prick her delicate cheeks; for indeed she is passionately in love with thee. So be patient and thou shalt attain thine object." My brother *was* patient and did her bidding and let her shave

41

off his beard and, when he was brought back to the lady, lo! he appeared dyed red as to his eyebrows, plucked of both mustachios, shorn of his beard, rouged on both cheeks. At first she was affrighted at him; then she made mockery of him and, laughing till she fell upon her back, said, "O my lord, thou hast indeed won my heart by thy good nature!" Then she conjured him, by her life, to stand up and dance, and he

arose, and capered about, and there was not a cushion in the house but she threw it at his head, and in like manner did all her women who also kept pelting him with oranges and lemons and citrons till he fell down senseless from the cuffing on the nape of the neck, the pillowing and the fruit-pelting.

"Now thou hast attained thy wish," said the old woman when he came round; "there are no more blows in store for thee and there remaineth but one little thing to do. It is her wont, when she is in her cups, to let no one have her until she put off her dress and trousers and remain stark naked. Then she will bid thee doff thy clothes and run; and do thou follow her from place to place till thy prickle stands at fullest point, when she will yield to thee"; adding, "Strip off thy clothes at once." So he rose, wellnigh lost in ecstasy, and, doffing his raiment, showed himself mother-naked. Whereupon the lady stripped also and said to my brother, "If thou want anything run after me till thou catch me." Then she set out at a run and he ran after her while she rushed into room after room and rushed out of room after room, my brother scampering after her in a rage of desire like a veritable madman, with yard standing terribly tall. After much of this kind she dashed into a darkened place, and he dashed after her; but suddenly he trod upon a yielding spot, which gave way under his weight; and, before he was aware where he was, he found himself in the midst of a crowded market, part of the bazar of the leather-sellers who were crying the prices of skins and hides and buying and selling.

When they saw him in his plight, naked, with standing yard, shorn of beard and mustachios, with eyebrows dyed red, and cheeks ruddled with rouge, they shouted and clapped their hands at him, and set to flogging him with skins upon his bare body till a swoon came over him. Then they threw him on the back of an ass and carried him to the Chief of Police. Quoth the Chief, "What is this?" Quoth they, "This fellow fell suddenly upon us out of the Wazir's house in this state." So the Prefect gave him an hundred lashes and then banished him from Baghdad.

Tale of Ghanim Bin Ayyub,
the Distraught, the Thrall o' Love

IT hath reached me, O auspicious King, that in times of yore,
and in years and ages long gone before, there lived in
Damascus a merchant among the merchants, a wealthy man
who had a son like the moon on the night of his fullness and
withal sweet of speech, who was named Ghanim bin Ayyub,
surnamed the Distraught, the Thrall o' Love. He had also a
daughter, own sister to Ghanim, who was called Fitnah, a
damsel unique in beauty and loveliness. Their father died and
left them abundant wealth, and amongst other things an
hundred loads[1] of silks and brocades, musk-pods and mother
o' pearl; and there was written on every bale, "This is of the
packages intended for Baghdad," it having been his purpose to
make the journey hither, when Almighty Allah took him to
Himself, which was in the time of the Caliph Harun al-
Rashid.

After a while his son took the loads and, bidding farewell to
his mother and kindred and townsfolk, went forth with a
company of merchants, putting his trust in Allah Almighty,
who decreed him safety, so that he arrived without let or stay
at Baghdad. There he hired for himself a fair dwelling-house
which he furnished with carpets and cushions, curtains and
hangings; and therein stored his bales and stabled his mules
and camels, after which he abode a while resting. Presently the

---

[1] *I.e.* camel-loads about 300 lb.; and for long journeys 250 lb.

merchants and notables of Baghdad came and saluted him, after which he took a bundle containing ten pieces of costly stuffs, with the prices written on them, and carried it to the merchants' bazar, where they welcomed and saluted him and showed him all honour, and, making him dismount from his beast, seated him in the shop of the Syndic of the market, to whom he delivered the package. He opened it and, drawing out the pieces of stuff, sold them for him at a profit of two dinars on every dinar of prime cost. At this Ghanim rejoiced and kept selling his silks and stuffs one after another, and ceased not to do on this wise for a full year.

On the first day of the following year he went, as was his wont, to the Exchange which was in the bazar, but found the gate shut, and inquiring the reason was told, "One of the merchants is dead and all the others have gone to follow his bier. And why shouldst thou not win the meed of good deeds by walking with them?"[1] He replied, "Yes," and asked for the quarter where the funeral was taking place, and one directed him thereto. So he purified himself by the Wazu-ablution[2] and repaired with the other merchants to the oratory, where they prayed over the dead, then walked before the bier to the burial place; and Ghanim, who was a bashful man, followed them, being ashamed to leave them. They presently issued from the city and passed through the tombs until they reached the grave, where they found that the deceased's kith and kin had pitched a tent over the tomb and had brought thither lamps and wax candles. So they buried the body and sat down while the readers read out and recited the Koran over the grave; and Ghanim sat with them, being overcome with bashfulness, and saying to himself, "I cannot well go away till they do."

They tarried, listening to the Koranic perlection till nightfall, when the servants set supper and sweetmeats before them and they ate till they were satisfied; then they washed their hands and again took their places. But Ghanim's mind was preoccupied with his house and goods, being in fear of robbers, and he said to himself, "I am a stranger here and supposed to have money; if I pass the night abroad the thieves will steal my money-bags and my bales to boot." So, when he could no longer control his fear, he arose and left the assembly, having first asked leave to go about some urgent business; and following the signs of the road he soon came to the city gate. But it was midnight, and he found the doors locked and saw none

---

[1] It is meritorious to accompany the funeral cortège of a Moslem even for a few paces.
[2] Otherwise he could not have joined in the prayers.

going or coming nor heard aught but the hounds baying and the wolves howling. At this he exclaimed, "There is no Majesty and there is no Might save in Allah! I was in fear for my property and came back on its account, but now I find the gate shut and I am in mortal fear for my life!" Then he turned back and, looking out for a place where he could sleep till morning, presently found a Santon's tomb, a square of four walls with a date tree in the central court and a granite gateway. The door was wide open; so he entered and would fain have slept, but sleep came not to him; and terror and a sense of desolation oppressed him, for that he was alone amidst the tombs. So he rose to his feet and, opening the door, looked out, and lo! he was ware of a light afar off in the direction of the city gate; then, walking a little way towards it, he saw that it was on the road whereby he had reached the tomb. This made him fear for his life, so he hastily shut the door and climbed to the top of the date tree, where he hid himself in the heart of the fronds. The light came nearer and nearer till it was close to the tomb; then it stopped, and he saw three slaves, two bearing a chest and one with a lanthorn, an adze and a basket containing some mortar.

When they reached the tomb, one of those who were carrying the case said, "What aileth thee, O Sawab?"; and said the other, "What is the matter, O Kafur?"[1] Quoth he, "Were we not here at supper-tide and did we not leave the door open?" "Yes," replied the other, "that is true." "See," said Kafur, "now it is shut and barred." "How weak are your wits!" cried the third who bore the adze, and his name was Bukhayt, "know ye not that the owners of the gardens used to come out from Baghdad and tend them and, when evening closes upon them, they enter this place and shut the door, for fear lest the wicked black men, like ourselves, should catch them and roast 'em and eat 'em."[2] "Thou sayest sooth," said the two others, "but, by Allah, however that may be, none amongst us is weaker of wits than thou." "If ye do not believe me," said Bukhayt, "let us enter the tomb and I will rouse the rat for you; for I doubt not but that, when he saw the light and us making for the place, he ran up the date tree and hid there for fear of us."

When Ghanim heard this, he said in himself, "O curstest of slaves! May Allah not have thee in His holy keeping for this thy craft and keenness of wit! There is no Majesty and there is no Might save in Allah, the Glorious, the Great! How shall I win free of these blackamoors?" Then said the two who

---

1 *I.e.* "Camphor" to a negro as we say "Snowball," by the figure antiphrase.
2 There are, as I have shown, not a few cannibal tribes in Central Africa and these at times find their way into the slave-market.

bore the box to him of the adze, "Swarm up the wall and open the gate for us, O Bukhayt, for we are tired of carrying the chest on our necks; and when thou hast opened the gate thou shalt have one of these we catch inside, a fine fat rat which we will fry for thee after such excellent fashion that not a speck of his fat shall be lost." But Bukhayt answered, "I am afraid of somewhat which my weak wits have suggested to me; we should do better to throw the chest over the gateway, for it is our treasure." "If we throw it 'twill break," replied they; and he said, "I fear lest there be robbers within who murder folk and plunder their goods, for evening is their time of entering such places and dividing their spoil." "O thou weak o' wits," said both the bearers of the box, "how could they ever get in here!"[1] Then they set down the chest, and climbing over the wall, dropped inside and opened the gate, whilst the third slave (he that was called Bukhayt) stood by them holding the adze, the lanthorn and the hand-basket containing the mortar. After this they locked the gate and sat down; and presently one of them said, "O my brethren, we are wearied with walking and with lifting up and setting down the chest, and with unlocking and locking the gate; and now 'tis midnight, and we have no breath left to open a tomb and bury the box; so let us rest here two or three hours, then rise and do the job.

"Meanwhile each of us shall tell how he came to be castrated and all that befell him from first to last, the better to pass away our time while we take our rest." Thereupon the first, he of the lanthorn and whose name was Bukhayt, said, "I'll tell you my tale." "Say on," replied they; so he began as follows the

TALE OF THE FIRST EUNUCH, BUKHAYT

KNOW, O my brothers, that when I was a little one, some five years old, I was taken home from my native country by a slave-driver who sold me to a certain Apparitor. My purchaser had a daughter three years old, with whom I was brought up, and they used to make mock of me, letting me play with her and dance for her[2] and sing to her, till I reached the age of twelve and she that of ten; and even then they did not forbid me seeing her. One day I went in to her and found her sitting in an inner room, and she looked as if she had just come out of

---

[1] *I.e.* after we bar the door.

[2] This familiarity with blackamoor slave-boys is common in Egypt and often ends as in the story; Egyptian blood is sufficiently mixed with negro to breed inclination for miscegenation. But here the girl was wickedly neglected by her mother at such an age as ten.

the bath which was in the house; for she was scented with essences and reek of aromatic woods, and her face shone like the circle of the moon on the fourteenth night. She began to sport with me, and I with her. Now I had just reached the age of puberty; so my prickle stood at point, as it were a huge key. Then she threw me on my back and, mounting astraddle on my breast, fell a-wriggling and a-bucking me till she had uncovered my yard. When she saw it standing with head erect, she hent it in hand and began rubbing it upon the lips of her

little slit outside her petticoat-trousers. Thereat hot lust stirred in me and I threw my arms round her, while she wound hers about my neck and hugged me to her with all her might, till, before I knew what I did, my pizzle split up her trousers and entered her slit and did away her maidenhead.

When I saw this, I ran off and took refuge with one of my comrades. Presently her mother came in to her; and, seeing her in this case, fainted clean away. However, she managed the matter advisedly and hid it from the girl's father out of good will to me; nor did they cease to call to me and coax me, till they took me from where I was. After two months had passed by, her mother married her to a young man, a barber who used to shave her papa, and portioned and fitted her out of her own monies; whilst the father knew nothing of what had passed. On the night of consummation they cut the throat of a pigeon poult and sprinkled the blood on her shift.[1] After a while they seized me unawares and gelded me; and, when they brought her to her bridegroom, they made me her Agha,[2] her eunuch, to walk before her wheresoever she went, whether to the bath or to her father's house. I abode with her a long time, enjoying her beauty and loveliness by way of kissing and clipping and coupling with her,[3] till she died, and her husband and mother and father died also, when they seized me for the Royal Treasury as being the property of an intestate, and I found my way hither, where I became your comrade. This, then, O my brethren, is the cause of my cullions being cut off; and peace be with you!

He ceased, and his fellow began in these words the

TALE OF THE SECOND EUNUCH, KAFUR[4]

KNOW, O my brothers, that, when beginning service as a boy of eight, I used to tell the slave-dealers regularly and exactly one lie every year, so that they fell out with one another, till at last my master lost patience with me and, carrying me down to the market, ordered the brokers to cry, "Who will buy this slave, knowing his blemish and making allowance for it?" He did so, and they asked him, "Pray, what may be his blemish?" and he answered, "He telleth me one single lie every year." Now a man that was a merchant came up and said to the broker, "How much do they allow for him with his blemish?" "They allow six hundred dirhams," he replied; and said the other, "Thou shalt have twenty dirhams for thyself." So he arranged between him and the slave-dealer who took the coin from him and the broker carried me to the merchant's house and departed, after receiving his brokerage. The trader clothed me

---

1 This ancient and venerable practice of inspecting the marriage-sheet is still religiously preserved in most parts of the East; and in old-fashioned Moslem families it is publicly exposed in the Harim to prove that the "domestic calamity" (the daughter) went to her husband a clean maid. Also the general idea is that no blood will impose upon the experts, or jury of matrons, except that of a pigeon poult, which exactly resembles hymeneal blood—when not subjected to the microscope.

2 "Agha" Turk.=sir, gentleman; is politely addressed to a eunuch.

3 As Bukhayt tells us he lost only his testes, consequently his *erectio et distensio penis* was as that of a boy before puberty and it would last as long as his heart and circulation kept sound. Hence the eunuch who preserves his penis is much prized in the Zenanah where some women prefer him to the entire man on account of his long performance of the deed of kind.

4 The tale is interesting as well as amusing, excellently describing the extra-vagances still practised in middle-class Moslem families on the death of the pater familias.

with suitable dress, and I stayed in his service the rest of my twelve-month, until the new year began happily.

It was a blessed season, plenteous in the produce of the earth, and the merchants used to feast every day at the house of some one among them, till it was my master's turn to entertain them in a flower garden without the city. So he and the other merchants went to the garden, taking with them all that they required of provaunt and else beside, and sat eating and carousing and drinking till mid-day, when my master, having need of some matter from his home, said to me, "O slave, mount

the she-mule and hie thee to the house and bring from thy mistress such and such a thing and return quickly." I obeyed his bidding and started for the house but, as I drew near it, I began to cry out and shed tears, whereupon all the people of the quarter collected, great and small; and my master's wife and daughters, hearing the noise I was making, opened the door and asked me what was the matter. Said I, "My master was sitting with his friends beneath an old wall, and it fell on one and all of them; and when I saw what had happened to them, I mounted the mule and came hither in haste to tell you."

When my master's daughters and wife heard this, they screamed and rent their raiment and beat their faces, whilst the neighbours came around them. Then the wife overturned the furniture of the house, one thing upon another, and tore down the shelves and broke the windows and the lattices and smeared the walls with mud and indigo, saying to me, "Woe to thee, O Kafur! come help me to tear down these cupboards and break up these vessels and this china-ware, and the rest of it." So I went to her and aided her to smash all the shelves in the house and whatever stood upon them, after which I went round about the terrace roofs and every part of the place, spoiling all I could and leaving no china in the house unbroken, till I had laid waste the whole, crying out the while, "Wellaway! my master!" Then my mistress fared forth bare faced wearing a handkerchief and naught else, and her daughters and the children sallied out with her, and said to me, "O Kafur, go thou before us and show us the place where thy master lieth dead, that we may take him from under the fallen wall and lay him on a bier and bear him to the house and give him a fine funeral."

So I went forth before them crying out, "Alack, my master!"; and they after me with faces and heads bare and all shrieking, "Alas! Alas for the man!" Now there remained none in the quarter, neither man nor woman, nor epicene, nor youth nor maid, nor child nor old trot, but went with us smiting their faces and weeping bitterly and I led them leisurely through the whole city. The folk asked them what was the matter, whereupon they told them what they had heard from me, and all exclaimed, "There is no Majesty and there is no Might save in Allah!" Then said one of them, "He was a personage of consequence; so let us go to the Governor and tell him what hath befallen him." When they told the Governor, he rose and mounted and, taking with him labourers, with spades and baskets, went on my track, with many people behind him; and I ran on before them, howling and casting dust on my head and beating my face, followed by my mistress and her children keening for the dead. But I got ahead of them and entered the garden before them, and when my master saw me in this state, I smiting my face and saying, "Wellaway! my mistress! Alas! Alas! Alas! Who is left to take pity on me, now that my mistress is gone? Would I had been a sacrifice for her!" he stood aghast and his colour waxed yellow and he said to me, "What aileth thee, O Kafur! What *is* the matter?"

"O my lord," I replied, "when thou sentest me to the house, I found that the saloon wall had given way and had fallen like a layer upon my mistress and her children!" "And did not thy mistress escape?" "No, by Allah, O my master; not one of them was saved; the first to die was my mistress, thine elder daughter!" "And did not my younger daughter escape?"

"No, she did not!" "And what became of the mare-mule I
used to ride? Is she safe?" "No, by Allah, O my master, the
house walls and the stable walls buried every living thing that
was within doors, even to the sheep and geese and poultry, so
that they all became a heap of flesh, and the dogs and cats are
eating them and not one of them is left alive." "And hath not
thy master, my elder son, escaped?" "No, by Allah! not one
of them was saved, and now there is naught left of house or
household, nor even a sign of them; and, as for the sheep and
geese and hens, the cats and dogs have devoured them."

When my master heard this the light became night before
his sight; his wits were dazed and he so lost command of his
senses that he could not stand firm on his feet; he was as one
struck with a sudden palsy and his back was like to break. Then
he rent his raiment and plucked out his beard and casting, his
turband from off his head, buffeted his face till the blood ran
down and he cried aloud, "Alas, my children! Alas, my wife!
Alas, my calamity! To whom ever befell that which hath
befallen me?" The merchants, his friends, also cried aloud at
his crying and wept for his weeping and tore their clothes,
being moved to pity of his case; and so my master went out
of the garden, smiting his face with such violence that from
excess of pain he staggered like one drunken with wine. As he
and the merchants came forth from the garden gate, behold,
they saw a great cloud of dust and heard a loud noise of crying
and lamentation; so they looked, and lo! it was the Governor
with his attendants and the townsfolk, a world of people, who
had come out to look on, and my master's family following
them, all screaming and crying aloud and weeping exceeding
sore weeping.

The first to address my owner were his wife and children;
and when he saw them he was confounded and laughed[1] and
said to them, "How is it with all of you and what befell you
in the house and what hath come to pass to you?" When they
saw him they exclaimed, "Praise be to Allah for thy preservation!" and threw themselves upon him and his children hung
about him crying, "Alack, our father! Thanks to Allah for
thy safety, O our father!" And his wife said to him, "Art
thou indeed well? Laud to Allah who hath shown us thy face
in safety!" And, indeed, she was confounded and her reason
fled when she saw him, and she asked, "O, my lord, how didst
thou escape, thou and thy friends and merchants?"; and he
answered her, "And how fared it with thee in the house?"
Quoth they, "We were all well, whole and healthy, nor hath

---

1 The usual hysterical laughter of this nervous race.

aught of evil befallen us in the house, save that thy slave Kafur came to us, bareheaded, with torn garments, and howling, 'Alas, the master! Alas, the master!' So we asked him, 'What tidings, O Kafur?' and he answered, 'A wall of the garden hath fallen on my master and his friends the merchants, and they are all crushed and dead!'" "By Allah," said my master, "he came to me but now, howling, 'Alas, my mistress! Alas, the children of the mistress!' and said, 'My mistress and her children are all dead, every one of them!'"

Then he looked round, and seeing me with my turband rent in rags round my neck, howling and weeping with exceeding weeping and throwing dust upon my head, he cried out at me. So I came to him and he said, "Woe to thee, O ill-omened slave! O whoreson knave! O thou damned breed! What mischief hast thou wrought? By Allah! I will flog thy skin from thy flesh and cut thy flesh from thy bones!" I rejoined, "By Allah, thou canst do nothing of the kind with me, O my lord, for thou boughtest me with my blemish; and there are honest men to bear witness against thee that thou didst so accepting the condition, and that thou knewest of my fault, which is to tell one lie every year. Now this is only a half-lie, but by the end of the year I will tell the other half, then will the lie stand whole and complete." "O dog, son of a dog!" cried my master, "O most accursed of slaves, is this all of it but a half-lie? Verily, if it be a half-lie 'tis a whole calamity! Get thee from me, thou art free in the face of Allah!" "By Allah," rejoined I, "if thou free me, I will not free thee till my year is completed and I have told thee the half-lie which is left. When this is done, go down with me to the slave-market and sell me as thou boughtest me to whoso will buy me with my blemish; but thou shalt not manumit me, for I have no handicraft whereby to gain my living;[1] and this my demand is a matter of law which the doctors have laid down in the Chapter of Emancipation."

While we were at these words, up came the crowd of people, and the neighbours of the quarter, men, women and children, together with the Governor and his suite, offering condolence. So my master and the other merchants went up to him and informed him of the adventure, and how this was but a half-lie, at which all wondered, deeming it a whole lie and a big one. And they cursed me and reviled me, while I stood laughing and grinning at them, till at last I asked, "How shall my master slay me when he bought me with this blemish?" Then my master returned home and found his house in ruins, and it

---

[1] Here the slave refuses to be set free and starve. For a master to do so without ample reason is held disgraceful.

was I who had laid waste the greater part of it,[1] having broken things which were worth much money, as also had done his wife, who said to him, " 'Twas Kafur who broke the vessels and chinaware." Thereupon his rage redoubled and he struck hand upon hand, explaining, "By Allah! in my life never saw I a whoreson like this slave; and he saith this is but a half-lie! How, then, if he had told me a whole lie? He would ruin a city, aye, or even two." Then in his fury he went to the Governor, and they gave me a neat thing in the bastinado line and made me eat stick till I was lost to the world and a fainting fit came on me; and, whilst I was yet senseless, they brought the barber who docked me and gelded me and cauterised the wound.

When I revived I found myself a clean eunuch with nothing left, and my master said to me, "Even as thou hast burned my heart for the things I held dearest, so have I burnt thy heart for that of thy members whereby thou settest most store!" Then he took me and sold me at a profit, for that I was become an eunuch. And I ceased not bringing trouble upon all, wherever I was sold, and was shifted from lord to lord and from notable to notable, being sold and being bought, till I entered the palace of the Commander of the Faithful. But now my spirit is broken and my tricks are gone from me, so—alas!—are my ballocks.

When the two slaves heard his history, they laughed at him and chaffed him and said, "Truly thou art skite and skite-son! Thou liedest an odious lie." Then quoth they to the third slave, "Tell us thy tale." "O sons of my uncle," quoth he, "all that ye have said is idle; I will tell you the cause of my losing my testicles, and indeed I deserved to lose even more, for I futtered both my mistress and my master's eldest son and heir; but my story is a long one and this is not the time to tell it; for the dawn, O my cousins, draweth near and if morning come upon us with this chest still unburied, we shall get into sore disgrace and our lives will pay for it. So up with you and open the door and, when we get back to the palace, I will tell you my story and the cause of my losing my precious stones."

Then he swarmed up and dropped down from the wall inside and opened the door, so they entered and, setting down the lantern, dug between four tombs a hole as long as the chest and of the same breadth. Kafur plied the spade and Sawab removed the earth by baskets-full till they reached the depth of the stature of a man, when they laid the chest in the hole

---

1 This is quite true to nature. The most remarkable thing in the wild Central African is his enormous development of "destructiveness". At Zanzibar I never saw a slave break a glass or plate without a grin or a chuckle of satisfaction.

and threw back the earth over it; then they went forth and, shutting the door, disappeared from Ghanim's eyes. When all was quiet and he felt sure that he was left alone in the place, his thought was busied about what the chest contained, and he said to himself, "Would that I knew the contents of that box!" However, he waited till day broke, when morning shone and showed her sheen; whereupon he came down from the date tree and scooped away the earth with his hands, till the box was laid bare and disengaged from the ground. Then he took a

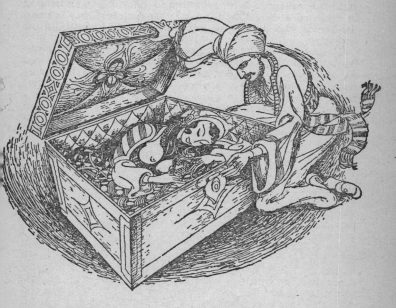

large stone and hammered at the lock till he broke it and, opening the lid, beheld a young lady, a model of beauty and loveliness, clad in the richest of garments and jewels of gold and such necklaces of precious stones that, were the Sultan's country evened with them, it would not pay their price. She had been drugged with Bhang, but her bosom, rising and falling, showed that her breath had not departed.

When Ghanim saw her, he knew that some one had played her false and hocussed her; so he pulled her out of the chest and laid her on the ground with her face upwards. As soon as she smelt the breeze, and the air entered her nostrils, mouth and lungs, she sneezed and choked and coughed, when there fell from out her throat a pill of Cretan Bhang; had an elephant smelt it, it would have slept from night to night. Then she opened her eyes and glancing around said, in sweet voice and gracious words, "Woe to thee, O wind! there is naught in thee to satisfy the thirsty, nor aught to gratify one whose thirst is satisfied! Where is Zahr al-Bostan?" But no one answered her, so she turned her and cried out, "Ho, Sabibah! Shajarat al-Durr! Nur al-Huda! Najmat al-Subh! be ye awake? Shahwah, Nuzhah, Halwa, Zarifah, out on you, speak!" But no one answered her, so she looked all around and said, "Woe's me! have they entombed me in the tombs. O thou who knowest what man's thoughts enwombs and who givest compensation on the Day of Doom, who can have brought me from amid hanging screens and curtains veiling the harim-rooms and set me down between four tombs?"

All this while Ghanim was standing by: then he said to her, "O my lady, here are neither screened rooms nor palace harims nor yet tombs; only the slave henceforth devoted to thy love, Ghanim bin Ayyub, sent to thee by the Omniscient One above, that all thy troubles He may remove and win for thee every wish that doth behove!" Then he held his peace. She was reassured by his words and cried, "I testify that there is no god but *the* God, and I testify that Mohammed is the Apostle of God!"; then she turned to Ghanim and, placing her hands before her face, said to him in the sweetest speech, "O blessed youth, who brought me hither? See, I am now come to myself." "O my lady," he replied, "three slave-eunuchs came here bearing this chest"; and related to her the whole of what had befallen him, and how evening having closed upon him had proved the cause of her preservation, otherwise she had died smothered.[1] Then he asked her who she was and what was her story, and she answered, "O youth, thanks be to Allah who hath cast me into the hands of the like of thee! But now rise and put me back into the box; then fare forth upon the road and hire the first camel-driver or muleteer thou findest to carry it to thy house. When I am there, all will be well and I will tell thee my tale and acquaint thee with my adventures, and great shall be thy gain by means of me."

At this he rejoiced and went outside the tomb. The day was now dazzling bright and the firmament shone with light and the folk had begun to circulate; so he hired a man with a mule and, bringing him to the tomb, lifted the chest wherein he

---

[1] This mode of disposing of a rival was very common in harims. But it had its difficulties and the river was (and is) preferred.

had put the damsel and set it on the mule. Her love now engrossed his heart and he fared homeward with her rejoicing, for that she was a girl worth ten thousand gold pieces and her raiment and ornaments would fetch a mint of money. As soon as he arrived at his house he carried in the chest and opened it and took out the young lady, who looked about her and, seeing that the place was handsome, spread with carpets and dight with cheerful colours and other deckings, and noting the stuffs up-piled and packed bales and other else than that, knew that he was a substantial merchant and a man of much money. Thereupon she uncovered her face and looked at him, and lo! he was a fair youth; so when she saw him she loved him and said, "O my lord, bring up something to eat." "On my head and mine eyes!" replied he; and, going down to the bazar, bought a roasted lamb and a dish of sweetmeats, and with these dry fruits and wax candles, besides wine and whatsoever was required of drinking-materials, not forgetting perfumes. With all this gear he returned to the house; and when the damsel saw him she laughed and kissed him and clàsped his neck. Then she began caressing him, which made his love wax hotter till it got the mastery of his heart.

They ate and drank and each had conceived the fondest affection; for indeed the two were one in age and one in loveliness; and when night came on Ghanim bin Ayyub, the Distraught, the Thrall o' Love, rose and lit the wax candles and lamps till the place blazed with light; after which he produced the wine service and spread the table. Then both sat down again, he and she, and he kept filling and giving her to drink, and she kept filling and giving him to drink, and they played and toyed and laughed and recited verses; whilst their joy increased and they clove in closer love each to each (glory be to the Uniter of Hearts!). They ceased not to carouse after this fashion till near upon dawn when drowsiness overcame them and they slept where they were, apart each from other, till the morning.[1] Then Ghanim arose, and going to the market bought all they required of meat and vegetables and wine and what not, and brought them to the house; whereupon both sat down to eat and ate their sufficiency, when he set on wine. They drank, and each played with each, till their cheeks flushed red and their eyes took a darker hue and Ghanim's soul longed to kiss the girl and to lie with her and he said, "O my lady, grant me one kiss of that dear mouth: perchance 'twill quench the fire of my heart." "O Ghanim," replied she, "wait till I am drunk and dead to the world; then steal a kiss of me, secretly

---

[1] He did not sleep with her because he suspected some palace mystery which suggested prudence; she also had her reasons.

and on such wise that I may not know thou hast kissed me."
Then she rose, and taking off her upper dress sat in a thin
shift of fine linen and a silken headkerchief.

At this, passion inflamed Ghanim and he said to her, "O my
lady, wilt thou not vouchsafe me what I asked of thee?" "By
Allah," she replied, "that may not be thine, for there is written
upon my trouser-string a hard word!" Thereupon Ghanim's
heart sank and desire grew on him as its object offered difficulties. Then his affection increased and love fires rose hotter
in his heart, while she refused herself to him, saying, "Thou
canst not possess me." They ceased not to make love and enjoy
their wine and wassail, whilst Ghanim was drowned in the sea
of love and longing; but she redoubled in coyness and cruelty
till the night brought on the darkness and let fall on them the
skirts of sleep.

Thereupon Ghanim rose and lit the lamps and wax candles
and refreshed the room and removed the table; then he took,
her feet and kissed them and, finding them like fresh cream,
pressed his face on them[1] and said to her, "O my lady, take
pity on one thy love hath ta'en and thine eyes hath slain; for
indeed I were heart-whole but for thy bane!" And he wept
somewhat. "O my lord, and light of my eyes," quoth she, "by
Allah, I love thee in very sooth and I trust to thy truth, but I
know that I may not be thine." "And what is the obstacle?"
asked he; when she answered, "To-night I will tell thee my
tale, that thou mayst accept my excuse." Then she threw herself upon him and, winding her arms like a necklace about
his neck, kissed him and caressed him and promised him her
favours; and they ceased not playing and laughing till love
gat the firmest hold upon both their hearts. And so it continued a whole month, both passing the night on a single
carpet-bed, but whenever he would enjoy her, she put him off;
whilst mutual love increased upon them and each could hardly
abstain from other.

One night, as he lay by her side, and both were warm with
wine, Ghanim passed his hand over her breasts and stroked
them; then he slipped it down to her waist as far as her navel.
She awoke and, sitting up, put her hand to her trousers, and
finding them fast tied once more fell asleep. Presently, he
again felt her, and sliding his hand down to her trouser-
string, began pulling at it, whereupon she awoke and sat upright. Ghanim also sat up by her side and she asked him,
"What dost thou want?" "I want to lie with thee," he answered, "and that we may deal openly and frankly with each

---

1 Like a fawning dog Ghanim is a "softy" lover, a favourite character in Arab tales;
and by contrast the girl is masterful enough.

other." Quoth she, "I must now declare to thee my case, that thou mayst know my quality; then will my secret be disclosed to thee and my excuse become manifest to thee." Quoth he, "So be it!" Thereat she opened the skirt of her shift and, taking up her trouser-string,[1] said to him, "O my lord, read what is worked on the flat of this string"; so he took it in hand, and saw these words broidered on it in gold, "I AM THINE, AND THOU ART MINE, O COUSIN OF THE APOSTLE!"[2] When he read this, he withdrew his hand and said to her, "Tell me who thou art!"

"So be it," answered she; "know that I am one of the concubines of the Commander of the Faithful, and my name is Kut al-Kulub—the Food of Hearts. I was brought up in his palace and, when I grew to woman's estate, he looked on me and, noting what share of beauty and loveliness the Creator had given me, loved me with exceeding love, and assigned me a separate apartment, and gave me ten slave-girls to wait on me and all these ornaments thou seest me wearing. On a certain day he set out for one of his provinces, and the Lady Zubaydah came to one of the slave-girls in my service and said to her, 'I have something to require of thee.' 'What is it, O my lady?' asked she, and the Caliph's wife answered, 'When thy mistress, Kut al-Kulub, is asleep, put this piece of Bhang into her nostrils or drop it into her drink, and thou shalt have of me as much money as will satisfy thee.' 'With love and gladness,' replied the girl, and took the Bhang from her, being a glad woman because of the money and because aforetime she had been one of Zubaydah's slaves. So she put the Bhang in my drink, and when it was night I drank, and the drug had no sooner settled in my stomach than I fell to the ground, my head touching my feet, and knew naught of my life but that I was in another world. When her device succeeded, she bade put me in this chest, and secretly brought in the slaves and the doorkeepers and bribed them; and, on the night when thou wast perched upon the date tree, she sent the blacks to do with me as thou sawest. So my delivery was at thy hands, and thou broughtest me to this house and hast entreated me honourably and with thy kindest. This is my story, and I wot not what is become of the Caliph during my absence. Know then my condition and divulge not my case."

When Ghanim heard her words and knew that she was a concubine of the Caliph, he drew back, for awe of the Caliphate beset him, and sat apart from her in one of the corners of the

---

[1] It would be a broad, ribbon-like band, on which the letters could be worked.
[2] Because the Abbaside Caliphs descend from Al-Abbas, paternal uncle of Mohammed. The text means more explicitly, "O descendant of the Prophet's uncle."

place, blaming himself and brooding over his affair and patiencing his heart, bewildered for love of one he could not possess. Then he wept for excess of longing, and plained him of Fortune and her injuries, and the world and its enmities (and praise be to Him who causeth generous hearts to be troubled with love and the beloved, and who endoweth not the minds of the mean and miserly with so much of it as eveneth a grain-weight!).

Thereupon, Kat al-Kulub arose and took him to her bosom and kissed him; for the love of him was firm fixed in her heart, so that she disclosed to him her secret and all the affection she felt; and, throwing her arms round Ghanim's neck like a collar of pearls, kissed him again and yet again. But he held off from her in awe of the Caliph. Then they talked together a long while (and indeed both were drowned in the sea of their mutual love); and, as the day broke, Ghanim rose and donned his clothes and, going to the bazar, as was his wont, took what the occasion required and returned home. He found her weeping; but when she saw him she checked herself and, smiling through her tears, said, "Thou hast desolated me, O beloved of my heart. By Allah, this hour of absence hath been to me like a year! I have explained to thee my condition in the excess of my eager love for thee; so come now near me, and forget the past and have thy will of me." But he interrupted her, crying, "I seek refuge with Allah! This thing may never be. How shall the dog sit in the lion's stead? What is the lord's is unlawful to the slave!" So he withdrew from her, and sat down on a corner of the mat. Her passion for him increased with his forbearance; so she seated herself by his side and caroused and played with him, till the two were flushed with wine and she was mad for her own dishonour.

Thereupon, Ghanim wept, and she wept at his weeping, and they ceased not drinking till nightfall, when he rose and spread two beds, each in its place. "For whom is this second bed?" asked she, and he answered her, "One is for me and the other is for thee; from this night forth we must not sleep save thus, for that which is the lord's is unlawful to the thrall." "O my master!" cried she, "let us have done with this, for all things come to pass by Fate and Fortune." But he refused, and the fire was lighted in her heart and, as her longing waxed fiercer, she clung to him and cried, "By Allah, we will not sleep save side by side!" "Allah forfend!" he replied, and prevailed against her and lay apart till the morning, when love and longing redoubled on her and distraction and eager thirst of passion. They abode after this fashion three full-told months, which were long and longsome indeed, and every time she made

60

advances to him, he would refuse himself and say, "Whatever belongeth to the master is unlawful to the man."

They abode in this state a long time, and fear kept Ghanim aloof from her.

So far concerning these two; but as regards the Lady Zubaydah, when, in the Caliph's absence, she had done this deed by Kut al-Kulub she became perplexed, saying to herself, "What shall I tell my cousin when he comes back and asks for her? What possible answer can I make to him?" Then she called an old woman, who was about her and discovered her secret, to her saying, "How shall I act, seeing that Kut al-Kulub died by such untimely death?" "O my lady," quoth the old crone, "the time of the Caliph's return is near; so do thou send for a carpenter and bid him make thee a figure of wood in the form of a corpse. We will dig a grave for it midmost the palace, and there bury it; then do thou build an oratory over it and set therein lighted candles and lamps, and order each and every in the palace to be clad in black. Furthermore, command thy handmaids and eunuchs, as soon as they know of the Caliph's returning from his journey, to spread straw over the vestibule floors and, when the Commander of the Faithful enters and asks what is the matter, let them say: Kut al-Kulub is dead, and may Allah abundantly compensate thee for the loss of her![1] and, for the high esteem in which she was held of our mistress, she hath buried her in her own palace. When he hears this he will weep and it shall be grievous to him; then will he cause perlections of the Koran to be made for her and he will watch by night at her tomb. Should he say to himself: Verily, Zubaydah, the daughter of my uncle, hath compassed in her jealousy the death of Kut al-Kulub; or, if love-longing overcome him and he bid her be taken out of her tomb, fear thou not; for when they dig down and come to the image in human shape he will see it shrouded in costly grave-clothes; and, if he wish to take off the winding-sheet that he may look upon her, do thou forbid him or let some other forbid him, saying: The sight of her nakedness is unlawful. The fear of the world to come will restrain him and he will believe that she is dead and will restore the figure to its place and thank thee for thy doings; and thus thou shalt escape, please Almighty Allah, from this slough of despond."

When the Lady Zubaydah heard her words, she commended the counsel and gave her a dress of honour and a large sum of money, ordering her to do all she had said. So the old woman set about the business forthright and bade the carpenter make

---

[1] Koran, Chapter IV. In the East, as elsewhere, the Devil quotes scripture.

her the aforesaid image; and, as soon as it was finished, she brought it to the Lady Zubaydah, who shrouded it and buried it and built a sepulchre over it, wherein they lighted candles and lamps, and laid down carpets about the tomb. Moreover, she put on black, and she spread abroad in the harim that Kut al-Kulub was dead. After a time the Caliph returned from his journey and went up to the palace, thinking only of Kut al-Kulub. He saw all the pages and eunuchs and handmaids habited in black, at which his heart fluttered with extreme fear; and, when he went in to the Lady Zubaydah, he found her also garbed in black. So he asked the cause of this and they gave him tidings of the death of Kut al-Kulub, whereon he fell a-swooning. As soon as he came to himself, he asked for her tomb, and the Lady Zubaydah said to him, "Know, O Prince of the Faithful, that for especial honour I have buried her in my own palace." Then he repaired in his travelling-garb to the tomb that he might wail over her, and found the carpets spread and the candles and lamps lighted.

When he saw this, he thanked Zubaydah for her good deed, and abode perplexed, halting between belief and unbelief, till at last suspicion overcame him and he gave order to open the grave and take out the body. When he saw the shroud and would have removed it to look upon her, the fear of Allah Almighty restrained him, and the old woman (taking advantage of the delay) said, "Restore her to her place." Then he sent at once for Fakirs and Koran readers, and caused perlections to be made over her tomb and sat there by the side of the grave, weeping till he fainted; and he continued to frequent the tomb and sit there for a whole month, at the end of which time it so happened one day that he entered the Serraglio, after dismissing the Emirs and Wazirs, and lay down and slept awhile; and there sat at his head a slave-girl fanning him, and at his feet a second, rubbing and shampooing them. Presently he awoke and, opening his eyes, shut them again and heard the handmaid at his head saying to her who was at his feet, "A nice business this, O Khayzaran!" and the other answered her, "Well, O Kazib al-Ban?" "Verily," said the first, "our lord knoweth naught of what hath happened and sitteth waking and watching by a tomb wherein is only a log of wood carved by the carpenter's art." "And Kut al-Kulub," quoth the other, "what hath befallen her?" She replied, "Know that the Lady Zubaydah sent a pellet of Bhang by one of the slave-women who was bribed to drug her; and when sleep overpowered her she put her in a chest, and ordered Sawab and Kafur and Bukhayt to throw her amongst the tombs." "What dost thou say, O Kazib al-

Ban," asked Khayzaran, "is not the lady Kut al-Kulub dead?" "Nay, by Allah!" she answered, "and long may her youth be saved from death! but I have heard the Lady Zubaydah say that she is in the house of a young merchant named Ghanim bin Ayyub of Damascus hight, the Distraught, the Thrall o' Love; and she hath been with him these four months, whilst our lord is weeping and watching by night at a tomb wherein is no corpse."

They kept on talking this sort of talk, and the Caliph gave ear to their words; and, by the time they had ceased speaking, he knew right well that the tomb was a feint and a fraud, and that Kut al-Kulub had been in Ghanim's house for four months. Whereupon he was angered with exceeding anger and, rising up, he summoned the Emirs of his state; and his Wazir, Ja-afar the Barmaki, came also and kissed the ground between his hands. The Caliph said to him in fury, "Go down, O Ja-afar, with a party of armed men and ask for the house of Ghanim, son of Ayyub; fall upon it and spoil it and bring him to me with my slave-girl, Kut al-Kulub, for there is no help but that I punish him!" "To hear is to obey," said Ja-afar; and, setting out with the Governor and the guards and a world of people, repaired to Ghanim's house. Now about that time the youth happened to have brought back a pot of dressed meat and was about to put forth his hand to eat of it, he and Kut al-Kulub, when the lady, happening to look out, saw calamity surrounding the house on every side; for the Wazir and the Governor, the night guard and the Mamelukes, with swords drawn, had girt it as the white of the eye girdeth the black. At this she knew that tidings of her had reached the Caliph, her lord; and she made sure of ruin, and her colour paled and her fair features changed and her favour faded.

Then she turned to Ghanim and said to him, "O my love, fly for thy life!" "What shall I do," asked he, "and whither shall I go, seeing that my money and means of maintenance are all in this house?"; and she answered, "Delay not lest thou be slain and lose life as well as wealth." "O my loved one and the light of mine eyes!" he cried. "How shall I do to get away when they have surrounded the house?" Quoth she, "Fear not"; and, stripping off his fine clothes, dressed him in ragged old garments, after which she took the pot and, putting in it bits of broken bread and a saucer of meat, placed the whole in a basket, and setting it upon his head said, "Go out in this guise and fear not for me who wotteth right well what thing is in my hand for the Caliph."[1] So he went out amongst them,

[1] *I.e.* "I will know how to deal with him."

bearing the basket with its contents, and the Protector vouch-safed him His protection and he escaped the snares and perils that beset him, by the blessing of his good conscience and pure conduct.

Meanwhile, Ja-afar dismounted and, entering the house, saw Kut al-Kulub who had dressed and decked herself in splendid raiments and ornaments and filled a chest with gold and jewellery and precious stones and rarities and what else was light to bear and of value rare. When she saw Ja-afar come in, she rose and, kissing the ground before him, said, "O my lord, the Reed hath written of old the rede which Allah decreed!"[1] "By Allah, O my lady," answered Ja-afar, "he gave me an order to seize Ghanim, son of Ayyub"; and she rejoined, "O my lord, he made ready his goods and set out therewith for Damascus and I know nothing more of him; but I desire thee take charge of this chest and deliver it to me in the harim of the Prince of the Faithful." "Hearing and obedience," said Ja-afar, and bade his men bear it away to the headquarters of the Caliphate, together with Kut al-Kulub, commanding them to entreat her with honour as one in high esteem. They did his bidding after they had wrecked and plundered Ghanim's house.[2] Then Ja-afar went in to the Caliph and told him all that had happened, and he ordered Kut al-Kulub to be lodged in a dark chamber and appointed an old woman to serve her, feeling convinced that Ghanim had debauched her and slept with her. Then he wrote a man-date to the Emir Mohammed bin Sulayman 'al-Zayni, his viceroy in Damascus, to this effect: "The instant thou shalt receive this our letter, seize upon Ghanim bin Ayyub and send him to us."

When the missive came to the viceroy, he kissed it and laid it on his head; then he let proclaim in the bazars, "Whoso is desirous to plunder, away with him to the house of Ghanim, son of Ayyub." So they flocked thither, when they found that Ghanim's mother and sister had built him a tomb in the midst of the house and sat by it weeping for him; whereupon they seized the two without telling them the cause and, after spoil-ing the house, carried them before the viceroy. He questioned them concerning Ghanim and both replied, "For a year or more we have had no news of him." So they restored them to their place.

---

[1] The Pen (title of the Koranic, Chapter LXVIII) and the Preserved Tablet.
[2] These plunderings were sanctioned by custom. But a few years ago, when the Turkish soldiers mutinied about arrears of pay (often delayed for years) the governing Pasha would set fire to the town and allow the men to loot what they pleased during a stated time.

Thus far concerning them; but as regards Ghanim, when he saw his wealth spoiled and his ruin utterest he wept over himself till his heart wellnigh brake. Then he fared on at random till the last of the day, and hunger grew hard on him and walking wearied him. So, coming to a village, he entered a mosque, where he sat down upon a mat and propped his back against the wall; but presently he sank to the ground in his extremity of famine and fatigue. There he lay till dawn, his heart fluttering for want of food; and, owing to his sweating, the lice coursed over his skin; his breath waxed fetid and his whole condition was changed. When the villagers came to pray the dawn-prayer, they found him prostrate, ailing, hunger-lean, yet showing evident signs of former affluence. As soon as prayers were over, they drew near him; and, understanding that he was starved with hunger and cold, they gave him an old robe with ragged sleeves and said to him, "O stranger, whence art thou and what sickness is upon thee?" He opened his eyes and wept, but returned no answer; whereupon one of them, who saw that he was starving, brought him a saucer of honey and two barley scones. He ate a little and they sat with him till sunrise when they went to their work.

He abode with them in this state for a month, whilst sickness and weakliness grew upon him; and they wept for him and, pitying his condition, took counsel with one another upon his case and agreed to forward him to the hospital in Baghdad.[1] Meanwhile, behold, two beggar-women,[2] who were none other than Ghanim's mother and sister, came into the mosque and, when he saw them, he gave them the bread that was at his head; and they slept by his side that night, but he knew them not. Next day the villagers brought a camel and said to the cameleer, "Set this sick man on thy beast and carry him to Baghdad and put him down at the Spital door; so haply he may be medicined and be healed and thou shalt have thy hire." "To hear is to comply," said the man. So they brought Ghanim, who was asleep, out of the mosque and set him, mat and all, on the camel; and his mother and sister came out among the crowd to gaze upon him, but they knew him not. However, after looking at him and considering him carefully, they said, "Of a truth he favours our Ghanim, poor boy! Can this sick man be he?"

Presently, he woke, and finding himself bound with ropes

[1] The Moslem peasant is a kind-hearted man and will make any sacrifices for a sick stranger, even of another creed.

[2] Such treatment of innocent women was only too common under the Caliphate and in contemporary Europe.

on a camel's back he began to weep and complain,[1] and the
village people saw his mother and sister weeping over him,
albeit they knew him not. Then they fared forth for Baghdad,
but the camel-man forwent them and, setting Ghanim down
at the Spital gate, went away with his beast. The sick man lay
there till dawn and, when the folk began to go about the streets,
they saw him and stood gazing on him, for he had become as
thin as a tooth-pick, till the Syndic of the bazar came up and
drove them away from him, saying, "I will gain Paradise
through this poor creature; for if they take him into the
hospital, they will kill him in a single day."[2] Then he made
his young men carry him to his house, where they spread him
a new bed with a new pillow, and he said to his wife, "Tend
him carefully"; and she replied, "Good! on my head be it!"
Thereupon she tucked up her sleeves and, warming some
water, washed his hands, feet and body; after which she
clothed him in a robe belonging to one of her slave-girls and
made him drink a cup of wine and sprinkled rose water over
him. So he revived and complained, and the thought of his
beloved Kut al-Kulub made his grief redouble.

Thus far concerning him; but as regards Kut al-Kulub,
when the Caliph was angered against her, he ordered her to a
dark chamber where she abode eighty days, at the end of
which the Caliph, happening to pass on a certain day the
place where she was, heard her repeating poetry, and after she
ceased reciting her verse, saying, "O my darling, O my
Ghanim! how great is thy goodness and how chaste is thy
nature! thou didst well by one who did ill by thee and thou
guardest his honour who garred thine become dishonour, and
his Harim thou didst protect who to enslave thee and thine
did elect! But thou shalt surely stand, thou and the Commander of the Faithful, before the Just Judge, and thou shalt
be justified of him on the Day when the Lord (to whom be
honour and glory!) shall be Kazi and the Angels of Heaven
shall be witnesses!" When the Caliph heard her complaint, he
knew that she had been wronged and, returning to the palace,
sent Masrur the Eunuch for her. She came before him with
bowed head and eyes tearful and heart sorrowful; and he said
to her, "O Kut al-Kulub, I find thou accusest me of tyranny
and oppression, and thou avouchest that I have done ill by one
who did well by me. Who is this who hath guarded my honour
while I garred his become dishonour? Who protected my
Harim and whose Harim I wrecked?"

"He is Ghanim, son of Ayyub," replied she, "for he never

---
[1] He felt that he was being treated like a corpse.
[2] A common enough idea even in twentieth-century Cairo (P. H. N.)

approached me in wantonness or with lewd intent, I swear by thy munificence, O Commander of the Faithful!" Then said the Caliph, "There is no Majesty and there is no Might save in Allah! Ask what thou wilt of me, O Kut al-Kulub." "O Prince of the Faithful!" answered she, "I require of thee only my beloved Ghanim, son of Ayyub." He did as she desired, whereupon she said, "O Lord of the Moslems, if I bring him to thy presence, wilt thou bestow me on him?"; and he replied, "If he come into my presence, I will give thee to him as the gift of the generous who revoketh not his largesse." "O Prince of True Believers," quoth she, "suffer me to go and seek him; haply Allah may unite me with him"; and quoth he, "Do even as thou wilt." So she rejoiced and, taking with her a thousand dinars in gold, went out and visited the elders of the various faiths and gave alms in Ghanim's name.[1] Next day she walked to the merchants' bazar, and disclosed her object to the Syndic and gave him money, saying, "Bestow this in charity to the stranger!" On the following Friday she fared to the bazar (with other thousand dinars) and, entering the goldsmiths' and jewellers' market street, called the Chief and presented to him a thousand dinars with these words, "Bestow this in charity to the stranger!" The Chief looked at her (and he was the Syndic who had taken in Ghanim) and said, "O my lady, wilt thou come to my house and look upon a youth, a stranger I have there, and see how goodly and graceful he is?"

Now the stranger was Ghanim, son of Ayyub, but the Chief had no knowledge of him and thought him to be some wandering pauper, some debtor whose wealth had been taken from him, or some lover parted from his beloved. When she heard his words her heart fluttered and her vitals yearned, and she said to him, "Send with me one who shall guide me to thy house." So he sent a little lad who brought her to the house wherein was the head man's stranger-guest and she thanked him for this. When she reached the house, she went and saluted the Syndic's wife, who rose and kissed the ground between her hands, for she knew her. Then quoth Kut al-Kulub, "Where is the sick man who is with thee?" She wept and replied, "He is here, O my lady; by Allah, he is come of good folk and he beareth the signs of gentle breeding; you see him lying on yonder bed." So she turned and looked at him; and she saw something like him, but he was worn and wasted till he had become lean as a toothpick, so his identity was doubtful to her and she could not be certain that it was he. Yet pity for him possessed her and she wept, saying, "Verily

---

[1] That they might pray for him.

the stranger is unhappy, even though he be a prince in his own land!"; and his case was grievous to her and her heart ached for him, yet she knew him not to be Ghanim. Then she furnished him with wine and medicines and she sat awhile by his head, after which she mounted and returned to her palace and continued to visit every bazar in quest of her lover.

Meanwhile, Ghanim's mother and sister Fitnah arrived at Baghdad and met the Syndic, who carried them to Kut al-Kulub and said to her, "O princess of beneficent ladies, there came to our city this day a woman and her daughter, who are fair of favour and signs of good breeding and dignity are apparent in them, though they be dressed in haircloth and have each one a wallet hanging to her neck; and their eyes are tearful and their hearts are sorrowful. So I have brought them to thee that thou mayst give them refuge, and rescue them from beggary, for they are not of asker-folk and, if it please Allah, we shall enter Paradise through them." "By Allah, O my master," cried she, "thou makest me long to see them! Where are they?" adding, "Here with them to me!" So he bade the eunuch bring them in; and, when she looked on them and saw that they were both of distinguished beauty, she wept for them and said, "By Allah, these are people of condition and show plain signs of former opulence." "O my lady," said the Syndic's wife, "we love the poor and the destitute, more especially as reward in Heaven will recompense our love; and, as for these persons, haply the oppressor hath dealt hardly with them and hath plundered their property and harried their houses."

Then Ghanim's mother and sister wept with sore weeping, remembering their former prosperity and contrasting it with their present poverty and miserable condition; and their thoughts dwelt upon son and brother, whilst Kut al-Kulub wept for their weeping; and they said, "We beseech Allah to reunite us with him whom we desire, and he is none other but my son named Ghanim bin Ayyub!" When Kut al-Kulub heard this, she knew them to be the mother and sister of her lover and wept till a swoon came over her. When she revived she turned to them and said, "Have no fear and sorrow not, for this day is the first of your prosperity and the last of your adversity!"

When Kut al-Kulub had consoled them she bade the Syndic lead them to his house and let his wife carry them to the Hammam and dress them in handsome clothes and take care of them and honour them with all honour; and she gave him a sufficient sum of money. Next day, she mounted and, riding to his house, went in to his wife who rose up and kissed her

hands and thanked her for her kindness. There she saw
Ghanim's mother and sister whom the Syndic's wife had
taken to the Hammam and clothed afresh, so that the traces
of their former condition became manifest upon them. She
sat talking with them awhile, after which she asked the wife
about the sick youth who was in her house and she replied,
"He is in the same state." Then said Kut al-Kulub, "Come, let
us go and visit him." So she arose, she and the Chief's wife
and Ghanim's mother and sister, and went in to the room
where he lay and sat down near him.

Presently, Ghanim bin Ayyub, the Distraught, the Thrall
o' Love, heard them mention the name of Kut al-Kulub;
whereupon life returned to him, emaciated and withered as he
was, and he raised his head from the pillow and cried aloud,
"O Kut al-Kulub!" She looked at him and made certain it
was he and shrieked rather than said, "Yes, O my beloved!"
"Draw near to me," said he, and she replied, "Surely thou art
Ghanim bin Ayyub?"; and he rejoined, "I am indeed!" Hereupon a swoon came upon her; and, as soon as Ghanim's
mother and his sister Fitnah heard these words, both cried out,
"O our joy!" and fainted clean away. When they all recovered,
Kut al-Kulub exclaimed, "Praise be to Allah who hath brought
us together again and who hath reunited thee with thy mother
and thy sister!" And she related to him all that had befallen
her with the Caliph and said, "I have made known the truth
to the Commander of the Faithful, who believed my words
and was pleased with thee; and now he desireth to see thee,"
adding, "He hath given me to thee."

Threat he rejoiced with extreme joy, when she said, "Quit
not this place till I come back," and, rising forthwith, betook
herself to her palace. There she opened the chest which she
had brought from Ghanim's house and, taking out some of the
dinars, gave them to the Syndic, saying, "Buy with this money
for each of them four complete suits of the finest stuffs and
twenty kerchiefs, and else beside of whatsoever they require";
after which she carried all three to the baths and had them
washed and bathed and made ready for them consommes, and
galangale-water and cider against their coming out. When they
left the Hammam, they put on the new clothes, and she abode
with them three days, feeding them with chicken meats and
bouillis, and making them drink sherbet of sugar candy. After
three days their spirits returned; and she carried them again
to the baths, and when they came out and had changed their
raiment, she led them back to the Syndic's house and left
them there, whilst she returned to the palace and craved permission to see the Caliph. When he ordered her to come in,

she entered and, kissing the ground between his hands, told him the whole story and how her lord, Ghanim bin Ayyub, yclept the Distraught, the Thrall o' Love, and his mother and sister were now in Baghdad. When the Caliph heard this, he turned to the eunuchs and said, "Here with Ghanim to me." So Ja-afar went to fetch him; but Kut al-Kulub forewent him and told Ghanim, "The Caliph hath sent to fetch thee before him," and charged him to show readiness of tongue and firmness of heart and sweetness of speech.

Then she robed him in a sumptuous dress and gave him dinars in plenty, saying, "Be lavish of largesse to the Caliph's household as thou goest in to him." Presently Ja-afar, mounted on his Nubian mule, came to fetch him; and Ghanim advanced to welcome the Wazir and, wishing him long life, kissed the ground before him. Now the star of his good fortune had risen and shone brightly; and Ja-afar took him; and they ceased not faring together, he and the Minister, till they went in to the Commander of the Faithful. When he stood in the presence, he looked at the Wazirs and Emirs and Chamberlains, and Viceroys and Grandees and Captains, and then at the Caliph. Hereupon he sweetened his speech and his eloquence and, bowing his head to the ground, broke out in these extempore couplets:

> May that Monarch's life span a mighty span,
> Whose lavish of largesse all lieges scan:
> None other but he shall be Kaysar hight,
> Lord of lordly hall and of haught Divan:
> Kings lay their gems on his threshold-dust
> As they bow and sala m to the mighty man;
> And his glances foil them and all recoil,
> Bowing beards aground and with faces wan:
> Yet they gain the profit of royal grace,
> The rank and station of high soldan.
> Earth's plain is scant for thy world of men,
> Camp there in Kaywan's Empyrean!
> May the King of Kings ever hold thee dear;
> Be counsel thine and right steadfast plan,
> Till thy justice spread o'er the wide-spread earth
> And the near and the far be of equal worth.

When he ended his improvisation the Caliph was pleased by it and marvelled at the eloquence of his tongue and the sweetness of his speech, and he said to him, "Draw near to me." So he drew near, and quoth the King, "Tell me thy tale and declare to me thy case." So Ghanim sat down and related to him what had befallen him in Baghdad, of his sleeping in the tomb and of his opening the chest after the three slaves had departed, and informed him, in short, of everything that had happened to him from commencement to conclusion—none of which we will repeat for interest fails in twice-told tales.

The Caliph was convinced that he was a true man; so he invested him with a dress of honour, and placed him near himself in token of favour, and said to him, "Acquit me of the responsibility I have incurred."[1] And Ghanim so did, saying, "O our lord the Sultan, of a truth thy slave and all things his two hands own are his master's." The Caliph was pleased at this and gave orders to set apart a palace for him and assigned to him pay and allowances, rations and donations, which amounted to something immense. So he removed thither with sister and mother; after which the Caliph, hearing that his sister Fitnah was in beauty a very "fitnah," a mere seduction, demanded her in marriage of Ghanim, who replied, "She is thy handmaid as I am thy slave." The Caliph thanked him and gave him an hundred thousand dinars, then summoned the witnesses and the Kazi, and on one and the same day they wrote out the two contracts of marriage between the Caliph and Fitnah and between Ghanim bin Ayyub and Kut al-Kulub; and the two marriages were consummated on one and the same night. When it was morning, the Caliph gave orders to record the history of what had befallen Ghanim from first to last and to deposit it in the royal muniment-rooms, that those who came after him might read it and marvel at the dealings of Destiny and put their trust in Him who created the night and the day.

---

[1] *I.e.* "Pardon me if I have injured thee"—a popular phrase.

The Ebony Horse

THERE was once in times of yore and ages long gone before, a great and puissant King, of the Kings of the Persians, Sabur by name, who was the richest of all the Kings in store of wealth and dominion and surpassed each and every in wit and wisdom. He was generous, openhanded and beneficent, and he gave to those who sought him and repelled not those who resorted to him; and he comforted the broken-hearted and honourably entreated those who fled to him for refuge. Moreover, he loved the poor and was hospitable to strangers and did the oppressed justice upon the oppressor.

He had three daughters, like full moons of shining light or flower gardens blooming bright; and a son as he were the moon; and it was his wont to keep two festivals in the twelve-month, those of the Nau-Roz, or New Year, and Mihrgan, the Autumnal Equinox, on which occasions he threw open his palaces and gave largesse and made proclamation of safety and security and promoted his chamberlains and viceroys; and the people of his realm came in to him and saluted him and gave him joy of the holy day, bringing him gifts and servants and eunuchs.

Now, he loved science and geometry, and one festival day, as he sat on his kingly throne, there came in to him three wise men, cunning artificers and past masters in all manner of craft and inventions, skilled in making things curious and rare, such as confound the wit; and versed in the knowledge

72

of occult truths and perfect in mysteries and subtleties. And they were of three different tongues and countries: the first a Hindi, or Indian, the second a Roumi, or Greek, and the third a Farsi, or Persian. The Indian came forward and, prostrating himself before the King, wished him joy of the festival and laid before him a present befitting his dignity; that is to say, a man of gold, set with precious gems and jewels of price and hending in hand a golden trumpet. When Sabur saw this, he asked, "O sage, what is the virtue of this figure?" and the Indian answered, "O my lord, if this figure be set at the gate of thy city, it will be a guardian over it; for, if an enemy enter the place, it will blow this clarion against him and he will be seized with a palsy and drop down dead." Much the King marvelled at this and cried, "By Allah, O sage, an this thy word be true, I will grant thee thy wish and thy desire."

Then came forward the Greek and, prostrating himself before the King, presented him with a basin of silver, in whose midst was a peacock of gold, surrounded by four-and-twenty chicks of the same metal. Sabur looked at them and, turning to the Greek, said to him, "O sage, what is the virtue of this peacock?" "O my lord," answered he, "as often as an hour of the day or night passeth, it pecketh one of its young and crieth out and flappeth its wings, till the four-and-twenty hours are accomplished, and when the month cometh to an end, it will open its mouth and thou shalt see the crescent therein." And the King said, "An thou speak sooth, I will bring thee to thy wish and thy desire."[1]

Then came forward the Persian sage and, prostrating himself before the King, presented him with a horse of the blackest ebony wood, inlaid with gold and jewels, and ready harnessed with saddle, bridle and stirrups, such as befit Kings; which, when Sabur saw, he marvelled with exceeding marvel and was confounded at the beauty of its form and the ingenuity of its fashion. So he asked, "What is the use of this horse of wood, and what is its virtue and what the secret of its movement?"; and the Persian answered, "O my lord, the virtue of this horse is that, if one mount him, it will carry him whither he will and fare with its rider through the air and cover the space of a year in a single day." The King marvelled and was amazed at these three wonders, following thus hard upon one another on the same day and, turning to the sage, said to him, "By Allah the Omnipotent, and our Lord the Beneficent, who created all creatures and feedeth them with meat and drink, an thy

---

[1] All moslems, except those of the Maliki school, hold that the maker of an image representing anything of life will be commanded on the Judgment Day to animate it, and failing will be duly sent to the Fire.

speech be veritable and the virtue of thy contrivance appear, I will assuredly give thee whatsoever thou lustest for and will bring thee to thy desire and thy wish!" Then he entertained the sages three days, that he might make trial of their gifts; after which they brought the figures before him and each took the creature he had wroughten and showed him the mystery of its movement. The trumpeter blew the trump; the peacock pecked its chicks; and the Persian sage mounted the ebony horse, whereupon it soared with him high in air and descended again. When King Sabur saw all this, he was amazed and perplexed and felt like to fly for joy and said to the three sages, "Now I am certified of the truth of thy words and it behoveth me to quit me of my promise. Ask ye, therefore, what ye will, and I will give you that same."

Now the report of the King's daughters had reached the sages, so they answered, "If the King be content with us and accept our gifts and allow us to prefer a request to him, we crave of him that he give us his three daughters in marriage, that we may be his sons-in-law; for that the stability of Kings may not be gainsaid." Quoth the King, "I grant you that which you wish and you desire," and bade summon the Kazi forthright, that he might marry each of the sages to one of his daughters. Now it fortuned that the Princesses were behind a curtain, looking on; and when they heard this, the youngest considered her husband-to-be and, behold, he was an old man[1] an hundred years of age, with hair frosted, forehead drooping, eyebrows mangy, ears slitten, beard and mustachios stained and dyed; eyes red and goggle; cheeks bleached and hollow; flabby nose like a brinjail, or egg-plant; face like a cobbler's apron, teeth overlapping and lips like a camel's kidneys, loose and pendulous; in brief a terror, a horror, a monster, for he was of the folk of his time the unsightliest, and of his age the frightfullest; sundry of his grinders had been knocked out and his eye-teeth were like the tusks of the Jinni who frighteneth poultry in hen-houses. Now the girl was the fairest and most graceful of her time, more elegant than the gazelle however tender, than the gentlest zephyr blander and brighter than the moon at her full; for amorous fray right suitable; confounding in graceful sway the waving bough, and outdoing in swimming gait the pacing roe; in fine, she was fairer and sweeter by far than all her sisters. So, when she saw her suitor, she went to her chamber and strewed dust on her head and tore her clothes and fell to buffeting her face and weeping and wailing.

---

[1] This description of ugly old age is written with true Arab verve.

Now the Prince, her brother, Kamar al-Akmar, or the Moon of Moons hight, was then newly returned from a journey and, hearing her weeping and crying, came in to her (for he loved her with fond affection, more than his other sisters) and asked her, "What aileth thee? What hath befallen thee? Tell me and conceal naught from me." So she smote her breast and answered, "O my brother and my dear one, I have nothing to hide. If the palace be straitened upon thy father, I will go out; and if he be resolved upon a foul thing, I will separate myself from him, though he consent not to make provision for me; and my Lord will provide." Quoth he, "Tell me what meaneth this talk and what hath straitened thy breast and troubled thy temper." "O my brother and my dear one," answered the Princess, "know that my father hath promised me in marriage to a wicked magician who brought him, as a gift, a horse of black wood, and hath bewitched him with his craft and his egromancy; but, as for me, I will none of him, and would, because of him, I had never come into this world!"

Her brother soothed and solaced her, then fared to his sire and said, "What be this wizard to whom thou hast given my youngest sister in marriage, and what is this present which he hath brought thee, so that thou hast killed my sister with chagrin? It is not right that this should be." Now the Persian was standing by and, when he heard the Prince's words, he was mortified and filled with fury, and the King said, "O my son, an thou sawest this horse, thy wit would be confounded and thou wouldst be amated with amazement." Then he bade the slaves bring the horse before him and they did so; and, when the Prince saw it, it pleased him. So (being an accomplished cavalier) he mounted it forthright and struck its sides with the shovel-shaped stirrup-irons; but it stirred not, and the King said to the sage, "Go show him its movement, that he also may help thee to win thy wish." Now the Persian bore the Prince a grudge because he willed not he should have his sister; so he showed him the pin of ascent on the right side of the horse, and saying to him, "Trill this," left him.

Thereupon, the Prince trilled the pin, and lo! the horse forthwith soared with him high in æther, as it were a bird, and gave not over flying till it disappeared from men's espying, whereat the King was troubled and perplexed about his case and said to the Persian, "O sage, look how thou mayst make him descend." But he replied, "O my lord, I can do nothing, and thou wilt never see him again till Resurrection Day, for he, of his ignorance and pride, asked me not of the pin of descent and I forgot to acquaint him therewith." When the King heard this he was enraged with sore rage, and bade bastinado the sorcerer and clap him in jail, whilst he himself cast the crown from his head and beat his face and smote his breast. Moreover, he shut the doors of his palaces and gave himself up to weeping and keening, he and his wife and daughters and all the folk of the city; and thus their joy was turned to annoy, and their gladness changed into sore affliction and sadness.

Thus far concerning them; but as regards the Prince, the horse gave not over soaring with him till he drew near the sun, whereat he gave himself up for lost and saw death in the skies, and was confounded at his case, repenting him of having mounted the horse and saying to himself, "Verily, this was a device of the sage to destroy me on account of my youngest sister; but there is no Majesty and there is no Might save in Allah, the Glorious, the Great! I am lost without recourse; but I wonder, did not he who made the ascent-pin make also a descent-pin?" Now, he was a man of wit and knowledge and intelligence; so he fell to feeling all the parts of the horse, but saw nothing save a screw, like a cock's head, on its right shoulder and the like on the left, when quoth he to himself, "I see no sign save these things like buttons." Presently he turned the right-hand pin, whereupon the horse flew heavenwards with increased speed. So he left it, and looking at the sinister shoulder and finding another pin he wound it up, and immediately the steed's upward motion slowed and ceased and it began to descend, little by little, towards the face of the earth, while the rider became yet more cautious and careful of his life. And when he saw this and knew the uses of the horse, his heart was filled with joy and gladness and he thanked Almighty Allah for that He had deigned deliver him from destruction. Then he began to turn the horse's head whithersoever he would, making it rise and fall at pleasure, till he had gotten complete mastery over its every movement.

He ceased not to descend the whole of that day, for that the steed's ascending flight had borne him afar from the earth; and, as he descended, he diverted himself with viewing the various cities and countries over which he passed and which he knew not, never having seen them in his life. Amongst the rest, he descried a city ordered after the fairest fashion in the midst of a verdant and riant land, rich in trees and streams, with gazelles pacing daintily over the plains; whereat he fell a-musing, and said to himself, "Would I knew the name of yon town and in what land it is!" And he took to circling about it and observing it right and left. By this time, the day began to decline and the sun drew near to its downing; and he said in his mind, "Verily, I find no goodlier place to night in than this city; so I will lodge here, and early on the morrow I will return to my kith and kin and my kingdom and tell my father and family what hath passed and acquaint him with what mine eyes have seen."

Then he addressed himself to seeking a place wherein he might safely bestow himself and his horse and where none should descry him, and presently, behold, he espied amiddle-most of the city a palace rising high in upper air surrounded by a great wall with lofty crenelles and battlements, guarded by forty black slaves, clad in complete mail, and armed with spears and swords, bows and arrows. Quoth he, "This is a goodly place," and turned the descent-pin, whereupon the horse sank down with him like a weary bird, and alighted gently on the terrace roof of the palace. So the Prince dismounted and, ejaculating "Alhamdolillah"—praise be to Allah[1] —he began to go round about the horse and examine it, saying, "By Allah, he who fashioned thee with these perfections was a cunning craftsman, and if the Almighty extend the term of my life and restore me to my country and kinsfolk in safety and reunite me with my father, I will assuredly bestow upon him all manner of bounties and benefit him with the utmost beneficence." By this time night had overtaken him and he sat on the roof till he was assured that all in the palace slept; and, indeed, hunger and thirst were sore upon him, for that he had not tasted food nor drunk water since he parted from his sire. So he said within himself, "Surely the like of this palace will not lack of victual"; and, leaving the horse above, went down in search of somewhat to eat.

Presently, he came to a staircase and, descending it to the bottom, found himself in a court paved with white marble and alabaster, which shone in the light of the moon. He marvelled at the place and the goodliness of its fashion, but sensed no sound of speaker and saw no living soul and stood in perplexed surprise, looking right and left and knowing not whither he should wend. Then said he to himself, "I may not do better than return to where I left my horse and pass the night by it; and as soon as day shall dawn I will mount and ride away." However, as he tarried talking to himself, he espied a light within the palace and, making towards it, found that it came from a candle that stood before a door of the harim, at the head of a sleeping eunuch, as he were one of

_____

[1] *I.e.* for fear of the evil eye injuring the palace and, haply, himself.

the Ifrits of Solomon or a tribesman of the Jinn, longer than lumber and broader than a bench. He lay before the door, with the pommel of his sword gleaming in the flame of the candle, and at his head was a bag of leather[1] hanging from a column of granite. When the Prince saw this, he was affrighted and said, "I crave help from Allah the Supreme! O mine Holy One, even as Thou hast already delivered me from destruction, so vouchsafe me strength to quit myself of the adventure of this palace!" So saying, he put out his hand to the budget and, taking it, carried it aside and opened it and

found in it food of the best. He ate his fill and refreshed himself and drank water, after which he hung up the provision-bag in its place, and drawing the eunuch's sword from its sheath, took it, whilst the slave slept on, knowing not whence destiny should come to him.

Then the Prince fared forwards into the palace and ceased not till he came to a second door, with a curtain drawn before it; so he raised the curtain and, behold, on entering he saw a couch of the whitest ivory, inlaid with pearls and jacinths and jewels, and four slave-girls sleeping about it. He went up to the couch, to see what was thereon, and found a young lady

---

1 The "Sufrah," an acting provision-bag and table-cloth.

lying asleep, chemised with her hair[1] as she were the full moon rising over the Eastern horizon, with flower-white brow and shining hair-parting, and cheeks like blood-red anemones and dainty moles thereon. He was amazed at her as she lay in her beauty and loveliness, her symmetry and grace, and he recked no more of death. So he went up to her, trembling in every nerve and, shuddering with pleasure, kissed her on the right cheek; whereupon she awoke forthright and opened her eys, and seeing the Prince standing at her head, said to him, "Who art thou and whence comest thou?" Quoth he, "I am thy slave and lover." Asked she, "And who brought thee hither?" and he answered, "My Lord and my fortune." Then said Shams al-Nahar (for such was her name), "Haply thou art he who demanded me yesterday of my father in marriage and he rejected thee, pretending that thou wast foul of favour. By Allah, my sire lied in his throat when he spoke this thing, for thou art not other than beautiful." Now the son of the King of Hind had sought her in marriage, but her father had rejected him, for that he was ugly and uncouth, and she thought the Prince was he. So, when she saw his beauty and grace (for indeed he was like the radiant moon) the syntheism[2] of love gat hold of her heart as it were a flaming fire, and they fell to talk and converse.

Suddenly, her waiting-women awoke and, seeing the Prince with their mistress, said to her, "O my lady, who is this with thee?" Quoth she, "I know not; I found him sitting by me, when I woke up; haply 'tis he who seeketh me in marriage of my sire." Quoth they, "O my lady, by Allah the All-Father, this is not he who seeketh thee in marriage, for he is hideous and this man is handsome and of high degree. Indeed, the other is not fit to be his servant." Then the handmaidens went out to the eunuch, and finding him slumbering awoke him, and he started up in alarm. Said they, "How happeth it that thou art on guard at the palace and yet men come in to us, whilst we are asleep?" When the black heard this, he sprang in haste to his sword, but found it not; and fear took him and trembling. Then he went in, confounded, to his mistress, and seeing the Prince sitting at talk with her, said to him, "O my lord, art thou man or Jinni?" Replied the Prince, "Woe to thee, O unluckiest of slaves; how darest thou even the sons of the royal Chosroes with one of the unbelieving Satans?" And he was as a raging lion. Then he took the

---

[1] Eastern women in hot weather lie mother-nude under a sheet here represented by the hair.
[2] Arab. "Shirk"=worshipping more than one God. A theological term here most appropriately used.

sword in his hand and said to the slave, "I am the King's son-in-law, and he hath married me to his daughter and bidden me go in to her." And when the eunuch heard these words he replied, "O my lord, if thou be indeed of kind a man as thou avouchest, she is fit for none but for thee, and thou art worthier of her than any other."

Thereupon the eunuch ran to the King, shrieking loud and rending his raiment and heaving dust upon his head; and when the King heard his outcry, he said to him, "What hath befallen thee? Speak quickly and be brief, for thou hast fluttered my heart." Answered the eunuch, "O King, come to thy daughter's succour; for a devil of the Jinn, in the likeness of a King's son, hath got possession of her; so up and at him!" When the King heard this, he thought to kill him and said, "How camest thou to be careless of my daughter and let this demon come at her?" Then he betook himself to the Princess's palace, where he found her slave-women standing to await him and asked them, "What is come to my daughter?" "O King," answered they, "slumber overcame us and, when we awoke, we found a young man sitting upon her couch in talk with her, as he were the full moon; never saw we aught fairer of favour than he. So we questioned him of his case and he declared that thou hadst given him thy daughter in marriage. More than this we know not, nor do we know if he be a man or a Jinni; but he is modest and well bred, and doth nothing unseemly or which leadeth to disgrace."

Now, when the King heard these words, his wrath cooled and he raised the curtain little by little and, looking in, saw sitting at talk with his daughter a Prince of the goodliest with a face like the full moon for sheen. At this sight he could not contain himself of his jealousy for his daughter's honour and, putting aside the curtain, rushed in upon them, drawn sword in hand, like a furious Ghul. Now, when the Prince saw him he asked the Princess, "Is this thy sire?"; and she answered, "Yes." Whereupon he sprang to his feet and, seizing his sword, cried out at the King with so terrible a cry that he was confounded. Then the youth would have fallen on him with the sword; but the King, seeing that the Prince was doughtier than he, sheathed his scymitar and stood till the young man came up to him, when he accosted him courteously and said to him, "O youth, art thou a man or a Jinni?" Quoth the Prince, "Did I not respect thy right as mine host and thy daughter's honour, I would spill thy blood! How darest thou fellow me with devils, me that am a Prince of the sons of the royal Chosroës who, had they wished to take thy kingdom, could shake thee like an earth-quake from thy glory and thy dominions and spoil thee of all thy possessions?"

Now, when the King heard his words, he was confounded with awe and bodily fear of him and rejoined, "If you indeed be of the sons of the Kings, as thou pretendest, how cometh it that thou enterest my palace without my permission, and smirchest mine honour, making thy way to my daughter and feigning that thou art her husband and claiming that I have given her to thee to wife, I that have slain Kings and Kings' sons, who sought her of me in marriage? And now who shall save thee from my might and majesty when, if I cried out to my slaves and servants and bade them put thee to the vilest of deaths they would slay thee forthright? Who shall deliver thee out of my hand?" When the Prince heard this speech of the King he answered, "Verily, I wonder at thee and at the shortness and denseness of thy wit! Say me, canst covet for thy daughter a mate comelier than myself, and hast ever seen a stouter-hearted man or one better fitted for a Sultan or a more glorious in rank and dominion than I?" Rejoined the King, "Nay, by Allah! but I would have had thee, O youth, act after the custom of Kings and demand her from me to wife before witnesses, that I might have married her to thee publicly; and now, even were I to marry her to thee privily, yet hast thou dishonoured me in her person." Rejoined the Prince, "Thou sayest sooth, O King, but if thou summon thy slaves and thy soldiers and they fall upon me and slay me, as thou pretendeth, thou wouldst but publish thine own disgrace, and the folk would be divided between belief in thee and disbelief in thee. Wherefore, O King, thou wilt do well, meseemeth, to turn from this thought to that which I shall counsel thee."

Quoth the King, "Let me hear what thou hast to advise"; and quoth the Prince, "What I have to propose to thee is this: either do thou meet me in combat singular, I and thou; and he who slayeth his adversary shall be held the worthier, and having a better title to the kingdom; or else, let me be this night and, whenas dawns the morn, draw out against me thy horsemen and footmen and servants; but first tell me their number." Said the King, "They are forty thousand horse, besides my own slaves and their followers,[1] who are the like of them in number." Thereupon said the Prince,

---

[1] The dearest ambition of a slave is not liberty but to have a slave of his own. This was systematised by the servile rulers known in history as the Mameluke Beys. Each had his household of servile pages and squires who looked forward to filling the master's place as knight or baron.

"When the day shall break, do thou array them against me and say to them, 'This man is a suitor to me for my daughter's hand, on condition that he shall do battle single-handed against you all; for he pretendeth that he will overcome you and put you to the rout and, indeed, that ye cannot prevail against him.' After which, leave me to do battle with them; if they slay me, then is thy secret the surer guarded and thine honour the better warded; and if I overcome them and see their backs, then is it the like of me a King should covet to his son-in-law."

So the King approved of his opinion and accepted his proposition, despite his awe at the boldness of his speech and amaze at the pretensions of the Prince to meet in fight his whole host, such as he had described it to him, being at heart assured that he would perish in the fray and so he should be quit of him and freed from the fear of dishonour. Thereupon he called the eunuch and bade him go to his Wazir without stay and delay and command him to assemble the whole of the army and cause them don their arms and armour and mount their steeds. So the eunuch carried the King's orders to the Minister, who straightway summoned the Captains of the host and the Lords of the realm and bade them don their harness of derring-do and mount horse and sally forth in battle array. Such was their case; but as regards the King, he sat a long while conversing with the young Prince, being pleased with his wise speech and good sense and fine breeding. And when it was daybreak he returned to his palace and, seating himself on his throne, commanded his merry men to mount, and bade them saddle one of the best of the royal steeds with handsome selle and housings and trappings and bring it to the Prince. But the youth said, "O King, I will not mount horse, till I come in view of the troops and review them." "Be it as thou wilt," replied the King.

Then the two repaired to the parade-ground, where the troops were drawn up, and the young Prince looked upon them and noted their great number; after which the King cried out to them, saying, "Ho, all ye men, there is come to me a youth who seeketh my daughter in marriage; and in very sooth never have I seen a goodlier than he; no, nor a stouter of heart nor a doughtier of arm, for he pretendeth that he can overcome you, single-handed, and force you to flight, and that, were ye an hundred thousand in number, yet for him would ye be but few. Now, when he chargeth down on you, do ye receive him upon point of pike and sharp of sabre; for, indeed, he hath undertaken a mighty matter."

Then quoth the King to the Prince. "Up, O my son, and do thy devoir on them." Answered he, "O King, thou dealest not justly and fairly by me; how shall I go forth against them, seeing that I am afoot and the men be mounted?" The King retorted, "I bade thee mount, and thou refusedst; but choose thou which of my horses thou wilt." Then he said, "Not one of thy horses pleaseth me, and I will ride none but that on which I came." Asked the King, "And where is thy horse?" "Atop of thy palace." "In what part of my palace?" "On the roof."

Now, when the King heard these words, he cried, "Out on thee! this is the first sign thou hast given of madness. How can the horse be on the roof? But we shall at once see if thou speak truth or lies." Then he turned to one of his chief officers and said to him, "Go to my palace and bring me what thou findest on the roof." So all the people marvelled at the young Prince's words, saying one to other, "How can a horse come down the steps from the roof? Verily, this is a thing whose like we never heard." In the meantime the King's messenger repaired to the palace and, mounting to the roof, found the horse standing there, and never had he looked on a handsomer; but when he drew near and examined it, he saw that it was made of ebony and ivory. Now the officer was accompanied by other high officers, who also looked on, and they laughed to one another, saying, "Was it of the like of this horse that the youth spake? We cannot deem him other than mad; however, we shall soon see the truth of his case. Peradventure herein is some mighty matter, and he is a man of high degree." Then they lifted up the horse bodily and, carrying it to the King, set it down before him, and all the lieges flocked round to look at it, marvelling at the beauty of its proportions and the richness of its saddle and bridle. The King also admired it and wondered at it with extreme wonder; and he asked the Prince, "O youth, is this thy horse?" He answered, "Yes, O King, this is my horse, and thou shalt soon see the marvel it showeth." Rejoined the King, "Then take and mount it," and the Prince retorted, "I will not mount till the troops withdraw afar from it." So the King bade them retire a bowshot from the horse; whereupon quoth its owner, "O King, see thou; I am about to mount my horse and charge upon thy host and scatter them right and left and split their hearts asunder." Said the King, "Do as thou wilt; and spare not their lives, for they will not spare thine."

Then the Prince mounted, whilst the troops ranged themselves in ranks before him, and one said to another, "When the youth cometh between the ranks, we will take him on the points of our pikes and the sharps of our sabres." Quoth another, "By Allah, this is a mere misfortune; how shall we slay a youth so comely of face and shapely of form?" And a third continued, "Ye will have hard work to get the better of him; for the youth had not done this, but for what he knew of his own prowess and pre-eminence of valour." Meanwhile having settled himself in his saddle, the Prince turned the pin of ascent, whilst all eyes were strained to see what he would do, whereupon the horse began to heave and rock and sway to and fro and make the strangest of movements steed ever made, till its belly was filled with air and it took flight with its rider and soared high into the sky. When the King saw this he cried out to his men, saying, "Woe to you! catch him, catch him, ere he 'scape you!" But his Wazirs and Viceroys said to him, "O King, can a man overtake the flying bird? This is surely none but some mighty magician or Marid of the Jinn or devil, and Allah save thee from him. So praise thou the Almighty for deliverance of thee and of all thy host from his hand."

Then the King returned to his palace after seeing the feat of the Prince and, going in to his daughter, acquainted her with what had befallen them both on the parade-ground. He found her grievously afflicted for the Prince and bewailing her separation from him; wherefore she fell sick with violent sickness and took to her pillow. Now, when her father saw her on this wise, he pressed her to his breast and, kissing her between the eyes, said to her, "O my daughter, praise Allah Almighty and thank Him for that He hath delivered us from this crafty enchanter, this villain, this low fellow, this thief who thought only of seducing thee!" And he repeated to her the story of the Prince and how he had disappeared in the firmament; and he abused him and cursed him knowing not how dearly his daughter loved him. But she paid no heed to his words and did but redouble in her tears and wails, saying to herself, "By Allah, I will neither eat meat nor drain drink till Allah reunite me with him!" Her father was greatly concerned for her case and mourned much over her plight; but, for all he could do to soothe her, love-longing only increased on her.

Thus far concerning the King and Princess Shams al-Nahar; but as regards Prince Kamar al-Akmar, when he had risen high in air, he turned his horse's head towards his native land and, being alone, mused upon the beauty of the Princess and her loveliness. Now he had inquired of the King's people the name of the city and of its King and his daughter; and men had told him that it was the city of Sana'a. So he journeyed with all speed, till he drew near his father's capital and, making an airy circuit about the city, alighted on the roof of the King's palace, where he left his horse, whilst he descended into the palace, and, seeing its threshold strewn with ashes, thought that one of his family was dead. Then he entered, as of wont, and found his father and mother and sisters clad in mourning raiment of black, all pale of faces and lean of frames. When his sire descried him and was assured that it was indeed his son, he cried out with a great cry and fell down in a fit, but after a time coming to himself, threw himself upon him and embraced him, clipping him to his bosom and rejoicing in him with exceeding joy and extreme gladness. His mother and sisters heard this; so they came in and, seeing the Prince, fell upon him, kissing him and weeping, and joying with exceeding joyance. Then they questioned him of his case; so he told them all that had past from first to last, and his father said to him, "Praised be Allah for thy safety, O coolth of my eyes and core of my heart!"

Then the King bade hold high festival, and the glad tidings flew through the city. So they beat drums and cymbals and, doffing the weed of mourning, they donned the gay garb of gladness and decorated the streets and markets; whilst the folk vied with one another who should be the first to give the King joy, and the King proclaimed a general pardon and, opening the prisons, released those who were therein prisoned. Moreover, he made banquets for the people, with great abundance of eating and drinking, for seven days and nights, and all creatures were gladsomest; and he took horse with his son and rode out with him, that the folk might see him and rejoice. After a while the Prince asked about the maker of the horse, saying, "O my father, what hath fortune done with him?"; and the King answered, "Allah never bless him nor the hour wherein I set eyes on him! For he was the cause of thy separation from us, O my son, and he hath lain in jail since the day of thy disappearance." Then the King bade release him from prison and, sending for him, invested him in a dress of satisfaction and entreated him with the utmost favour and munificence, save that he would not give him his daughter to wife; whereat the sage raged with sore rage and repented of that which he had done, knowing that the Prince had secured the secret of the steed and the manner of its motion. Moreover, the King said to his son, "I reck thou wilt do well not to go near the horse henceforth and, more especially, not to mount it after this day; for thou knowest not its properties, and belike thou art in error about it."

Now the Prince had told his father of his adventure with the King of Sana'a and his daughter and he said, "Had the King intended to kill thee, he had done so; but thine hour was not yet come." When the rejoicings were at an end the people returned to their places and the King and his son to the palace, where they sat down and fell to eating and drinking and making merry. Now the King had a handsome handmaiden who was skilled in playing the lute; so she took it and began to sweep the strings and sing thereto before the King and his son of separation of lovers, and she chanted the following verses:

Deem not that absence breeds in me aught of forgetfulness;
What should remember I did you fro' my remembrance wane?
Time dies but never dies the fondest love for you we bear;
And in your love I'll die and in your love I'll rise again.

When the Prince heard these verses, the fires of longing flamed up in his heart and pine and passion redoubled upon him. Grief and regret were sore upon him and his bowels yearned in him for love of the King's daughter of Sana'a; so he rose forthright and, escaping his father's notice, went forth the palace to the horse and, mounting it, turned the pin of ascent, whereupon bird-like it flew with him high in air and soared towards the upper regions of the sky. In early morning his father missed him and, going up to the pinnacle of the palace, in great concern, saw his son rising into the firmament; whereat he was sore afflicted and repented in all penitence that he had not taken the horse and hidden it; and he said to himself, "By Allah, if but my son return to me, I will destroy the horse, that my heart may be at rest concerning my son." And he fell again to weeping and bewailing himself for his son.

Such was his case; but as regards the Prince, he ceased not flying on through air till he came to the city of Sana'a and alighted on the roof as before. Then he crept down stealthily and, finding the eunuch asleep, as of wont, raised the curtain and went on little by little, till he came to the door of the Princess's alcove-chamber and stopped to listen; when lo! he heard her shedding her plenteous tears and reciting verses, whilst her women slept around her. Presently, overhearing her weeping and wailing, quoth they, "O our mistress, why wilt thou mourn for one who mourneth not for thee?" Quoth she, "O ye little of wit, is he for whom

I mourn of those who forget or who are forgotten?" And she fell again to wailing and weeping, till sleep overcame her. Hereat the Prince's heart melted for her and his gall-bladder was like to burst, so he entered and, seeing her lying asleep without covering, touched her with his hand; whereupon she opened her eyes and espied him standing by her. Said he, "Why all this crying and mourning?" And when she knew him, she threw herself upon him, and took him around the neck and kissed him and answered, "For thy sake and because of my separation from thee." Said he, "O my lady, I have been made desolate by thee all this long time!" But she replied, "'Tis thou who hast desolated *me*; and hadst thou tarried longer, I had surely died!" Rejoined he, "O my lady, what thinkest thou of my case with thy father and how he dealt with me? Were it not for my love of thee, O temptation and seduction of the Three Worlds, I had certainly slain him and made him a warning to all beholders; but, even as I love thee, so I love him for thy sake." Quoth she, "How couldst thou leave me: can my life be sweet to me after thee?" Quoth he, "Let what hath happened suffice; I am now hungry, and thirsty."

So she bade her maidens make ready meat and drink, and they sat eating and drinking and conversing till night was wellnigh ended; and when day broke he rose to take leave of her and depart, ere the eunuch should awake. Shams al-Nahar asked him, "Whither goest thou?"; and he answered, "To my father's house, and I plight thee my troth that I will come to thee once in every week." But she wept and said, "I conjure thee, by Allah the Almighty, take me with thee whereso thou wendest and make me not taste anew the bitter-gourd of separation from thee." Quoth he, "Wilt thou indeed go with me?" and quoth she, "Yes." "Then," said he, "arise that we depart." So she rose forthright and, going to a chest, arrayed herself in what was richest and dearest to her of her trinkets of gold and jewels of price, and she fared forth, her handmaids recking naught. So he carried her up to the roof of the palace and, mounting the ebony horse, took her up behind him and made her fast to himself, binding her with strong bonds; after which he turned the shoulder-pin of ascent, and the horse rose with him high in air. When her slave-women saw this they shrieked aloud and told her father and mother, who in hot haste ran to the palace roof and, looking up, saw the magical horse flying away with the Prince and Princess. At this the King was troubled with ever-increasing trouble and cried out, saying, "O King's son, I conjure thee, by Allah, have ruth on me and my wife and bereave us not of our daughter!" The Prince made him no reply; but, thinking in himself that the maiden repented of leaving father and mother, asked her, "O ravishment of the age, say me, wilt thou that I restore thee to thy mother and father?"; whereupon she answered, "By Allah, O my lord, that is not my desire; my only wish is to be with thee, wherever thou art; for I am distracted by the love of thee from all else, even from my father and mother."

Hearing these words the Prince joyed with great joy, and made the horse fly and fare softly with them, so as not to disquiet her; nor did they stay their flight till they came in sight of a green meadow, wherein was a spring of running water. Here they alighted and ate and drank; after which the Prince took horse again and set her behind him, binding her in his fear for her safety; after which they fared on till they came in sight of his father's capital. At this, the Prince was filled with joy and bethought himself to show his beloved the seat of his dominion and his father's power and dignity and give her to know that it was greater than that of her sire. So he set her down in one of his father's gardens without the city where his parent was wont to take his pleasure; and, carrying her into a domed summer-house prepared there for the King, left the ebony horse at the door and charged the damsel keep watch over it, saying, "Sit here, till my messenger come to thee; for I go now to my father, to make ready a palace for thee and show thee my royal estate." She was delighted when she heard these words and said to him, "Do as thou wilt"; for she thereby understood that she should not enter the city but with due honour and worship, as became her rank.

Then the Prince left her and betook himself to the palace of the King his father, who rejoiced in his return and met and welcomed him; and the Prince said to him, "Know that I have brought with me the King's daughter of whom I told thee; and have left her without the city in such a garden and come to tell thee, that thou mayst make ready the procession of estate and go forth to meet her and show her thy royal dignity and troops and guards." Answered the King, "With joy and gladness"; and straightway bade decorate the town with the goodliest adornment. Then he took horse and rode out in all magnificence and majesty, he and his host, high officers and household, with drums and kettledrums, fifes and clarions and all manner instruments; whilst the Prince drew forth of his treasuries jewellery and apparel and what else of the things which kings hoard and made a rare display of wealth and splendour; moreover he got ready for the Princess a canopied litter of brocades, green, red and yellow, wherein he set Indian and Greek and Abyssinian slave-girls. Then he left the litter and those who were therein and preceded them to the pavilion where he had set her down; and searched but found naught, neither Princess nor horse.

When he saw this, he beat his face and rent his raiment and began to wander round about the garden, as he had lost his wits; after which he came to his senses and said to himself, "How could she have come at the secret of this horse, seeing I told her nothing of it? Maybe the Persian sage who made the horse hath chanced upon her and stolen her away, in revenge for my father's treatment of him." Then he sought the guardians of the garden and asked them if they had seen any pass the precincts; and said, "Hath anyone come in here? Tell me the truth and the whole truth or I will at once strike off your heads." They were terrified by his threats; but they answered with one voice, "We have seen no man enter save the Persian sage, who came to gather healing herbs." So the Prince was certified that it was indeed he who had taken away the maiden and abode confounded and perplexed concerning his case. And he was abashed before the folk and, turning to his sire, told him what had happened and said to him, "Take the troops and march them back to the city. As for me, I will never return till I have cleared up this affair." When the King heard this, he wept and beat his breast and said to him, "O my son, calm thy choler and master thy chagrin and come home with us and look what King's daughter thou wouldst fain have, that I may marry thee to her." But the Prince paid no heed to his words and, farewelling him, departed, whilst the King returned to the city and their joy was changed into sore annoy.

Now, as Destiny issued her decree, when the Prince left the Princess in the garden-house and betook himself to his father's palace, for the ordering of his affair, the Persian entered the garden to pluck certain simples and, scenting the sweet savour of musk and perfumes that exhaled from the Princess and impregnated the whole place, followed it till he came to the pavilion and saw standing at the door the horse which he had made with his own hands. His heart was filled with joy and gladness, for he had bemourned its loss much since it had gone out of his hand; so he went up to it and, examining its every part, found it whole and sound; whereupon he was about to mount and ride away, when he bethought himself and said, "Needs must I first look what the Prince hath brought and left here with the horse." So he entered the pavilion, and seeing the Princess sitting there, as she were the sun shining sheen in the sky serene, knew her at the first glance to be some high-born lady and doubted not but the Prince had brought her thither on the horse and left her in the pavilion, whilst he went to the city, to make ready for her entry in state procession with all splendour.

Then he went up to her and kissed the earth between her hands; whereupon she raised her eyes to him and, finding him exceedingly foul of face and favour, asked, "Who art thou?"; and he answered, "O my lady, I am a messenger sent by the Prince who hath bidden me bring thee to another pleasance nearer the city; for that my lady the Queen cannot walk so far and is unwilling, of her joy in thee, that another should forestall her with thee." Quoth she, "Where is the Prince?"; and quoth the Persian, "He is in the city, with his sire, and forthwith he shall come for thee in great state." Said she, "O thou! say me, could he find none handsomer to send to me?"; whereat loud laughed the sage and said; "Yea, verily, he hath not a Mameluke as ugly as I am; but, O my lady, let not the ill-favour of my face and the foulness of my form deceive thee. Hadst thou profited of me as hath the Prince, verily thou wouldst praise my affair. Indeed, he chose me as his messenger to thee, because of my uncomeliness and loathsomeness in his jealous love of thee; else hath he Mamelukes and negro slaves, pages, eunuchs and attendants out of number, each goodlier than other." When as she heard this, it commended itself to her reason and she believed him; so she rose forthright; and, putting her hand in his, said, "O my father, what hast thou brought me to ride?" He replied, "O my lady, thou shalt ride the horse thou camest on"; and she, "I cannot ride it by myself." Whereupon he smiled and knew that he was her master and said, "I will ride with thee myself."

So he mounted and, taking her up behind him, bound her to himself with firm bonds, while she knew not what he would with her. Then he turned the ascent-pin, whereupon the belly of the horse became full of wind and it swayed to and fro like a wave of the sea, and rose with them high in air nor slackened in its flight, till it was out of sight of the city. Now, when Shams al-Nahar saw this, she asked him, "Ho, thou! what is become of that thou toldst me of my Prince, making me believe that he sent thee to me?" Answered the Persian, "Allah damn the Prince! he is a mean and skinflint knave." She cried, "Woe to thee! How darest thou disobey thy lord's commandment?" Whereto the Persian

replied, "He is no lord of mine; knowest thou who I am?"
Rejoined the Princess, "I know nothing of thee save what
thou toldest me"; and retorted he, "What I told thee was a
trick of mine against thee and the King's son; I have long
lamented the loss of this horse which is under us; for I
constructed it and made myself master of it. But now I
have gotten firm hold of it and of thee too, and I will burn
his heart even as he hath burnt mine; nor shall he ever have
the horse again; no, never! So be of good cheer and keep
thine eyes cool and clear; for I can be of more use to thee
than he; and I am generous as I am wealthy; my servants
and slaves shall obey thee as their mistress; I will robe thee
in finest raiment and thine every wish shall be at thy will."

When she heard this, she buffeted her face and cried out,
saying, "Ah, well-away! I have not won my beloved and I
have lost my father and mother!" And she wept bitter tears
over what had befallen her, whilst the sage fared on with
her, without ceasing, till he came to the land of the Greeks
and alighted in a verdant mead, abounding in streams and
trees. Now this meadow lay near a city wherein was a King
of high puissance, and it chanced that he went forth that
day to hunt and divert himself. As he passed by the meadow,
he saw the Persian standing there, with the damsel and the
horse by his side; and, before the sage was ware, the King's
slaves fell upon him and carried him and the lady and the
horse to their master who, noting the foulness of the man's
favour and his loathsomeness and the beauty of the girl and
her loveliness, said, "O my lady, what kin is this oldster
to thee?" The Persian made haste to reply, saying, "She is
my wife and the daughter of my father's brother." But the
lady at once gave him the lie and said, "O King, by Allah,
I know him not, nor is he my husband; nay, he is a wicked
magician who hath stolen me away by force and fraud."
Thereupon the King bade bastinado the Persian and they
beat him till he was wellnigh dead; after which the King
commanded to carry him to the city and cast him into jail;
and, taking from him the damsel and the ebony horse (though
he knew not its properties nor the secret of its motion), set
the girl in his Serraglio and the horse amongst his hoards.

Such was the case with the sage and the lady; but as regards
Prince Kamar al-Akmar, he garbed himself in travelling
gear and taking what he needed of money, set out tracking
their trail in very sorry plight; and journeyed from country
to country and city to city seeking the Princess and inquiring
after the ebony horse, whilst all who heard him marvelled
at him and deemed his talk extravagant. Thus he continued

doing a long while; but, for all his inquiry and quest, he could hit on no news of her. At last he came to her father's city of Sana'a and there asked for her, but could get no tidings of her and found her father mourning her loss. So he turned back and made for the land of the Greeks, continuing to inquire concerning the twain as he went along, till, as chance would have it, he alighted at a certain Khan and saw a company of merchants sitting at talk. So he sat down near them and heard one say, "O my friends, I lately witnessed a wonder of wonders." They asked, "What was that?" and he answered, "I was visiting such a district in such a city (naming the city wherein was the Princess), and I heard its people chatting of a strange thing which had lately befallen. It was that their King went out one day hunting and coursing with a company of his courtiers and the lords of his realm; and, issuing from the city, they came to a green meadow where they espied an old man standing, with a woman sitting hard by a horse of ebony. The man was foulest-foul of face and loathy of form, but the woman was a marvel of beauty and loveliness and elegance and perfect grace; and as for the wooden horse, it was a miracle, never saw eyes aught goodlier than it nor more gracious than its make." Asked the others, "And what did the King with them?"; and the merchant answered, "As for the man the King seized him and questioned him of the damsel and he pretended that she was his wife and the daughter of his paternal uncle; but she gave him the lie forthright and declared that he was a sorcerer and a villain. So the King took her from the old man and bade bear him and cast him into the trunk-house. As for the ebony horse, I know not what became of it."

When the Prince heard these words, he drew near to the merchant and began questioning him discreetly and courteously touching the name of the city and of its King; which when he knew, he passed the night full of joy. And as soon as dawned the day he set out and travelled sans surcease till he reached that city; but, when he would have entered, the gatekeepers laid hands on him, that they might bring him before the King to question him of his condition and the craft in which he skilled and the cause of his coming thither —such being the usage and custom of their ruler. Now it was supper-time when he entered the city, and it was then impossible to go in to the King or take counsel with him respecting the stranger. So the guards carried him to the jail, thinking to lay him by the heels there for the night; but, when the warders saw his beauty and loveliness, they could not find it in their hearts to imprison him: they made him sit with them without the walls; and, when food came to them, he ate with them what sufficed him.

As soon as they had made an end of eating, they turned to the Prince and said, "What countryman art thou?" "I come from Fars," answered he, "the land of the Chosroës." When they heard this they laughed and one of them said, "O Chosroan,[1] I have heard the talk of men and their histories and I have looked into their conditions; but never saw I or heard I a bigger liar than the Chosroan which is with us in the jail." Quoth another, "And never did I see aught fouler than his favour or more hideous than his visnomy." Asked the Prince, "What have ye seen of his lying?"; and they answered, "He pretendeth that he is one of the wise! Now the King came upon him, as he went a-hunting, and found with him a most beautiful woman and a horse of the blackest ebony, never saw I a handsomer. As for the damsel, she is with the King, who is enamoured of her and would fain marry her; but she is mad, and were this man a leach as he claimeth to be, he would have healed her, for the King doth his utmost to discover a cure for her case and a remedy for her disease, and this whole year past hath he spent treasures upon physicians and astrologers, on her account; but none can avail to cure her. As for the horse, it is in the royal hoard-house, and the ugly man is here with us in prison; and as soon as night falleth, he weepeth and bemoaneth himself and will not let us sleep."

When the warders had recounted the case of the Persian egromancer they held in prison and his weeping and wailing, the Prince at once devised a device whereby he might compass his desire; and presently the guards of the gate, being minded to sleep, led him into the jail and locked the door. So he overheard the Persian weeping and bemoaning himself, in his own tongue, and saying, "Alack, and alas for my sin, that I sinned against myself and against the King's son, in that which I did with the damsel; for I neither left her nor won my will of her! All this cometh of my lack of sense, in that I sought for myself that which I deserved not and which befitted not the like of me; for whoso seeketh what suiteth him not at all, falleth with the like of my fall." Now when the King's son heard this, he accosted him in Persian, saying, "How long will this weeping and wailing last? Say me, thinkest thou that hath befallen thee that which never befell other than thou?" Now when the Persian heard this, he made friends with him and began to complain to him of his case

[1] "Fars" is the origin of Persia; and there is a hit at the prodigious lying of the modern race.

and misfortunes. And as soon as the morning morrowed, the warders took the Prince and carried him before their King, informing him that he had entered the city on the previous night, at a time when audience was impossible. Quoth the King to the Prince, "Whence comest thou and what is thy name and trade and why hast thou travelled hither?" He replied, "As to my name I am called in Persian Harjah; as to my country I come from the land of Fars; and I am of the men of art and especially of the art of medicine and healing the sick and those whom the Jinn drive mad. For this I go round about all countries and cities, to profit by adding knowledge to my knowledge, and whenever I see a patient I heal him and this is my craft."

Now when the King heard this, he rejoiced with exceeding joy and said; "O excellent sage, thou hast indeed come to us at a time when we need thee." Then he acquainted him with the case of the Princess, adding, "If thou cure her and recover her from her madness, thou shalt have of me everything thou seekest." Replied the Prince, "Allah save and favour the King: describe to me all thou hast seen of her insanity and tell me how long it is since the access attacked her; also how thou camest by her and the horse and the sage." So the King told him the whole story, from first to last, adding, "The sage is in jail." Quoth the Prince, "O auspicious King, and what hast thou done with the horse?" Quoth the King, "O youth, it is with me yet, laid up in one of my treasure-chambers," whereupon said the Prince within himself, "The best thing I can do is first to see the horse and assure myself of its condition. If it be whole and sound, all will be well and end well; but, if its motor-works be destroyed, I must find some other way of delivering my beloved."

Thereupon he turned to the King and said to him, "O King, I must see the horse in question: haply I may find in it somewhat that will serve me for the recovery of the damsel." "With all my heart," replied the King, and taking him by the hand, showed him into the place where the horse was. The Prince went round about it, examining its condition, and found it whole and sound, whereat he rejoiced greatly and said to the King, "Allah save and exalt the King! I would fain go in to the damsel, that I may see how it is with her; for I hope in Allah to heal her by my healing hand through means of the horse." Then he bade them take care of the horse and the King carried him to the Princess's apartment, where her lover found her wringing her hands and writhing and beating herself against the ground, and tearing her garments to tatters as was her wont; but there was no madness of

94

Jinn in her, and she did this but that none might approach her.

When the Prince saw her thus he said to her, "No harm shall betide thee, O ravishment of the three worlds"; and went on to soothe her and speak her fair, till he managed to whisper, "I am Kamar al-Akmar"; whereupon she cried out with a loud cry and fell down fainting for excess of joy; but the King thought this was epilepsy brought on by her fear of him, and by her suddenly being startled. Then the Prince put his mouth to her ear and said to her, "O Shams al-Nahar, O seduction of the universe, have a care for thy life and mine and be patient and constant; for this our position needeth sufferance and skilful contrivance to make shift for our delivery from this tyrannical King. My first move will be now to go out to him and tell him that thou art possessed of a Jinni and hence thy madness; but that I will engage to heal thee and drive away the evil spirit, if he will at once unbind thy bonds. So when he cometh in to thee, do thou speak him smooth words, that he may think I have cured thee, and all will be done for us as we desire." Quoth she, "Hearkening and obedience"; and he went out to the King in joy and gladness, and said to him, "O august King, I have, by thy good fortune, discovered her disease and its remedy, and have cured her for thee. So now do thou go in to her and speak her softly and treat her kindly; and promise her what may please her; so shall all thou desirest of her be accomplished to thee."

Thereupon the King went in to her and when she saw him, she rose and kissing the ground before him, bade him welcome and said, "I admire how thou hast come to visit thy handmaid this day"; whereat he was ready to fly for joy and bade the waiting-women and the eunuchs attend her and carry her to the Hammam and make ready for her dresses and adornment. So they went in to her and saluted her, and she returned their salams with the goodliest language and after the pleasantest fashion; whereupon they clad her in royal apparel and, clasping a collar of jewels about her neck, carried her to the bath and served her there. Then they brought her forth, as she were the full moon; and, when she came into the King's presence, she saluted him and kissing the ground before him; whereupon he joyed in her with joy exceeding and said to the Prince, "O sage, O philosopher, all this is of thy blessing. Allah increase to us the benefit of thy healing breath!" The Prince replied, "O King, for the completion of her cure it behoveth that thou go forth, thou and all thy troops and guards, to the place where thou foundest her, not forgetting the beast of black wood which was with her; for therein is a devil; and, unless I exorcise him, he will return to her and afflict her at the head of every month." "With love and gladness," cried the King, "O thou Prince of all philosophers and most learned of all who see the light of day."

Then he brought out the ebony horse to the meadow in question and rode thither with all his troops and the Princess, little weeting the purpose of the Prince. Now when they came to the appointed place, the Prince, still habited as a leach, bade them set the Princess and the steed as far as eye could reach from the King and his troops, and said to him, "With thy leave, and at thy word, I will now proceed to the fumigations and conjurations, and here imprison the adversary of mankind, that he may never more return to her. After this, I shall mount this wooden horse which seemeth to be made of ebony, and take the damsel up behind me; whereupon it will shake and sway to and fro and fare forwards, till it come to thee, when the affair will be at an end; and after this thou mayst do with her as thou wilt." When the King heard his words, he rejoiced with extreme joy; so the Prince mounted the horse, and, taking the damsel up behind him, whilst the King and his troops watched him, bound her fast to him. Then he turned the ascending-pin and the horse took flight and soared with them high in air, till they disappeared from every eye.

After this the King abode half the day, expecting their return; but they returned not. So when he despaired of them, repenting him greatly of that which he had done and grieving sore for the loss of the damsel, he went back to the city with his troops. He then sent for the Persian who was in prison and said to him, "O thou traitor, O thou villain, why didst thou hide from me the mystery of the ebony horse? And now a sharper hath come to me and hath carried it off, together with a slave-girl whose ornaments are worth a mint of money, and I shall never see anyone or anything of them again!" So the Persian related to him all his past, first and last, and the King was seized with a fit of fury which wellnigh ended his life. He shut himself up in his palace for a while, mourning and afflicted; but at last his Wazirs came in to him and applied themselves to comfort him, saying, "Verily, he who took the damsel is an enchanter, and praised be Allah who hath delivered thee from his craft and sorcery!" And they ceased not from him, till he was comforted for her loss.

Thus far concerning the King; but as for the Prince, he

continued his career towards his father's capital in joy and cheer, and stayed not till he alighted on his own palace, where he set the lady in safety; after which he went in to his father and mother and saluted them and acquainted them with her coming, whereat they were filled with solace and gladness. Then he spread great banquets for the townsfolk and they held high festival a whole month, at the end of which time he went in to the Princess and they took their joy of each other with exceeding joy. But his father brake the ebony horse in pieces and destroyed its mechanism for flight; moreover the Prince wrote a letter to the Princess's father, advising him of all that had befallen her and informing him how she was now married to him and in all health and happiness, and sent it by a messenger, together with costly presents and curious rarities. And when the messenger arrived at the city which was Sana'a and delivered the letter and the presents to the King, he read the missive and rejoiced greatly thereat and accepted the presents, honouring and rewarding the bearer handsomely. Moreover, he forwarded rich gifts to his son-in-law by the same messenger, who returned to his master and acquainted him with what had passed; whereat he was much cheered. And after this the Prince wrote a letter every year to his father-in-law and sent him presents till, in course of time, his sire King Sabur deceased and he reigned in his stead, ruling justly over his lieges and conducting himself well and righteously towards them, so that the land submitted to him and his subjects did him loyal service; and Kamar al-Akmar and his wife Shams al-Nahar abode in the enjoyment of all satisfaction and solace of life, till there came to them the Destroyer of Delights and Sunderer of Societies; the Plunderer of Palaces, the Caterer for Cemeteries, and the Garnerer of Graves. And now glory be to the Living One who dieth not and in whose hand is the dominion of the worlds visible and invisible!

How Abu Hasan Brake Wind

THEY recount that in the City Kaukaban of Al-Yaman there
was a man of the Fazli tribe who had left Badawi life, and
become a townsman for many years and was a merchant of
the most opulent merchants. His wife had deceased when
both were young; and his friends were instant with him to
marry again, ever quoting to him the words of the poet:

> Go, gossip! re-wed thee, for Prime draweth near:
> A wife is an almanac—good for the year.

So being weary of contention, Abu Hasan entered into negotia-
tions with the old women who procure matches, and married
a maid like Canopus when he hangeth over the seas of
Al-Hind. He made high festival therefor, bidding to the
wedding-banquet kith and kin, Olema and Fakirs; friends
and foes and all his acquaintances of that countryside. The
whole house was thrown open to feasting: there were rices
of five several colours, and sherbets of as many more; and
kids stuffed with walnuts and almonds and pistachios, and
a camel-colt[1] roasted whole. So they ate and drank and

---

[1] A favourite Badawi dish, but too expensive unless some accident happens to the
animal.

made mirth and merriment; and the bride was displayed in her seven dresses and one more, to the women, who could not take their eyes off her.

At last, the bridegroom was summoned to the chamber where she sat enthroned; and he rose slowly and with dignity from his divan; but in so doing, for that he was over-full of meat and drink, lo and behold! he let fly a fart, great and terrible. Thereupon each guest turned to his neighbour and talked aloud and made as though he had heard nothing, fearing for his life. But a consuming fire was lit in Abu Hasan's heart; so he pretended a call of nature; and, in lieu of seeking the bride-chamber, he went down to the house-court and saddled his mare and rode off, weeping bitterly, through the shadow of the night. In time he reached Lahej where he found a ship ready to sail for India; so he shipped on board and made Calicut of Malabar. Here he met with many Arabs, especially Hazramis,[1] who recommended him to the King; and this King (who was a Kafir) trusted him and advanced him to the captainship of his bodyguard. He remained ten years in all solace and delight of life; at the end of which time he was seized with homesickness; and the longing to behold his native land was that of a lover pining for his beloved; and he came near to die of yearning desire.

But his appointed day had not dawned; so, after taking the first bath of health, he left the King without leave, and in due course landed at Makalla of Hazramaut. Here he donned the rags of a religious; and, keeping his name and case secret, fared for Kaukaban afoot; enduring a thousand hardships of hunger, thirst and fatigue; and braving a thousand dangers from the lion, the snake and the Ghul. But when he drew near his old home, he looked down upon it from the hills with brimming eyes, and said in himself, "Haply they might know thee; so I will wander about the outskirts, and hearken to the folk. Allah grant that my case be not remembered by them!" He listened carefully for seven nights and seven days, till it so chanced that, as he was sitting at the door of a hut, he heard the voice of a young girl saying, "O my mother, tell me the day when I was born; for such an one of my companions is about to take an omen for me."[2] And the mother answered, "Thou was born, O my daughter, on the very night when Abu Hasan farted."

---

[1] *I.e.* of the province of Hazramaut, the Biblical Hazarmaveth (Gen. x. 26).
[2] Alluding to the *Sortes Coranicæ* and other silly practices known to the English servant-girl when curious about her future.

Now the listener no sooner heard these words than he rose up from the bench, and fled away saying to himself, "Verily thy fart hath become a date, which shall last for ever and ever; even as the poet said:

As long as palms shall shift the flower;
As long as palms shall sift the flour. [1]

And he ceased not travelling and voyaging and returned to India; and there abode in self-exile till he died; and the mercy of Allah be upon him! [2]

---

[1] *I.e.* in Arab-land (where they eat dates) and Ajam, or lands non-Arab (where bread is the staff of life); that is, all the world over.

[2] The Badawi who eructates as a civility has a mortal hatred of a *crepitus ventris*; and were a by-stander to laugh at its accidental occurrence he would at once be cut down as a "pundonor."

The Lady and her Five Suitors

A WOMAN of the daughters of the merchants was married
to a man who was a great traveller. It chanced once that
he set out for a far country and was absent so long that
his wife, from pure ennui, fell in love with a handsome
young man of the sons of the merchants, and they loved
each other with exceeding love. One day the youth quarrelled
with another man, who lodged a complaint against him with
the Chief of Police, and he cast him into prison. When the
news came to the merchant's wife his mistress, she wellnigh
lost her wits; then she arose and donning her richest clothes
repaired to the house of the Chief of Police. She saluted
him and presented a written petition to this purport: "He
thou hast clapped in jail is my brother such and such, who
fell out with such an one; and those who testified against
him bore false witness. He hath been wrongfully imprisoned,
and I have none other to come in to me nor to provide for my
support; therefore I beseech thee of thy grace to release him."
When the magistrate had read the paper, he cast his eyes
on her and fell in love with her forthright; so he said to
her, "Go into the house, till I bring him before me; then I
will send for thee and thou shalt take him." "O my lord,"
replied she, "I have none to protect me save Almighty Allah!
I am a stranger and may not enter any man's abode." Quoth
the Wali, "I will not let him go, except thou come to my
home and I take my will of thee." Rejoined she, "If it must
be so, thou must needs come to my lodging and sit and
sleep the siesta and rest the whole day there." "And where
is thy abode?" asked he; and she answered, "In such a place,"
and appointed him for such a time. Then she went out from
him, leaving his heart taken with love of her, and she
repaired to the Kazi of the city to whom she said, "O our
lord the Kazi!" He exclaimed, "Yes!" and she continued,
"Look into my case, and thy reward be with Allah the Most
High!" Quoth he, "Who hath wronged thee?" and quoth she,

101

"O my lord, I have a brother and I have none but that one, and it is on his account that I come to thee; because the Wali hath imprisoned him for a criminal and men have borne false witness against him that he is a wrong-doer; and I beseech thee to intercede for him with the Chief of Police."

When the Kazi looked on her, he fell in love with her forthright and said to her, "Enter the house and rest awhile with my handmaids whilst I send to the Wali to release thy brother. If I knew the money-fine which is upon him, I would pay it out of my own purse, so I may have my desire of thee, for thou pleasest me with thy sweet speech." Quoth she, "If thou, O my lord, do thus, we must not blame others." Quoth he, "An thou wilt not come in, wend thy ways." Then said she, "An thou wilt have it so, O our lord, it will be privier and better in my place than in thine, for here are slave-girls and eunuchs and goers-in and comers-out, and indeed I am a woman who wotteth naught of this fashion; but need compelleth." Asked the Kazi, "And where is thy house?"; and she answered, "In such a place," and appointed him for the same day and time as the Chief of Police. Then she went out from him to the Wazir, to whom she preferred her petition for the release from prison of her brother who was absolutely necessary to her; but he also required her of herself, saying, "Suffer me to have my will of thee and I will set thy brother free." Quoth she, "An thou wilt have it so, be it in my house, for there it will be privier both for me and for thee. It is not far distant and thou knowest that which behoveth us women of cleanliness and adornment." Asked he, "Where is thy house?" "In such a place," answered she and appointed him for the same time as the two others.

Then she went out from him to the King of the city and told him her story and sought of him her brother's release. "Who imprisoned him?" inquired he; and she replied, " 'Twas thy Chief of Police." When the King heard her speech, it transpierced his heart with the arrows of love and he bade her enter the palace with him, that he might send to the Kazi and release her brother. Quoth she, "O King, this thing is easy to thee, whether I will or nill; and if the King will indeed have this of me, it is of my good fortune; but, if he come to my house, he will do me the more honour by setting step therein." Quoth the King, "We will not cross thee in this." So she appointed him for the same time as the three others, and told him where her house was.

Then she left him and, betaking herself to a man which was a carpenter, said to him, "I would have thee make me a cabinet with four compartments one above other, each with its door for locking up. Let me know thy hire and I will give it thee." Replied he, "My price will be four dinars; but, O noble lady and well-protected, if thou wilt vouchsafe me thy favours, I will ask nothing of thee." Rejoined she, "An there be no help but that thou have it so, then make thou five compartments with their padlocks"; and she appointed him to bring it exactly on the day required. Said he, "It is well; sit down, O my lady, and I will make it for thee forthright, and after I will come to thee at my leisure." So she sat down by him, whilst he fell to work on the cabinet, and when he had made an end of it she chose to see it at once carried home and set up in the sitting-chamber. Then she took four gowns and carried them to the dyer, who dyed them each of a different colour; after which she applied herself to making ready meat and drink, fruits, flowers and perfumes.

Now, when the appointed trysting-day came, she donned her costliest dress and adorned herself and scented herself, then spread the sitting-room with various kinds of rich carpets and sat down to await who should come. And behold, the Kazi was the first to appear, devancing the rest; and when she saw him, she rose to her feet and kissed the ground before him; then, taking him by the hand, made him sit down by her on the couch and lay with him and fell to jesting and toying with him. By and by, he would have her do his desire, but she said, "O my lord, doff thy clothes and turband and assume this yellow cassock and this headkerchief,[1] whilst I bring thee meat and drink; and after thou shalt win thy will." So saying, she took his clothes and turband and clad him in the cassock and the kerchief; but hardly had she done this, when lo! there came a knocking at the door. Asked he, "Who is that rapping at the door?" and she answered, "My husband." Quoth the Kazi, "What is to be done, and where shall I go?" Quoth she, "Fear nothing, I will hide thee in this cabinet"; and he, "Do as seemeth good to thee." So she took him by the hand and, pushing him into the lowest compartment, locked the door upon him.

Then she went to the house-door, where she found the Wali; so she kissed the ground before him and, taking his hand, brought him into the saloon, where she made him sit down and said to him, "O my lord, this house is thy house; this place is thy place, and I am thy handmaid; thou shalt pass all this day with me; wherefore do thou doff thy clothes

---

[1] When Easterns sit down to a drinking-bout, which means to get drunk as speedily and pleasantly as possible, they put off dresses of dull colours and robe themselves in clothes supplied by the host, of the brightest he may have, especially yellow, green and red of different shades. So the lady's proceeding was not likely to breed suspicion.

and don this red gown, for it is a sleeping-gown." So she took away his clothes and made him assume the red gown and set on his head an old patched rag she had by her; after which she sat by him on the divan and she sported with him while he toyed with her awhile, till he put out his hand to her. Whereupon she said to him, "O our lord, this day is thy day and none shall share in it with thee; but first, of thy favour and benevolence, write me an order for my brother's release from jail that my heart may be at ease." Quoth he, "Hearkening and obedience; on my head and eyes be it!"; and wrote a letter to his treasurer, saying: "As soon as this communication shall reach thee, do thou set such an one free, without stay or delay; neither answer the bearer a word." Then he sealed it and she took it from him, after which she began to toy again with him on the divan when, behold, someone knocked at the door. He asked, "Who is that?" and she answered, "My husband." "What shall I do?" said he, and she, "Enter this cabinet, till I send him away and return to thee." So she clapped him into the second compartment from the bottom and padlocked the door on him; and meanwhile the Kazi heard all they said.

Then she went to the house-door and opened it, whereupon, lo! the Wazir entered. She kissed the ground before him and received him with all honour and worship, saying, "O my lord, thou exaltest us by thy coming to our house; Allah never deprive us of the light of thy countenance!" Then she seated him on the divan and said to him, "O my lord, doff thy heavy dress and turband and don these lighter vestments." So he put off his clothes and turband and she clad him in a blue cassock and a tall red bonnet, and said to him, "Erst thy garb was that of the Wazirate; so leave it to its own time and don this light gown, which is better fitted for carousing and making merry and sleep." Thereupon she began to play with him and he with her, and he would have done his desire of her; but she put him off, saying, "O my lord, this shall not fail us." As they were talking there came a knocking at the door, and the Wazir asked her, "Who is that?"; to which she answered, "My husband." Quoth he, "What is to be done?" Quoth she, "Enter this cabinet, till I get rid of him and come back to thee and fear thou nothing." So she put him in the third compartment and locked the door on him, after which she went out and opened the house door when, lo and behold! in came the King.

As soon as she saw him she kissed the ground before him and, taking him by the hand, led him into the saloon and seated him on the divan at the upper end. Then said she to him, "Verily, O King, thou dost us high honour, and if we brought thee to gift the world and all that therein is, it would not be worth a single one of thy steps us-wards." And when he had taken his seat upon the divan she said, "Give me leave to speak one word." "Say what thou wilt," answered he, and she said, "O my lord, take thine ease and doff thy dress and turband." Now his clothes were worth a thousand dinars; and when he put them off she clad him in a patched gown, worth at the very most ten dirhams, and fell to talking and jesting with him; all this while the folk in the cabinet hearing everything that passed, but not daring to say a word. Presently, the King put his hand to her neck and sought to do his desire of her; when she said, "This thing shall not fail us, but I had first promised myself to entertain thee in this sitting-chamber, and I have that which shall content thee." Now, as they were speaking, someone knocked at the door and he asked her, "Who is that?" "My husband," answered she; and he, "Make him go away of his own good will, or I will fare forth to him and send him away perforce." Replied she, "Nay, O my lord, have patience till I send him away by my skilful contrivance." "And I, how shall I do?" inquired the King; whereupon she took him by the hand and, making him enter the fourth compartment of the cabinet, locked it upon him. Then she went out and opened the house-door, when behold, the carpenter entered and saluted her.

Quoth she, "What manner of thing is this cabinet thou hast made me?" "What aileth it, O my lady?" asked he, and she answered, "The top compartment is too strait." Rejoined he, "Not so"; and she, "Go in thyself and see; it is not wide enough for thee." Quoth he, "It is wide enough for four," and entered the fifth compartment, whereupon she locked the door on him. Then she took the letter of the Chief of Police and carried it to the treasurer who, having read and understood it, kissed it and delivered her lover to her. She told him all she had done and he said, "And how shall we act now?" She answered, "We will remove hence to another city, for after this work there is no tarrying for us here." So the twain packed up what goods they had and, loading them on camels, set out forthright for another city.

Meanwhile, the five abode each in his compartment of the cabinet without eating or drinking three whole days, during which time they held their water, until at last the carpenter could retain his no longer; so he staled on the King's head, and the King urined on the Wazir's head, and the Wazir piddled on the Wali and the Wali pissed on the head of the

Kazi; whereupon the Judge cried out and said, "What nastiness is this? Doth not what strait we are in suffice us, but you must make water upon us?" The Chief of Police recognised the Kazi's voice and answered, saying aloud, "Allah increase thy reward, O Kazi!" And when the Kazi heard him, he knew him for the Wali. Then the Chief of Police lifted up his voice and said, "What means this nastiness?" and the Wazir answered, saying, "Allah increase thy reward, O Wali!" whereupon he knew him to be the Minister. Then the Wazir lifted up his voice and said, "What means this nastiness?" But when the King heard and recognised his Minister's voice, he held his peace and concealed his affair. Then said the Wazir, "May God damn this woman for her dealing with us! She hath brought hither all the Chief Officers of the State, except the King." Quoth the King, "Hold your peace, for I was the first to fall into the toils of this lewd strumpet." Whereat cried the carpenter, "And I, what have I done? I made her a cabinet for four gold pieces, and when I came to seek my hire, she tricked me into entering this compartment and locked the door on me." And they fell to talking with one another, diverting the King and doing away his chagrin.

Presently the neighbours came up to the house and, seeing it deserted, said one to other, "But yesterday our neighbour, the wife of such an one, was in it; but now no sound is to be heard therein nor is soul to be seen. Let us break open the doors and see how the case stands, lest it come to the ears of the Wali or the King and we be cast into prison and regret not doing this thing before." So they broke open the doors and entered the saloon, where they saw a large wooden cabinet and heard men within groaning for hunger and thirst. Then said one of them, "Is there a Jinni in this cabinet?" and his fellow, "Let us heap fuel about it and burn it with fire." When the Kazi heard this, he bawled out to them, "Do it not!" And they said to one another, "Verily the Jinn make believe to be mortals and speak with men's voices." Thereupon the Kazi repeated somewhat of the Sublime Koran and said to the neighbours, "Draw near to the cabinet wherein we are." So they drew near, and he said, "I am so and so the Kazi, and ye are such an one and such an one, and we are here a company." Quoth the neighbours, "Who brought you here?" And he told them the whole case from beginning to end. Then they fetched a carpenter, who opened the five doors and let out Kazi, Wazir, Wali, King and carpenter in their queer disguises; and each, when he saw how the others were accoutred, fell a-laughing at them.

Julnar the Sea-Born and Her Son King Badr Basim of Persia

THERE was once in days of yore and in ages and times long
gone before, in Ajam-land, a King, Shahriman hight, whose
abiding-place was Khorasan. He owned an hundred concubines, but by none of them had he been blessed with boon
of child, male or female, all the days of his life. One day,
among the days, he bethought him of this and fell lamenting
for that the most part of his existence was passed and he had
not been vouchsafed a son to inherit the kingdom after him,
even as he had inherited it from his fathers and forbears;
by reason whereof there betided him sore cark and care and
chagrin exceeding. As he sat thus one of his Mamelukes came
in to him and said, "O my lord, at the door is a slave-girl with
her merchant, and fairer than she eye hath never seen." Quoth
the King, "Hither to me with merchant and maid!"; and
both came in to him. Now, when Shahriman beheld the girl,
he saw that she was like a Rudaynian lance, and she was
wrapped in a veil of gold-purfled silk. The merchant
uncovered her face, whereupon the place was illumined by
her beauty and her seven tresses hung down to her anklets
like horses' tails. She had Nature-kohl'd eyes, heavy hips and
thighs and waist of slenderest guise; her sight healed all
maladies and quenched the fire of sighs.

The King, seeing her, marvelled at her beauty and loveliness,
her symmetry and perfect grace, and said to the merchant,
"O Shaykh, how much for this maiden?" Replied the
merchant, "O my lord, I bought her for two thousand dinars
of the merchant who owned her before myself, since when I

have travelled with her three years and she hath cost me, up to the time of my coming hither, other three thousand gold pieces; but she is a gift from me to thee." The King robed him with a splendid robe of honour and ordered him ten thousand ducats, whereupon he kissed his hands, thanking him for his bounty and beneficence, and went his ways. Then the King committed the damsel to the tire-women, saying, "Amend ye the case of this maiden[1] and adorn her and furnish her a bower and set her therein." And he bade his chamberlains carry her everything she needed and shut all the doors upon her.

Now his capital wherein he dwelt was called the White City and was seated on the seashore; so they lodged her in a chamber whose latticed casements overlooked the main. Then Shahriman went in to her; but she spake not to him neither took any note of him. Quoth he, "'Twould seem she hath been with folk who have not taught her manners." Then he looked at the damsel and saw her surpassing beauty and loveliness and symmetry and perfect grace, with a face like the rondure of the moon at its full or the sun shining in the sheeny sky. So he marvelled at her charms of favour and figure and he praised Allah the Creator (magnified be His might!), after which he walked up to her and sat him down by her side; then he pressed her to his bosom and seating her on his thighs, sucked the dew of her lips which he found sweeter than honey. Presently he called for trays spread with richest viands of all kinds and ate and fed her by mouthfuls, till she had enough; yet she spoke not one word.

The King began to talk to her and asked her of her name; but she abode still silent and uttered not a syllable nor made him any answer, neither ceased to hang down her head groundwards; and it was but the excess of her beauty and loveliness and the amorous grace that saved her from the royal wrath. Quoth he to himself, "Glory be to God, the Creator of this girl! How charming she is, save that she speaketh not! But perfection belongeth only to Allah the Most High." And he asked the slave-girls whether she had spoken, and they said, "From the time of her coming until now she hath not uttered a word nor have we heard her address us." Then he summoned some of his women and concubines and bade them sing to her and make merry with her, so haply she might speak. Accordingly they played before her all manner instruments of music and sports and what not and sang, till the whole

---

1 *I.e.* bathe her and apply cosmetics to remove all traces of travel.

company was moved to mirth, except the damsel, who looked at them in silence, but neither laughed nor spoke. The King's breast was straitened; thereupon he dismissed the women and abode alone with that damsel: after which he doffed his clothes and disrobing her with his own hand, looked upon her body and saw it as it were a silvern ingot. So he loved her with exceeding love and falling upon her, took her maidenhead and found her a pure virgin; whereat he rejoiced with excessive joy and said in himself, "By Allah, 'tis a wonder that a girl so fair of form and face should have been left by the merchants a clean maid as she is!"

Then he devoted himself altogether to her, heeding none other and forsaking all his concubines and favourites, and tarried with her a whole year as it were a single day. Still she spoke not, till one morning he said to her (and indeed the love of her and longing waxed upon him), "O desire of souls, verily passion for thee is great with me, and I have forsaken for thy sake all my slave-girls and concubines and women and favourites and I have made thee my portion of the world and had patience with thee a whole year; and now I beseech Almighty Allah, of His favour, to soften thy heart to me, so thou mayst speak to me. Or, an thou be dumb, tell me by a sign, that I may give up hope of thy speech. I pray the Lord (extolled be He!) to vouchsafe me by thee a son child who shall inherit the kingdom after me; for I am old and lone and have none to be my heir. Wherefore, Allah upon thee, an thou love me, return me a reply." The damsel bowed her head awhile in thought, and presently raising it, smiled in his face; whereat it seemed to him as if lightning filled the chamber. Then she said, "O magnanimous liege lord, and valorous lion, Allah hath answered thy prayer, for I am with child by thee and the time of my delivery is near at hand, though I know not if the unborn babe be male or female. But, had I not conceived by thee, I had not spoken to thee one word."

When the King heard her speech, his face shone with joy and gladness and he kissed her head and hands for excess of delight, saying, "Alhamdolillah—laud to Lord—who hath vouchsafed me the things I desired!; first, thy speech, and secondly, thy tidings that thou art with child by me." Then he rose up and went forth from her and, seating himself on the throne of his kingship in an ecstasy of happiness, bade his Wazir distribute to the poor and needy and widows and others an hundred thousand dinars, by way of thank-offering to Allah Most High and alms on his own account. The Minister did as bidden by the King who, returning to the damsel, sat with her and embraced and pressed her to his breast, saying, "O my lady, my queen, whose slave I am, prithee what was the cause of this thy silence? Thou hast been with me a whole year, night and day, waking and sleeping, yet hast not spoken to me till this day." She replied, "Hearken, O King of the Age, and know that I am a wretched exile, broken-hearted and far-parted from my mother and my family and my brother." When the King heard her words, he knew her desire and said, "As for thy saying that thou art wretched, there is for such speech no ground, inasmuch as my kingdom and good and all I possess are at thy service and I also am become thy bondman; but, as for thy saying 'I am parted from my mother and brother and family,' tell me where they are and I will send and fetch them to thee."

Thereupon she answered, "Know, then, O auspicious King, that I am called Julnar the Sea-born and that my father was of the Kings of the Main. He died and left us his reign, but while we were yet unsettled, behold, one of the other Kings arose against us and took the realm from our hands. I have a brother called Salih, and my mother also is a woman of the sea; but I fell out with my brother, 'The Pious,' and swore that I would throw myself into the hands of a man of the folk of the land. So I came forth of the sea and sat down on the edge of an island in the moonshine, where a passer-by found me and, carrying me to his house, besought me of love-liesse; but I smote him on the head, so that he all but died; whereupon he carried me forth and sold me to the merchant from whom thou hadst me, and this was a good man and a virtuous; pious, loyal and generous. Were it not that thy heart loved me and that thou promotedest me over all thy concubines, I had not remained with thee a single hour, but had cast myself from this window into the sea and gone to my mother and family; but I was ashamed to fare themwards, being with child by thee; for they would have deemed evilly of me and would not have credited me, even although I swore to them, an I told them that a King had bought me with his gold and made me his portion of the world and preferred me over all his wives and every thing that his right hand possessed. This then is my story and—the Peace!"

The King thanked her and kissed her between the eyes, saying, "By Allah, O my lady and light of mine eyes, I cannot bear to be parted from thee one hour; and given thou leave me, I shall die forthright. What then is to be done?" Replied she, "O my lord, the time of my delivery is at hand and my family needs must be present, that they may tend me; for the women of the land know not the manner of child-bearing of the women of the sea, nor do the daughters of the ocean know the manner of the daughters of the earth; and when my people come, I shall be reconciled to them and they will be reconciled to me." Quoth the King, "How do the people of the sea walk therein, without being wetted?"; and quoth she, "O King of the Age, we walk in the waters with our eyes open, as do ye on the ground, by the blessing of the names graven upon the seal-ring of Solomon David-son (on whom be peace!). But, O King, when my kith and kin come, I will tell them how thou boughtest me with thy gold, and hast entreated me with kindness and benevolence. It behoveth that thou confirm my words to them and that they witness thine estate with their own eyes and they learn that thou art a King, son of a King." He rejoined, "O my lady, do what seemeth good to thee and what pleaseth thee; and I will consent to thee in all thou wouldst do."

The damsel continued, "Yes, we walk in the sea and see what is therein and behold the sun, moon, stars and sky, as it were on the surface of earth; and this irketh us naught. Know also that there be many peoples in the main and various forms and creatures of all kinds that are on the land, and that all that is on the land compared with that which is in the main is but a very small matter." And the King marvelled at her words. Then she pulled out from her bosom two bits of Comorin lignaloes and, kindling fire in a chafing-dish, chose somewhat of them and threw it in, then she whistled a loud whistle and spake words none understood. Thereupon arose a great smoke and she said to the King, who was looking on, "O my lord, arise and hide thyself in a closet, that I may show thee my brother and mother and family, whilst they see thee not; for I design to bring them hither, and thou shalt presently espy a wondrous thing and shalt marvel at the several creatures and strange shapes which Almighty Allah hath created." So he arose without stay or delay and entering a closet, fell awatching what she should do. She continued her fumigations and conjurations till the sea foamed and frothed turbid and there rose from it a handsome young man of a bright favour, as he were the moon at its full, with brow flower-white, cheeks of ruddy light and teeth like the marguerite. He was the likest of all creatures to his sister. After him there came forth of the sea an ancient dame with hair speckled grey and five maidens, as they were moons, bearing a likeness to the damsel hight Julnar.

The King looked upon them as they all walked upon the face of the water, till they drew near the window and saw

Julnar, whereupon they knew her and went in to her. She rose to them and met them with joy and gladness, and they embraced her and wept with sore weeping. Then said they to her, "O Julnar, how couldst thou leave us four years, and we unknowing of thine abiding place? By Allah the world hath been straitened upon us for stress of severance from thee, and we have had no delight of food or drink; no, not for one day, but have wept with sore weeping night and day for the excess of our longing after thee!" Then she fell to kissing the hands of the youth her brother and her mother and cousins, and they sat with her awhile, questioning her of her case and of what had betided her, as well as of her present estate. "Know," replied she, "that, when I left you, I issued from the sea and sat down on the shore of an island, where a man found me and sold me to a merchant, who brought me to this city and sold me for ten thousand dinars to the King of the country, who entreated me with honour and forsook all his concubines and women and favourites for my sake and was distracted by me from all he had and all that was in his city." Quoth her brother, "Praised be Allah, who hath reunited us with thee! But now, O my sister, 'tis my purpose that thou arise and go with us to our country and people."

When the King heard these words his wits fled him for fear lest the damsel accept her brother's words and he himself avail not to stay her, albeit he loved her passionately, and he became distracted with fear of losing her. But Julnar answered, "By Allah, O my brother, the mortal who bought me is lord of this city and he is a mighty King and a wise man, good and generous with extreme generosity. Moreover, he is a personage of great worth and wealth and hath neither son nor daughter. He hath entreated me with honour and done me all manner of favour and kindness; nor, from the day of his buying me to this time have I heard from him an ill-word to hurt my heart; but he hath never ceased to use me courteously; doing nothing save with my counsel, and I am in the best of case with him and in the perfection of fair fortune. Furthermore, were I to leave him, he would perish; for he cannot endure to be parted from me an hour; and if I left him I also should die, for the excess of love I bear him, by reason of his great goodness to me during the time of my sojourn with him; for, were my father alive, my estate with him would not be like my estate with this great and glorious and puissant potentate. And verily, ye see me with child by him and praise be to Allah, who hath made me a daughter of the Kings of the sea, and my husband the mightiest of the Kings of the land, and Allah, in very sooth, he hath compensated me whatso I lost. Now this King hath no issue, male of female, so I pray the Almighty to vouchsafe me a son who shall inherit of this mighty sovran that which the Lord hath bestowed upon him of the lands and palaces and possessions."

Now, when her brother and the daughters of her uncle heard this her speech, their eyes were cooled thereby and they said, "O Julnar, thou knowest thy value with us and thou wottest the affection we bear thee and thou art certified that thou art to us the dearest of all creatures and thou art assured that we seek but ease for thee, without travail or trouble. Wherefore, an thou be in unease, arise and go with us to our land and our folk; but, an thou be at thine ease here, in honour and happiness, this is our wish and and our will; for we desire naught save thy welfare in any case." Quoth she, "By Allah, I am here in the utmost ease and solace and honour and grace!" When the King heard what she said, he joyed with a heart set at rest and thanked her silently for this; the love of her redoubled on him and entered his heart-core and he knew that she loved him and he loved her and that she desired to abide with him, that she might see his child by her. Then Julnar bade her women lay the tables and set on all sorts of viands, which had been cooked in kitchen under her own eyes, and fruits and sweetmeats, whereof she ate, she and her kinsfolk.

But presently they said to her, "O Julnar, thy lord is a stranger to us, and we have entered his house, without his leave or weeting. Thou hast extolled to us his excellence and eke thou hast set before us of his victual whereof we have eaten; yet have we not companied with him nor seen him, neither hath he seen us nor come to our presence and eaten with us, so there might be between us bread and salt." And they all left eating and were wroth with her, and fire issued from their mouths, as from cressets; which, when the King saw, his wits fled for excess of fear of them. But Julnar arose and soothed them and, going to the closet where was the King her lord, said to him, "O my lord, hast thou seen and heard how I praised thee and extolled thee to my people, and hast thou noted what they said to me of their desire to carry me away with them?" Quoth he, "I both heard and saw. May the Almighty abundantly requite thee for me! By Allah, I knew not the full measure of thy fondness until this blessed hour, and now I doubt not of thy love to me!" Quoth she, "O my lord, is the reward of kindness aught but kindness? Verily, thou hast dealt generously with me and hast entreated me with worship and I have seen that thou lovest me with the utmost love, and thou hast done me all manner of honour and kindness and preferred me above all thou lovest and desirest. So how should my heart be content to leave thee and depart from thee, and how should I do thus after all thy goodness to me? But now I desire of thy courtesy that thou come and salute my family, so thou mayst see them and they thee and pure love and friendship may be between you; for know, O King of the Age, that my brother and mother and cousins love thee with exceeding love, by reason of my praises of thee to them, and they say, 'We will not depart from thee nor go to our homes till we have foregathered with the King and saluted him.' For indeed they desire to see thee and make acquaintance with thee."

The King replied, "To hear is to obey, for this is my very own wish." So saying, he rose and went in to them and saluted them with the goodliest salutation; and they sprang up to him and received him with the utmost worship, after which he sat down in the palace and ate with them; and he entertained them thus for the space of thirty days. Then, being desirous of returning home, they took leave of the King and Queen and departed with due permission to their own land, after he had done them all possible honour.

Awhile after this, Julnar completed the days of her pregnancy; and the time of her delivery being come, she bore a boy, as he were the moon at its full; whereat the utmost joy betided the King, for that he had never in his life been vouchsafed son or daughter. So they held high festival and decorated the city seven days, in the extreme of joy and jollity; and, on the seventh day, came Queen Julnar's mother, Farashah hight, and brother and cousins, whenas they knew of her delivery. The King received them with joy at their coming and said to them, "I said that I could not give my son a name till you should come and name him of your knowledge." So they named him Badr Basim, and all agreed upon this name. Then they showed the child to his uncle, Salih, who took him in his arms and, arising, began to walk about the chamber with him in all directions right and left. Presently he carried him forth of the palace and, going down to the salt sea, fared on with him, till he was hidden from the King's sight. Now, when Shahriman saw him take his son and disappear with him in the depth of the sea, he gave the child up for lost and fell to weeping and wailing; but Julnar said to him, "O King of the Age, fear not, neither grieve for thy son, for I love my child more than thou and he is with my brother; so reck thou not of the sea, neither fear for him drowning. Had my brother known that aught

114

of harm would betide the little one, he had not done this deed; and he will presently bring thee thy son safe, Inshallah!—an it please the Almighty."

Nor was an hour past before the sea became turbid and troubled and King Salih came forth and flew from the sea till he came up to them with the child lying quiet and showing a face like the moon on the night of fullness. Then, looking at the King, he said, "Haply thou fearedst harm for thy son, whenas I plunged into the sea with him?" Replied the father, "Yes, O my lord, I did indeed fear for him and thought he would never be saved therefrom." Rejoined Salih, "O King of the land, we pencilled his eyes with an eye-powder we know of and recited over him the names graven upon the seal-ring of Solomon David-son (on whom be the Peace!), for this is what we used to do with children newly born among us; and now thou needst not fear for him drowning or suffocation in all the oceans of the world, if he should go down into them; for, even as ye walk on the land, so walk we in the sea." Then he pulled out of his pocket a casket, graven and sealed, and, breaking open the seals, emptied it; whereupon there fell from it strings of all manner of jacinths and other jewels, besides three hundred bugles of emerald and other three hundred hollow gems, as big as ostrich eggs, whose light dimmed that of sun and moon. Quoth Salih, "O King of the Age, these jewels and jacinths are a present from me to thee. We never yet brought thee a gift, for that we knew not Julnar's abiding-place neither had we of her any tidings or trace; but now that we see thee to be united with her and we are all become one thing, we have brought thee this present; and every little while we will bring thee the like thereof, Inshallah! for that these jewels and jacinths are more plentiful with us than pebbles on the beach and we know the good and the bad of them and their whereabouts and the way to them, and they are easy to us."

When the King saw the jewels, his wits were bewildered and his sense was astounded and he said, "By Allah, one single gem of these jewels is worth my realm!" Then he thanked for his bounty Salih the Sea-born and, looking towards Queen Julnar, said, "I am abashed before thy brother, for that he hath dealt munificently by me and bestowed on me this splendid gift, which the folk of the land were unable to present." So she thanked her brother for his deed and he said, "O King of the Age, thou hast the prior claim on us and it behoves us to thank thee, for thou hast entreated our sister with kindness and we have entered thy dwelling and eaten of thy victual. And if we stood on our faces in thy service, O King of the Age, a thousand years, yet had we not the might to requite thee, and this were but a scantling of thy due." The King thanked him with heartiest thanks and the Merman and Merwomen abode with him forty days' space, at the end of which Salih arose and kissed the ground before his brother-in-law, who asked, "What wantest thou, O Salih?" He answered, "O King of the Age, indeed thou hast done us overabundant favours, and we crave of thy bounties that thou deal charitably with us and grant us permission to depart; for we yearn after our people and country and kins-folk and our homes; so we will never forsake thy service nor that of my sister and my nephew; and, by Allah, O King of the Age, 'tis not pleasant to my heart to part from thee, but how shall we do, seeing that we have been reared in the sea and that the sojourn of the shore liketh us not?" When the King heard these words he rose to his feet and farewelled Salih the Sea-born and his mother and his cousins, and all wept together, because of parting and presently they said to him, "Anon we will be with thee again, nor will we forsake thee, but will visit thee every few days." Then they flew off and, descending into the sea, disappeared from sight.

After this King Shahriman showed the more kindness to Julnar and honoured her with increase of honour; and the little one grew up and flourished, whilst his maternal uncle and grandam and cousins visited the King every few days and abode with him a month or two months at a time. The boy ceased not to increase in beauty and loveliness with increase of years, till he attained the age of fifteen and was unique in his perfection and symmetry. He learnt writing and Koran-reading; history, syntax and lexicography; archery, spearplay and horsemanship and what not else behoveth the sons of kings; nor was there one of the children of the folk of the city, men or women, but would talk of the youth's charms, for he was of surpassing beauty and perfection. And, indeed, the King loved him with exceeding love, and summoning his Wazir and Emirs and the Chief Officers of State and Grandees of his realm, required of them a binding oath that they would make Badr Basim King over them after his sire; and they sware the oath gladly, for the sovran was liberal to the lieges, pleasant in parley and a very compend of goodness, saying naught but that wherein was advantage for the people.

On the morrow Shahriman mounted, with all his troops and Emirs and Lords, and went forth into the city and returned. When they drew near the palace, the King dismounted, to wait upon his son who abode on horseback, and he and all the Emirs and Grandees bore the saddle-cloth of honour before him, each and every of them bearing it in his turn, till they came to the vestibule of the palace, where the Prince alighted and his father and the Emirs embraced him and seated him on the throne of Kingship, whilst they (including his sire) stood before him. Then Badr Basim judged the people, deposing the unjust and promoting the just and continued so doing till near upon noon, when he descended from the throne and went in to his mother, Julnar the Sea-born, with the crown upon his head, as he were the moon. When she saw him, with the King standing before him, she rose and, kissing him, gave him joy of the Sultanate and wished him and his sire length of life and victory over their foes. He sat with her and rested till the hour of mid-afternoon prayer, when he took horse and repaired, with the Emirs before him, to the Maydan-plain, where he played at arms with his father and his Lords, till nightfall, when he returned to the palace, preceded by all the folk.

He rode thus every day to the tilting-ground, returning to sit and judge the people and do justice between carl and churl; and thus he continued doing a whole year, at the end of which he began to ride out a-hunting and a-chasing and to go round about in the cities and countries under his rule, proclaiming security and satisfaction and doing after the fashion of Kings; and he was unique among the people of his day for glory and valour and just-dealing among the subjects.

And it chanced that one day the old King fell sick and his fluttering heart forebode him of translation to the Mansion of Eternity. His sickness grew upon him till he was nigh upon death, when he called his son and commended his mother and subjects to his care and caused all the Emirs and Grandees once more swear allegiance to the Prince and assured himself of them by strongest oaths; after which he lingered a few days and departed to the mercy of Almighty Allah. His son and widow and all the Emirs and Wazirs and Lords mourned over him, and they built him a tomb and buried him therein. They ceased not ceremonially to mourn for him a whole month, till Salih and his mother and cousins arrived and condoled with their grieving for the King and said, "O Julnar, though the King be dead, yet hath he left this noble and peerless youth, and not dead is whoso leaveth the like of him, the rending lion and the shining moon." Thereupon the Grandees and notables of the Empire went in to King Badr Basim and said to him, "O King, there is no harm in mourning for the late sovran; but over-mourning beseemeth none save women; wherefore occupy thou not thy heart and our hearts with mourning for thy sire; inasmuch as he hath left thee behind him, and whoso leaveth the like of thee is not dead." Then they comforted him and diverted him and lastly carried him to the bath.

When he came out of the Hammam, he donned a rich robe, purfled with gold and embroidered with jewels and jacinths; and, setting the royal crown on his head, sat down on his throne of kingship and ordered the affairs of the folk, doing equal justice between strong and weak, and exacting from the prince the dues of the pauper; wherefore the people loved him with exceeding love. Thus he continued doing for a full year, whilst, every now and then, his kinsfolk of the sea visited him, and his life was pleasant and his eye was cooled.

Now it came to pass that his uncle Salih went in one night of the nights to Julnar and saluted her; whereupon she rose and, embracing him, seated him by her side and asked him "O my brother, how art thou and my mother and my cousins." He answered, "O my sister, they are well and glad and in good case, lacking naught save a sight of thy face." Then she set somewhat of food before him and he ate, after which talk ensued between the twain and they spake of King Badr Basim and his beauty and loveliness, his symmetry and skill in cavalrice and cleverness and good breeding. Now Badr was propped upon his elbow hard by them; and, hearing his mother and uncle speak of him, he feigned sleep and listened to their talk. Presently Salih said to his sister, "Thy son is now seventeen years old and is unmarried, and I fear lest mishap befall him and he have no son; wherefore it is my desire to marry him to a Princess of the princesses of the sea, who shall be a match for him in beauty and loveliness." Quoth Julnar, "Name them to me for I know them all." So Salih proceeded to enumerate them to her, one by one, but to each she said, "I like not this one for my son; I will not marry him but to one who is his equal in beauty and loveliness and wit and piety and good breeding and magnanimity and dominion and rank and lineage." Quoth Salih, "I know none other of the daughters of the Kings of the sea, for I have numbered to thee more than an hundred girls and not one of them pleaseth thee: but see, O my sister, whether thy son be asleep or no."

So she felt Badr and finding on him the signs of slumber said to Salih, "He is asleep; what hast thou to say and what is thine object in making sure his sleeping?" Replied he, "O my sister, know that I have bethought me of a Mermaid of the mermaids who befitteth thy son; but I fear to name her, lest he be awake and his heart be taken with her love and maybe we shall be unable to win to her; so should he and we and the

118

Grandees of the realm be wearied in vain and trouble betide us through this." When she heard these words, she cried, "Tell me the condition of this girl, and her name for I know all the damsels of the sea, King's daughters and others; and, if I judge her worthy of him, I will demand her in marriage for him of her father, though I spend on her whatso my hand possesseth. So recount to me all anent her and fear naught, for my son sleepeth." Quoth Salih, "I fear lest he be awake." But Julnar said, "Speak out and be brief and fear not, O my brother." So he said, "By Allah, O my sister, none is worthy of thy son save the Princess Jauharah, daughter of King Al-Samandal, for that she is like unto him in beauty and loveliness and brilliancy and perfection; nor is there found, in sea or on land, a sweeter or pleasanter of gifts than she; for she is prime in comeliness and seemlihead of face and symmetrical shape of perfect grace; her cheek is ruddy dight, her brow flower-white, her teeth gem-bright, her eyes blackest black and whitest white, her hips of heavy weight, her waist slight and her favour exquisite. When she turneth she shameth the wild cattle and the gazelles and when she walketh, she breedeth envy in the willow branch: when she unveileth, her face outshineth sun and moon and all who look upon her she enslaveth soon: sweet-lipped and soft-sided indeed is she."

Now when Julnar heard what Salih said, she replied, "Thou sayest sooth, O my brother! By Allah, I have seen her many and many a time and she was my companion, when we were little ones; but now we have no knowledge of each other, for constraint of distance; nor have I set eyes on her for eighteen years. By Allah, none is worthy of my son but she!" Now Badr heard all they said and mastered what had passed, first and last, of these praises bestowed on Jauharah, daughter of King Al-Samandal; so he fell in love with her on hearsay, pretending sleep the while, wherefore fire was kindled in his heart on her account full sore and he was drowned in a sea without bottom or shore. Then Salih, looking at his sister, exclaimed, "By Allah, O my sister, there is no greater fool among the Kings of the sea than her father nor one more violent of temper than he! So name thou not the girl to thy son, till we demand her in marriage of her father. If he favour us with his assent, we will praise Allah Almighty; and if he refuse us and will not give her to thy son to wife, we will say no more about it and seek another match." Answered Julnar, "Right is thy rede"; and they parleyed no more; but Badr passed the night with a heart on fire with passion for Princess Jauharah. However he concealed his case and spake

119

not of her to his mother or his uncle, albeit he was on coals of fire for love of her.

Now when it was morning, the King and his uncle went to the Hammam bath and washed, after which they came forth and drank wine and the servants set food before them, whereof they and Julnar ate their sufficiency, and washed their hands. Then Salih rose and said to his nephew and sister, "With your leave, I would fain go to my mother and my folk for I have been with you some days and their hearts are troubled with awaiting me." But Badr Basim said to him, "Tarry with us this day"; and he consented. Then quoth the King, "Come, O my uncle, let us go forth to the garden." So they sallied forth and promenaded about the pastures and took their solace awhile, after which King Badr lay down under a shady tree, thinking to rest and sleep; but he remembered his uncle's description of the maiden and her beauty and loveliness and shed railing tears. When Salih saw this he smote hand upon hand and said, "There is no god but *the* God! Mohammed is the Apostle of God and there is no Majesty and there is no Might save in Allah, the Glorious, the Great!" adding, "O my son, heardest thou what passed between me and thy mother respecting Princess Jauharah?" Replied Badr Basim, "Yes, O my uncle, and I fell in love with her by hearsay through what I heard you say. Indeed, my heart cleaveth to her and I cannot live without her."

Rejoined his uncle, "O King, let us return to thy mother and tell her how the case standeth and crave her leave that I may take thee with me and seek the Princess in marriage of her sire; after which we will farewell her and I and thou will return. Indeed, I fear to take thee and go without her leave, lest she be wroth with me; and verily the right would be on her side, for I should be the cause of her separation from us. Moreover, the city would be left without king and there would be none to govern the citizens and look to their affairs; so should the realm be disordered against thee and the kingship depart from thy hands." But Badr Basim, hearing these words, cried, "O my uncle, if I return to my mother and consult her on such matter, she will not suffer me to do this; wherefore I will not return to my mother nor consult her." And he wept before him and presently added, "I will go with thee and tell her not and after will return." When Salih heard what his nephew said, he was confused anent his case and said, "I crave help of the Almighty in any event." Then, seeing that Badr Basim was resolved to go with him, whether his mother would let him or no, he drew from his finger a seal-ring whereon were graven certain of the names of Allah the

Most High, and gave it to him, saying, "Put this on thy finger, and thou shalt be safe from drowning and other perils and from the mischief of sea-beasts and great fishes." So King Badr Basim took the ring and set it on his finger. Then they drove into the deep and fared on till they came to Salih's palace, where they found Badr Basim's grandmother, the mother of his mother, seated with her kinsfolk; and, going in to them, kissed their hands.

When the old Queen saw Badr she rose to him and embracing him, kissed him between the eyes and said to him, "A blessed coming, O my son! How didst thou leave thy mother Julnar?" He replied, "She is well in health and fortune, and saluteth thee and her uncle's daughters. Then Salih related to his mother what had occurred between him and his sister and how King Badr Basim had fallen in love with the Princess Jauharah, daughter of Al-Samandal, by report, and told her the whole tale from beginning to end, adding, "He hath not come save to demand her in wedlock of her sire"; which when the old Queen heard, she was wroth against her son with exceeding wrath and sore troubled and concerned and said, "O Salih, O my son, in very sooth thou diddest wrong to name the Princess before thy nephew, knowing as thou dost, that her father is stupid and violent, little of wit and tyrannical of temper, grudging his daughter to every suitor; for all the Monarchs of the Main have sought her hand, but he rejected them all; nay, he would none of them, saying, 'Ye are no match for her in beauty or in loveliness or in aught else.' Wherefore we fear to demand her in wedlock of him lest he reject us, even as he hath rejected others; and we are a folk of high spirit and should return brokenhearted."

Hearing these words Salih answered, "O my mother, what is to do? For King Badr Basim saith, 'There is no help but that I seek her in marriage of her sire, though I expend my whole kingdom'; and he avoucheth that, an he take her not to wife, he will die of love for her and longing." And Salih continued, "He is handsomer and goodlier than she; his father was King of all the Persians, whose King he now is, and none is worthy of Jauharah save Badr Basim. Wherefore I purpose to carry her father a gift of jacinths and jewels befitting his dignity, and demand her of him in marriage. An he object to us that he is a King, behold, our man also is a King and the son of a King; or, if he object to us her beauty, behold our man is more beautiful than she; or, again, if he object to us the vastness of his dominion, behold our man's dominion is vaster than hers and her father's and numbereth more troops and guards, for that his kingdom is greater than that of Al-Samandal. Needs must I do my endeavour to further the desire of my sister's son, though it relieve me of my life; because I was the cause of whatso hath betided; and, even as I plunged him into the ocean of her love, so will I go about to marry him to her, and may Almighty Allah help me thereto!" Rejoined his mother, "Do as thou wilt, but beware of giving her father rough words, whenas thou speakest with him; for thou knowest his stupidity and violence and I fear lest he do thee a mischief, for he knoweth not respect for any." And Salih answered, "Hearkening and obedience."

Then he sprang up, and taking two bags full of gems such as rubies and bugles of emerald, noble ores and all manner jewels, gave them to his servants to carry and set out with his nephew for the palace of Al-Samandal. When they came thither, he sought audience of the King and being admitted to his presence, kissed the ground before him and saluted him with the goodliest salam. The King rose to him and honouring him with the utmost honour, bade him be seated. So he sat down and presently the King said to him, "A blessed coming: indeed thou has desolated us, O Salih! But what bringeth thee to us? Tell me thine errand that we may fulfil it to thee." Whereupon Salih arose and, kissing the ground a second time, said, "O King of the Age, my errand is to Allah and the magnanimous liege lord of the valiant lion, the report of whose good qualities the caravans far and near have dispread and whose renown for benefits and beneficence and clemency and graciousness and liberality to all climes and countries hath sped." Thereupon he opened the two bags and, displaying their contents before Al-Samandal, said to him, "O King of the Age, haply wilt thou accept my gift and, by showing favour to me, heal my heart." King Al-Samandal asked, "With what object dost thou gift me with this gift? Tell me thy tale and acquaint me with thy requirement. An its accomplishment be in my power I will straightway accomplish it to thee and spare thee toil and trouble; and if I be unable thereunto, Allah compelleth not any soul aught beyond its power."

So Salih rose and kissing the ground three times, said, "O King of the Age, that which I desire thou art indeed able to do; it is in thy power and thou art master thereof; and I impose not on the King a difficulty, nor am I Jinn-demented, that I should crave of the King a thing whereto he availeth not; for one of the sages saith, 'An thou wouldst be complied with, ask that which can be readily supplied.' Wherefore, that of which I am come in quest, the King (whom Allah preserve!) is able to grant." The King replied, "Ask what

thou wouldst have, and state thy case and seek thy need."
Then said Salih, "O King of the Age, know that I come as
a suitor, seeking the unique pearl and the hoarded jewel, the
Princess Jauharah, daughter of our lord the King; wherefore,
O King, disappoint thou not thy suitor." Now when the King
heard this, he laughed till he fell backwards, in mockery of
him and said, "O Salih, I had thought thee a man of worth
and a youth of sense, seeking naught save what was reasonable
and speaking not save advisedly. What then hath befallen thy
reason and urged thee to this monstrous matter and mighty
hazard, that thou seekest in marriage daughters of Kings,
lords of cities and climates? Say me, art thou of a rank to
aspire to this great eminence and hath thy wit failed thee to
this extreme pass that thou affrontest me with this demand?"
Replied Salih, "Allah amend the King! I seek her not for
myself (albeit, an I did, I am her match and more than her
match, for thou knowest that my father was King of the
Kings of the sea, for all thou art this day our King), but I
seek her for King Badr Basim, lord of the lands of the
Persians and son of King Shahriman, whose puissance thou
knowest. An thou object that thou art a mighty great King,
King Badr is a greater; and if thou object thy daughter's
beauty, King Badr is more beautiful than she and fairer of
form and more excellent of rank and lineage; and he is the
champion of the people of his day. Wherefore, if thou grant
my request, O King of the Age, thou wilt have set the thing
in its stead; but, if thou deal arrogantly with us, thou wilt
not use us justly nor travel with us the 'road which is straight.'
Moreover, O King, thou knowest that the Princess Jauharah,
the daughter of our lord the King, must needs be wedded and
bedded, for the sage saith, a girl's lot is either grace of marriage
or the grave. Wherefore, an thou mean to marry her, my
sister's son is worthier of her than any other man."

Now, when King Al-Samandal heard Salih's words, he was
wroth with exceeding wrath; his reason wellnigh fled and his
soul was like to depart his body for rage, and he cried, "O
dog, shall the like of thee dare to bespeak me thus and name
my daughter in the assemblies, saying that the son of thy
sister Julnar is a match for her? Who art thou and who is
this sister of thine and who is her son and who was his father,
that thou durst say to me such say and address me with such
address? What are ye all, in comparison with my daughter,
but dogs?" And he cried out to his pages, saying, "Take
yonder gallows-bird's head?" So they drew their swords and
made for Salih, but he fled and for the palace gate sped;
and, reaching the entrance, he found of his cousins and

kinsfolk and servants, more than a thousand horse armed cap-à-pie in iron and close-knitted mail-coats, hending in hand spears and naked swords glittering white. And these, when they saw Salih come running out of the palace (they having been sent by his mother to his succour), questioned him and he told them what was to do; whereupon they knew that the King was a fool and violent tempered to boot. So they dismounted and, baring their blades, went in to the King Al-Samandal, whom they found seated upon the throne of his Kingship, unaware of their coming and enraged against Salih with furious rage; and they beheld his eunuchs and pages and officers unprepared. When the King saw them enter, drawn brand in hand, he cried out to his people, saying, "Woe to you! Take me the heads of these hounds!" But ere an hour had sped Al-Samandal's party were put to the route and relied upon flight, and Salih and his kinsfolk seized upon the King and pinioned him.

Then Princess Jauharah awoke and knew that her father was a captive and his guards slain. So she fled forth the palace to a certain island and, climbing up into a high tree, hid herself in its summit. Now, when the two parties came to blows, some of King Al-Samandal's pages fled and Badr Basim, meeting them, questioned them of their case and they told him what had happened. But when he heard that the King was a prisoner, Badr feared for himself and fled, saying in his heart, "Verily, all this turmoil is on my account and none is wanted but I." So he sought safety in flight, security to sight, knowing not whither he went; but destiny from Eternity fore-ordained drave him to the very island where the Princess had taken refuge, and he came to the very tree whereon she sat and threw himself down, like a dead man, thinking to lie and repose himself and knowing not there is no rest for the pursued, for none knoweth what Fate hideth for him in the future. As he lay down, he raised his eyes to the tree and they met the eyes of the Princess. So he looked at her, and seeing her to be like the moon rising in the east, cried, "Glory to Him who fashioned yonder perfect form, Him who is the Creator of all things and who over all things is Almighty! Glory to the Great God, the Maker, the Shaper and Fashioner! By Allah, if my presentiments be true, this is Jauharah, daughter of King Al-Samandal! Methinks that, when she heard of our coming to blows with her father, she fled to this island and, happening upon this tree, hid herself on its head; but, if this be not the Princess herself, 'tis one yet goodlier than she." Then he bethought himself of her case and said in himself, "I will arise and lay hands on her and question her of her condition; and, if she be indeed the she, I will demand her in wedlock of herself and so win my wish."

So he stood up and said to her, "O end of all desire, who art thou and who brought thee hither?" She looked at Badr Basim, and seeing him to be as the full moon when it shineth from under the black cloud, slender of shape and sweet of smile, answered, "O fair of fashion, I am Princess Jauharah, daughter of King Al-Samandal, and I took refuge in this place, because Salih and his host came to blows with my sire and slew his troops and took him prisoner, with some of his men; wherefore I fled, fearing for my very life," presently adding, "And I weet not what fortune hath done with my father." When King Badr Basim heard these words he marvelled with exceeding marvel at this strange chance and thought, "Doubtless I have won my wish by the capture of her sire." Then he looked at Jauharah and said to her, "Come down. O my lady; for I am slain for love of thee and thine eyes have captivated me. On my account and thine are all these broils and battles; for thou must know that I am King Badr Basim, Lord of the Persians, and Salih is my mother's brother and he it is who came to thy sire to demand thee of him in marriage. As for me, I have quitted my kingdom for thy sake, and our meeting here is the rarest coincidence. So come down to me and let us twain fare for thy father's palace, that I may beseech Uncle Salih to release him and I may make thee my lawful wife."

When Jauharah heard his words, she said in herself. " 'Twas on this miserable gallows-bird's account, then, that all this hath befallen and that my father hath fallen prisoner and his chamberlains and suite have been slain and I have been departed from my palace, a miserable exile, and have fled for refuge to this island. But, an I devise not against him some device to defend myself from him, he will possess himself of me and take his will of me; for he is in love and for aught that he doeth a lover is not blamed." Then she beguiled him with winning words and soft speeches, whilst he knew not the perfidy against him she purposed, and asked him, "O my lord and light of my eyes, say me, art thou indeed King Badr Basim, son of Queen Julnar?" And he answered, "Yes, O my lady!" Then she, "May Allah cut off my father and gar his kingdom cease from him and heal not his heart, neither avert from him strangerhood, if he could desire a comelier than thou or aught goodlier than these fair qualities of thine! By Allah, he is of little wit and judgment!" presently adding, "But, O King of the Age, punish him not for that he hath done;

more by token that an thou love me a span, verily I love thee a cubit. Indeed, I have fallen into the net of thy love and am become of the number of thy slain. The love that was with thee hath transferred itself to me and there is left thereof with thee but a tithe of that which is with me."

So saying, she came down from the tree and, drawing near him, strained him to her bosom and fell to kissing him; whereat passion and desire for her redoubled on him and, doubting not but she loved him, he trusted in her, and returned her kisses and caresses. Presently he said to her, "By Allah, O Princess, my Uncle Salih set forth to me not a fortieth part

of thy charms; no, nor a quarter-carat of the four-and-twenty." Then Jauharah pressed him to her bosom and pronounced some unintelligible words; then spat on his face, saying, "Quit this form of man and take shape of bird, the handsomest of birds, white of robe, with red bill and legs." Hardly had she spoken, when King Badr Basim found himself transformed into a bird, the handsomest of birds, who shook himself and stood looking at her. Now Jauharah had with her one of her slave-girls, by name Marsinah; so she called her and said to her, "By Allah, but that I fear for the life of my father, who is his uncle's prisoner, I would kill him! Allah never requite him with good! How unlucky was his coming to us; for all this trouble is due to his hard-headedness! But do thou, O slave-girl, bear him to the Thirsty Island and leave him there to die of thirst." So Marsinah

n to the island in question and would have returned
him there; but she said in herself, "By Allah, the
such beauty and loveliness deserveth not to die of
So she went forth from that island and brought him
to another abounding in trees and fruits and rills and,
setting him down there, returned to her mistress and told her,
"I have left him on the Thirsty Island."

Such was the case of Badr Basim; but as regards King
Salih, he sought for Jauharah after capturing the King and
killing his folk; finding her not, returned to his palace
and said to his mother, "Where is my sister's son, King
Badr Basim?" "By Allah, O my son," replied she, "I know
nothing of him! For when it reached him that you and
King Al-Samandal had come to blows and that strife and
slaughter had betided between you, he was affrighted and fled."
When Salih heard this, he grieved for his nephew and said,
"O my mother, by Allah, we have dealt negligently by King
Badr and I fear lest he perish or lest one of King
Al-Samandal's soldiers or his daughter Jauharah fall in with
him. So should we come to shame with his mother and no
good betide us from her, for that I took him without her
leave." Then he despatched guards and scouts thoughout the
sea and elsewhere to seek for Badr; but they could learn no
tidings of him; so they returned and told King Salih, wherefore cark and care redoubled on him and his breast was
straitened for King Badr Basim.

So far concerning nephew and uncle, but as for Julnar
the Sea-born, after their departure, she abode in expectation
of them, but her son returned not and she heard no report of
him. So when many days of fruitless waiting had gone by, she
arose and, going down into the sea, repaired to her mother,
who, sighting her, rose to her and kissed her and embraced
her, as did the Mermaids her cousins. Then she questioned
her mother of King Badr Basim, and she answered, saying,
"O my daughter, of a truth he came hither with his uncle,
who took jacinths and jewels and, carrying them to the King
Al-Samandal, demanded his daughter in marriage for thy son;
but he consented not and was violent against thy brother in
words. Now, I had sent Salih nigh upon a thousand horse
and a battle befell between him and King Al-Samandal; but
Allah aided thy brother against him, and he slew his guards
and troops and took himself prisoner. Meanwhile, tidings
of this reached thy son, and it would seem as if he feared for
himself; wherefore he fled forth from us, without our will,
and returned not to us, nor have we heard any news of him."
Then Julnar inquired for King Salih, and his mother said,

"He is seated on the throne of his kingship, in the st
King Al-Samandal, and hath sent in all directions to seek
son and Princess Jauharah." When Julnar heard the materna.
words she mourned for her son with sad mourning and was
highly incensed against her brother Salih for that he had taken
him and gone down with him into the sea without her leave;
and she said, "O my mother, I fear for our realm; as I came
to thee without letting any know; and I dread tarrying with
thee, lest the state fall into disorder and the kingdom pass
from our hands. Wherefore I deem best to return and govern
the reign till it please Allah to order our son's affair for us.
But, look ye, forget him not, neither neglect his case; for
should he come to any harm, it would infallibly kill me, since
I see not the world save in him and delight but in his life."
She replied, "With love and gladness, O my daughter. Ask
not what we suffer by reason of his loss and absence." Then
she sent to seek for her grandson, whilst Julnar returned to
her kingdom, weeping-eyed and heavy-hearted, and indeed
the gladness of the world was straitened upon her.

So fared it with her; but as regards King Badr Basim, after
Princess Jauharah had ensorcelled him and had sent him with
her handmaid to the Thirsty Island, saying, "Leave him there
to die of thirst," and Marsinah had set him down in a green
islet, he abode days and nights in the semblance of a bird,
eating of its fruits and drinking of its waters and knowing
not whither to go nor how to fly; till, one day, there came a
certain fowler to the island to catch somewhat wherewithal to
get his living. He espied King Badr Basim in his form of a
white-robed bird, with red bill and legs, captivating the sight
and bewildering the thought; and, looking thereat, said in
himself, "Verily, yonder is a beautiful bird; never saw I its
like in fairness or form." So he cast his net over Badr and,
taking him, carried him to the town, mentally resolved to
sell him for a high price. On his way one of the townsfolk
accosted him and said, "For how much this fowl, O fowler?"
Quoth the fowler, "What wilt thou do with him an thou buy
him?" Answered the other, "I will cut his throat and eat him";
whereupon said the birder, "Who could have the heart to kill
this bird and eat him? Verily, I mean to present him to our
King, who will give me more than thou wouldst give me and
will not kill him, but will divert himself by gazing upon his
beauty and grace, for in all my life, since I have been a fowler,
I never saw his like among land game or water fowl. The
utmost thou wouldst give me for him, however much thou
covet him, would be a dirham, and, by Allah Amighty, I
will not sell him!"

Then he carried the bird up to the King's palace, and when the King saw it, its beauty and grace pleased him and the red colour of its beak and legs. So he sent an eunuch to buy it, who accosted the fowler and said to him, "Wilt thou sell this bird?" Answered he, "Nay, 'tis a gift from me to the King." So the eunuch carried the bird to the King and told him what the man had said; and he took it and gave the fowler ten dinars, whereupon he kissed the ground and fared forth. Then the eunuch carried the bird to the palace and, placing him in a fine cage, hung him up after setting meat and drink by him. When the King came down from the Divan, he said to the eunuch, "Where is the bird? Bring it to me, that I may look upon it; for, by Allah, 'tis beautiful!" So the eunuch brought the cage and set it between the hands of the King, who looked and, seeing the food untouched, said, "By Allah, I wist not what it will eat, that I may nourish it!" Then he called for food and they laid the tables the King ate.

Now when the bird saw the flesh and meats and fruits and sweetmeats, he ate of all that was upon the trays before the King, whereat the Sovran and all the by-standers marvelled and the King said to his attendants, eunuchs and Mamelukes, "In all my life I never saw a bird eat as doth this bird!" Then he sent an eunuch to fetch his wife that she might enjoy looking upon the bird, and he went in to summon her and said, "O my lady, the King desireth thy presence, that thou mayst divert thyself with the sight of a bird he hath bought. When we set on the food it flew down from its cage and perching on the table ate of all that was thereon. So arise, O my lady, and solace thee with the sight for it is goodly of aspect and is a wonder of the wonders of the age." Hearing these words she came in haste; but, when she noted the bird, she veiled her face and turned to fare away. The King rose up and looking at her, asked, "Why dost thou veil thy face when there is none in presence save the women and eunuchs who wait on thee and thy husband?" Answered she, "O King, this bird is no bird, but a man like thyself." He rejoined, "Thou liest, this is too much of a jest. How should he be other than a bird?"; and she, "O King, by Allah, I do not jest with thee nor do I tell thee aught but the truth; for verily this bird is King Badr Basim, son of King Shahriman, Lord of the land of the Persians, and his mother is Julnar the Sea-born." Quoth the King, "And how came he in this shape?"; and quoth she, "Princess Jauharah, daughter of King Al-Samandal, hath enchanted him": and told him all that had passed with King Badr Basim from first to last.

The King marvelled exceedingly at his wife's words and

conjured her, on his life, to free Badr from his enchantment (for she was the notablest enchantress of her age), and not leave him in torment, saying, "May Almighty Allah cut off Jauharah's hand, for a foul witch as she is! How little is her faith and how great her craft and perfidy!" Said the Queen, "Do thou say to him, 'O Badr Basim, enter yonder closet!'" So the King bade him enter the closet and he went in obediently. Then the Queen veiled her face and taking in her hand a cup of water, entered the closet, where she pronounced over the water certain incomprehensible words ending with, "By the virtue of these mighty names and holy verses and by the majesty of Allah Almighty, Creator of heaven and earth, the Quickener of the dead and Appointer of the means of daily bread and the terms determined, quit this thy form wherein thou art and return to the shape in which the Lord created thee!" Hardly had she made an end of her words, when the bird trembled once and became a man; and the King saw before him a handsome youth, than whom on earth's face was none goodlier. But when King Badr Basim found himself thus restored to his own form he cried, "There is no god but *the* God and Mohammed is the Apostle of God! Glory be to the Creator of all creatures and Provider of their provision, and Ordainer of their life-terms preordained!" Then he kissed the King's hand and wished him long life, and the King kissed his head and said to him, "O Badr Basim, tell me thy history from commencement to conclusion."

So he told him his whole tale, concealing naught; and the King marvelled thereat and said to him, "O Badr Basim, Allah hath saved thee from the spell: but what hath thy judgment decided and what thinkest thou to do?" Replied he, "O King of the Age, I desire of thy bounty that thou equip me a ship with a company of thy servants and all that is needful; for 'tis long since I have been absent and I dread lest the kingdom depart from me. And I misdoubt me my mother is dead of grief for my loss; and this doubt is the stronger for that she knoweth not what is come of me nor whether I am alive or dead. Wherefore, I beseech thee, O King, to crown thy favours to me by granting me what I seek." The King, after beholding the beauty and grace of Badr Basim and listening to his sweet speech, said "I hear and obey." So he fitted him out a ship, to which he transported all that was needful and which he manned with a company of his servants; and Badr Basim set sail in it, after having taken leave of the King.

They sailed over the sea ten successive days with a favouring wind; but, on the eleventh day, the ocean became troubled with exceeding trouble, the ship rose and fell and the sailors were powerless to govern her. So they drifted at the mercy of the waves, till the craft neared a rock in mid-sea which fell upon her and broke her up and all on board were drowned, save King Badr Basim who got astride one of the planks of the vessel, after having been nigh upon destruction. The plank ceased not to be borne by the set of the sea, whilst he knew not whither he went and had no means of directing its motion, as the wind and waves wrought for three whole days. But on the fourth the plank grounded with him on the seashore where he sighted a white city, as it were a dove passing white, builded upon a tongue of land that jutted out into the deep and it was goodly of ordinance, with high towers and lofty walls against which the waves beat. When Badr Basim saw this he rejoiced with exceeding joy, for he was well nigh dead of hunger and thirst, and dismounting from the plank, would have gone up the beach to the city; but there came down to him mules and asses and horses, in number as the sea-sands and fell to striking at him and staying him from landing. So he swam round to the back of the city, where he waded to shore and entering the place, found none therein and marvelled at this, saying, "Would I knew to whom doth this city belong, wherein is no lord nor any liege, and whence came these mules and asses and horses that hindered me from landing?" And he mused over his case.

Then he walked on at hazard till he espied an old man, a grocer. So he saluted him and the other returned his salam and seeing him to be a handsome young man, said to him, "O youth, whence comest thou and what brought thee to this city?" Badr told him his story; at which the old man marvelled and said, "O my son, didst thou see any on thy way?" He replied, "Indeed, O my father, I wondered in good sooth to sight a city void of folk." Quoth the Shaykh, "O my son, come up into the shop lest thou perish." So Badr Basim went up into the shop and sat down; whereupon the old man set before him somewhat of food, saying, "O my son, enter the inner shop; glory be to Him who hath preserved thee from yonder she-Sathanas!" King Badr Basim was sore affrighted at the grocer's words; but he ate his fill and washed his hands; then glanced at his host and said to him, "O my lord, what is the meaning of these words? Verily thou hast made me fearful of this city and its folk." Replied the old man, "Know, O my son, that this is the City of the Magicians and its Queen is as she were a she-Satan, a sorceress and a mighty enchantress, passing crafty and perfidious exceedingly. All thou sawest of horses and mules and asses were once sons of Adam like thee and me; they were also strangers, for whoever entereth this city, being a young man like thyself, this miscreant witch taketh him and hometh him for forty days, after which she enchanteth him, and he becometh a mule or a horse or an ass, of those animals thou sawest on the seashore. All these people hath she spelled; and, when it was thy intent to land they feared lest thou be transmewed like themselves; so they counselled thee by signs that said, 'Land not,' of their solicitude for thee, fearing that haply she should do with thee like as she had done with them. She possessed herself of this city and seized it from its citizens by sorcery and her name is Queen Lab, which being interpreted, meaneth in Arabic 'Almanac of the Sun.'"

When Badr Basim heard what the old man said, he was affrighted with sore affright and trembled like reed in wind saying in himself, "Hardly do I feel free from the affliction wherein I was by reason of sorcery, when Destiny casteth me into yet sorrier case!" And he fell a-musing over his condition and that which had betided him. When the Shaykh looked at him and saw the violence of his terror, he said to him, "O my son, come, sit at the threshold of the shop and look upon yonder creatures and upon their dress and complexion and that wherein they are by reason of gramarye and dread not; for the Queen and all in the city love and tender me and will not vex my heart or trouble my mind." So King Badr Basim came out and sat at the shop-door, looking out upon the folk; and there passed by him a world of creatures without number.

But when the people saw him, they accosted the grocer and said to him, "O elder, is this thy captive and thy prey gotten in these days?" The old man replied, "He is my brother's son, I heard that his father was dead; so I sent for him and brought him here that I might quench with him the fire of my home-sickness." Quoth they, "Verily, he is a comely youth; but we fear for him from Queen Lab, lest she turn on thee with treachery and take him from thee, for she loveth handsome young men." Quoth the Shaykh, "The Queen will not gainsay my commandment, for she loveth and tendereth me; and when she shall know that he is my brother's son, she will not molest him or afflict me in him neither trouble my heart on his account." Then King Badr Basim abode some months with the grocer, eating and drinking, and the old man loved him with exceeding love.

One day, as he sat in the shop according to his custom, behold, there came up a thousand eunuchs, with drawn swords and clad in various kinds of raiment and girt with jewelled girdles: all rode Arabian steeds and bore in baldrick Indian blades. They saluted the grocer, as they passed his shop and were followed by a thousand damsels like moons, clad in various raiments of silks and satins fringed with gold and embroidered with jewels of sorts, and spears were slung to their shoulders. In their midst rode a damsel mounted on a Rabite mare, saddled with a saddle of gold set with various kinds of jewels and jacinths; and they reached in a body the Shaykh's shop. The damsels saluted him and passed on, till, lo and behold! up came Queen Lab, in great state, and seeing King Badr Basim sitting in the shop, as he were the moon at its full, was amazed at his beauty and loveliness and became passionately enamoured of him, and distraught with desire of him. So she alighted and sitting down by King Badr Basim said to the old man, "Whence hadst thou this handsome one?"; and the Shaykh replied, "He is my brother's son, and is lately come to me." Quoth Lab, "Let him be with me this night, that I may talk with him"; and quoth the old man, "Wilt thou take him from me and not enchant him?" Said she, "Yes," and said he, "Swear to me." So she sware to him that she would not do him any hurt or ensorcell him, and bidding bring him a fine horse, saddled and bridled with a golden bridle and decked with trappings all of gold set with jewels, gave the old man a thousand dinars, saying, "Use this." Then she took Badr Basim and carried him off, as he were the full moon on its fourteenth night, whilst all the folk, seeing his beauty, were grieved for him and said, "By Allah, verily, this youth deserveth not to be bewitched by yonder sorceress, the accursed!"

Now King Badr Basim heard all they said, but was silent, committing his case to Allah Almighty, till they came to her palace gate, where the Emirs and eunuchs and Lords of the realm took foot and she bade the Chamberlains dismiss her Officers and Grandees, who kissed the ground and went away, whilst she entered the palace with Badr Basim and her eunuchs and women. Here he found a place, whose like he had never seen at all, for it was builded of gold and in its midst was a great basin brimful of water midmost a vast flower-garden. He looked at the garden and saw it abounding in birds of various kinds and colours, warbling in all manner tongues and voices, pleasurable and plaintive. And everywhere he beheld great state and dominion and said, "Glory be to God, who of His bounty and long-suffering provideth those who serve other than Himself!" The Queen sat down at a latticed window overlooking the garden on a couch of ivory, whereon was a high bed, and King Badr Basim seated himself by her side. She kissed him and pressing him to her breast, bade her women bring a tray of food. So they brought a tray of red gold, inlaid with pearls and jewels and spread with all manner of viands and he and she ate, till they were satisfied, and washed their hands; after which the waiting-women set on flagons of gold and silver and glass, together with all kinds of flowers and dishes of dried fruits. Then the Queen summoned the singing-women and there came ten maidens, as they were moons, hending all manner of musical instruments. Queen Lab crowned a cup and drinking it off, filled another and passed it to King Badr Basim, who took it and drank; and they ceased not to drink till they had their sufficiency. Then she bade the damsels sing, and they sang all manner modes till it seemed to Badr Basim as if the palace danced with him for joy.

His sense was ecstasied and his breast broadened, and he forgot his strangerhood and said in himself, "Verily, this Queen is young and beautiful and I will never leave her; for her kingdom is vaster than my kingdom and she is fairer than Princess Jauharah." So he ceased not to drink with her till eventide came, when they lighted the lamps and waxen candles and diffused censer-perfumes; nor did they leave drinking, till they were both drunken, and the singing-women sang the while. Then Queen Lab, being in liquor, rose from her seat and lay down on a bed and dismissing her women called to Badr Basim to come and sleep by her side. So he lay with her, in all delight of life till the morning. And when the Queen awoke she repaired to the Hammam bath in the palace, King Badr Basim being with her, and they bathed and were purified; after which she clad him in the finest of raiment and called for the service of wine. So the waiting-women brought the drinking-gear and they drank. Presently, the Queen arose and taking Badr Basim by the hand, sat down with him on chairs and bade bring food, whereof they ate, and washed their hands. Then the damsels fetched the drinking-gear and fruits and flowers and confections and they ceased not to eat and drink,[1] whilst the singing-girls sang various airs till the evening.

They gave not over eating and drinking and merry-making for a space of forty days, when the Queen said to him, "O Badr Basim, say me whether is the more pleasant, this place or the shop of thine uncle the grocer?" He replied, "By Allah, O Queen, this is the pleasanter, for my uncle is but a

[1] The heroes and heroines of Eastern love tales are always *bonnes fourchettes*; they eat and drink hard enough to scandalise the sentimental amourist of the West; but it is understood that this abundant diet is necessary to qualify them for the Herculean labours of the love-night.

beggarly man, who vendeth pot-herbs." She laughed at his words and the twain lay together in the pleasantest of case till the morning, when King Badr Basim awoke from sleep and found not Queen Lab by his side, so he said, "Would Heaven I knew where can she have gone!" And indeed he was troubled at her absence and perplexed about the case, for she stayed away from him a great while and did not return; so he donned his dress and went seeking her, but not finding her, and he said to himself, "Haply, she is gone to the flower garden." Thereupon he went out into the garden and came to a running rill beside which he saw a white she-bird and on the stream bank a tree full of birds of various colours, and he stood and watched the birds without their seeing him. And, behold, a black bird flew down upon that white she-bird and fell to billing her pigeon fashion, then he leapt on her and trod her three consecutive times, after which the bird changed and became a woman. Badr looked at her and lo! it was Queen Lab.

So he knew that the black bird was a man transmewed and that she was enamoured of him and had transformed herself into a bird, that he might enjoy her; wherefore jealousy got hold upon him and he was wroth with the Queen because of the black bird. Then he returned to his place and lay down on the carpet-bed and after an hour or so she came back to him and fell to kissing him and jesting with him; but, being sore incensed against her, he answered her not a word. She saw what was to do with him and was assured that he had witnessed what befell her when she was a white bird and was trodden by the black bird; yet she discovered naught to him but concealed what ailed her. When he had done her need, he said to her, "O Queen, I would have thee give me leave to go to my uncle's shop, for I long after him and have not seen him these forty days." She replied, "Go to him, but tarry not from me, for I cannot brook to be parted from thee, nor can I endure without thee an hour." He said, "I hear and I obey," and, mounting, rode to the shop of the Shaykh, the grocer, who welcomed him and rose to him, and, embracing him, said to him, "How hast thou fared with yonder idolatress?"

He replied, "I was well in health and happiness till this last night," and told him what had passed in the garden with the black bird. Now, when the old man heard his words, he said, "Beware of her, for know that the birds upon the trees were all young men and strangers, whom she loved and enchanted and turned into birds. That black bird thou sawest was one of her Mamelukes whom she loved with exceeding

135

love, till he cast his eyes upon one of her women, wherefore
she changed him into a black bird. And whenas she lusteth
after him she transformeth herself into a she-bird that he
may enjoy her, for she still loveth him with passionate love.
When she found that thou knewest of her case, she plotted
evil against thee, for she loveth thee not wholly. But no harm
shall betide thee from her, so long as I protect thee; therefore
fear nothing; for I am a Moslem, by name Abdallah, and
there is none in my day more magical than I; yet do I not
make use of gramarye save upon constraint. Many a time
have I put to naught the sorceries of yonder accursed and
delivered folk from her, and I care not for her, because she
can do me no hurt—nay, she feareth me with exceeding fear,
as do all in the city who, like her, are magicians and serve
the Fire, not the Omnipotent Sire. So to-morrow, come thou
to me and tell me what she doth with thee; for this very
night she will cast about to destroy thee, and I will tell thee
how thou shalt do with her, that thou mayst save thyself
from her malice."

Then King Badr Basim farewelled the Shaykh and returned
to the Queen whom he found awaiting him. When she saw
him, she rose and, seating him and welcoming him, brought
him meat and drink and the two ate till they had enough and
washed their hands; after which she called for wine and they
drank till the night was wellnigh half-spent, when she plied
him with cup after cup till he was drunken and lost sense
and wit. When she saw him thus, she said to him, "I conjure
thee by Allah and by whatso thou worshippest, if I ask thee
a question wilt thou inform me rightly and answer me truly?"
And he being drunken, answered, "Yes, O my lady." Quoth
she, "O my lord and light of mine eyes, when thou awokest
last night and foundest me not, thou soughtest me, till thou
sawest me in the garden, under the guise of a white she-bird,
and also thou sawest the black bird leap on me and tread me.
Now I will tell the truth of this matter. That black bird was
one of my Mamelukes, whom I loved with exceeding love;
but one day he cast his eyes upon a certain of my slave-girls,
wherefore jealousy gat hold upon me and I transformed him
by my spells into a black bird and her I slew. But now I
cannot endure without him a single hour; so, whenever I
lust after him, I change myself into a she-bird and go to
him, that he may leap me and enjoy me, even as thou hast
seen. Art thou not therefore incensed against me, because of
this, albeit, by the virtue of Fire and Light, Shade and Heat,
I love thee more than ever and have made thee my portion of
the world?"

He answered (being drunken), "Thy conjecture of the cause of my rage is correct, and it had no reason other than this." With this she embraced him and kissed him and made great show of love to him; then she lay down to sleep and he by her side. Presently, about midnight, she rose from the carpet-bed and King Badr Basim was awake; but he feigned sleep and watched stealthily to see what she would do. She took out of a red bag a something red, which she planted amiddle-most the chamber, and it became a stream, running like the sea; after which she took a handful of barley and, strewing it on the ground, watered it with water from the river; where-upon it became wheat in the ear, and she gathered it and ground it into flour. Then she set it aside and, returning to bed, lay down by Badr Basim till morning, when he arose and washed his face and asked her leave to visit the Shaykh his uncle. She gave him permission and he repaired to Abdallah and told him what had passed. The old man laughed and said, "By Allah, this miscreant witch plotteth mischief against thee; but reck thou not of her ever!" Then he gave him a pound of parched corn and said to him, "Take this with thee and know that, when she seeth it, she will ask thee, 'What is this and what wilt thou do with it?' Do thou answer, 'Abundance of good things is good'; and eat of it.

"Then she will bring forth to thee parched grain of her own and say to thee, 'Eat of this Sawik'; and do thou feign to her that thou eatest thereof, but eat of this instead, and beware and have a care lest thou eat of hers even a grain; for, an thou eat so much as a grain thereof, her spells will have power over thee and she will enchant thee and say to thee, 'Leave this form of a man.' Whereupon thou wilt quit thine own shape for what shape she will. But, an thou eat not thereof, her enchantments will be null and void and no harm will betide thee therefrom; whereat she will be shamed with shame exceeding and say to thee, 'I did but jest with thee!' Then will she make a show of love and fondness to thee; but this will all be but hypocrisy in her and craft. And do thou also make a show of love to her and say to her, 'O my lady and light of mine eyes, eat of this parched barley and see how delicious it is.' And if she eat thereof, though it be but a grain, take water in thy hand and throw it in her face, saying, 'Quit this human form' (for what form soever thou wilt have her take). Then leave her and come to me and I will counsel thee what to do."

So Badr Basim took leave of him and, returning to the palace, went in to the Queen, who said to him, "Welcome and well come and good cheer to thee!" And she rose and kissed him, saying, "Thou hast tarried long from me, O my lord." He replied, "I have been with my uncle, and he gave me to eat of this Sawik." Quoth she, "We have better than that." Then she laid his parched Sawik in one plate and hers in another and said to him, "Eat of this, for 'tis better than thine." So he feigned to eat of it and when she thought he had done so, she took water in her hand and sprinkled him therewith, saying, "Quit this form, O thou gallows-bird, thou miserable, and take that of a mule one-eyes and foul of favour." But he changed not; which, when she saw, she arose and went up to him and kissed him between the eyes, saying, "O my beloved, I did but jest with thee; bear me no malice because of this." Quoth he, "O my lady, I bear thee no whit of malice; nay, I am assured that thou lovest me; but eat of this my parched barley." So she ate a mouthful of Abdallah's Sawik; but no sooner had it settled in her stomach than she was convulsed; and King Badr Basim took water in his palm and threw it in her face, saying, "Quit this human form and take that of a dapple mule."

No sooner had he spoken than she found herself changed into a she-mule, whereupon the tears rolled down her cheeks and she fell to rubbing her muzzle against his feet. Then he would have bridled her, but she would not take the bit; so he left her and, going to the grocer, told him what had passed. Abdallah brought out for him a bridle and bade him rein her forthwith. So he took it to the palace, and when she saw him, she came up to him and he set the bit in her mouth and, mounting her, rode forth to find the Shaykh. But when the old man saw her, he rose and said to her, "Almighty Allah confound thee, O accursed woman!" Then quoth he to Badr, "O my son, there is no more tarrying for thee in this city; so ride her and fare with her whither thou wilt and beware lest thou commit the bridle to any."

King Badr thanked him and, farewelling him, fared on three days, without ceasing, till he drew near another city and there met him an old man, grey-headed and comely, who said to him. "Whence comest thou, O my son?" Badr replied, "From the city of this witch"; and the old man said, "Thou art my guest to-night." He consented and went with him; but by the way, behold, they met an old woman, who wept when she saw the mule, and said, "There is no god but *the* God! Verily, this mule resembleth my son's she-mule, which is dead, and my heart acheth for her; so, Allah upon thee, O my lord, do thou sell her to me!" He replied, "By Allah, O my mother, I cannot sell her." But she cried, "Allah upon thee, do not refuse my request, for my son will surely be a dead man except I buy him this mule." And she importuned him, till he exclaimed, "I will not sell her save for a thousand dinars," saying in himself, "Whence should this old woman get a thousand gold pieces?" Thereupon she brought out from her girdle a purse containing a thousand ducats, which when King Badr Basim saw, he said, "O my mother, I did but jest with thee; I cannot sell her." But the old man looked at him and said, "O my son, in this city none may lie, for whoso lieth they put to death."

So King Badr Basim dismounted from and delivered the mule to the old woman; she drew the bit from her mouth and, taking water in her hand, sprinkled the mule therewith, saying, "O my daughter, quit this shape for that form wherein thou wast aforetime!" Upon this she was straightway restored to her original semblance and the two women embraced and kissed each other. So King Badr Basim knew that the old woman was Queen Lab's mother and that he had been tricked and would have fled; when lo! the old woman whistled a loud whistle and her call was obeyed by an Ifrit as he were a great mountain, whereat Badr was affrighted and stood still. Then the old woman mounted on the Ifrit's back, taking her daughter behind her and King Badr Basim before her, and the Ifrit flew off with them; nor was it a full hour ere they were in the palace of Queen Lab who sat down on the throne of kingship and said to Badr, "Gallows-bird that thou art, now am I come hither and have attained to that I desired and soon will I show thee how I will do with thee and with yonder old man the grocer! How many favours have I shown him! Yet he doth me frowardness; for thou hast not attained thine end but by means of him." Then she took water and sprinkled him therewith, saying, "Quit the shape wherein thou art for the form of a foul-favoured fowl, the foulest of all fowls"; and she set him in a cage and cut off from him meat and drink; but one of her women, seeing this cruelty, took compassion on him and gave him food and water without her knowledge.

One day, the damsel took her mistress at unawares and going forth the palace, repaired to the old grocer, to whom she told the whole case, saying, "Queen Lab is minded to make an end of thy brother's son." The Shaykh thanked her and said, "There is no help but that I take the city from her and make thee Queen thereof in her stead." Then he whistled a loud whistle and there came forth to him an Ifrit with four wings, to whom he said, "Take up this damsel and carry her to the city of Julnar the Sea-born and her mother Farashah for they twain are the most powerful magicians on face of earth."

And he said to the damsel, "When thou comest thither, tell them that King Badr Basim is Queen Lab's captive." Then the Ifrit took up his load and, flying off with her, in a little while set her down upon the terrace roof of Queen Julnar's palace. So she descended and going in to the Queen, kissed the earth and told her what had passed to her son, first and last, whereupon Julnar rose to her and entreated her with honour and thanked her. Then she let beat the drums in the city and acquainted her lieges and the lords of her realm with the good news that King Badr Basim was found; after which she and her mother Farashah and her brother Salih assembled all the tribes of the Jinn and the troops of the main; for the Kings of the Jinn obeyed them since the taking of King Al-Samandal.

Presently they all flew up into the air and lighting down on the city of the sorceress, sacked the town and the palace and slew all the Unbelievers therein in the twinkling of an eye. Then said Julnar to the damsel, "Where is my son?" And the slave-girl brought her the cage and signing to the bird within, cried, "This is thy son." So Julnar took him forth of the cage and sprinkled him with water, saying, "Quit this shape for the form wherein thou wast aforetime"; nor had she made an end of her speech ere he shook and became a man as before: whereupon his mother, seeing him restored to human shape, embraced him and he wept with sore weeping. On likewise did his uncle Salih and his grandmother and the daughters of his uncle and fell to kissing his hands and feet. Then Julnar sent for Shaykh Abdallah and, thanking him for his kind dealing with her son, married him to the damsel whom he had despatched to her with news of him, and made him King of the city. Moreover, she summoned those who survived of the citizens (and they were Moslems), and made them swear fealty to him and take the oath of loyalty, whereto they replied, "Hearkening and obedience!" Then she and her company farewelled him and returned to their own capital. The townsfolk came out to meet them, with drums beating, and decorated the place three days and held high festival, of the greatness of their joy for the return of their King Badr Basim.

After this Badr said to his mother, "O my mother, naught remains but that I marry and we be all united." She replied, "Right is thy rede, O my son, but wait till we ask who befitteth thee among the daughters of the Kings." And his grandmother Farashah, and the daughters of both his uncles said, "O Badr Basim, we will help thee to win thy wish forthright." Then each of them arose and fared forth questing in the lands, whilst Julnar sent out her waiting-women on the necks of Ifrits, bidding them leave not a city nor a King's palace without noting all the handsome girls that were therein. But, when King Badr Basim saw the trouble they were taking in this matter, he said to Julnar, "O my mother, leave this thing, for none will content me save Jauharah, daughter of King Al-Samandal; for that she is indeed a jewel, according to her name." Replied Julnar, "I know that which thou seekest"; and bade forthright bring Al-Samandal the King. As soon as he was present she sent for Badr Basim and acquainted him with the King's coming, whereupon he went in to him.

Now when Al-Samandal was aware of his presence, he rose to him and saluted him and bade him welcome; and King Badr Basim demanded of him his daughter Jauharah in marriage. Quoth he, "She is thine handmaid and at thy service and disposition," and despatched some of his suite bidding them seek her abode and, after telling her that her sire was in the hands of King Badr Basim, to bring her forthright. So they flew up into the air and disappeared and they returned after a while, with the Princess who, as soon as she saw her father, went up to him and threw her arms round his neck. Then, looking at her, he said, "O my daughter, know that I have given thee in wedlock to this magnanimous Sovran, and valiant lion King Badr Basim, son of Queen Julnar the Sea-born, for that he is the goodliest of the folk of his day and most powerful and the most exalted of them in degree and the noblest in rank; he befitteth none but thee, and thou none but him." Answered she, "I may not gainsay thee, O my sire; do as thou wilt, for indeed chagrin and despite are at an end, and I am one of his handmaids." So they summoned the Kazi and the witnesses who drew up the marriage contract between King Badr Basim and the Princess Jauharah, and the citizens decorated the city and beat the drums of rejoicing, and they released all who were in the jails, whilst the King clothed the widows and orphans and bestowed robes of honour upon the Lords of the Realm and Emirs and Grandees: and they made bride-feasts and held high festival night and morn ten days, at the end of which time they displayed the bride, in nine different dresses, before King Badr Basim who bestowed an honourable robe upon King Al-Samandal and sent him back to his country and people and kinsfolk. And they ceased not from living the most delectable of life and the most solaceful of days, eating and drinking and enjoying every luxury, till there came to them the Destroyer of Delights and the Sunderer of Societies; and this is the end of their story, may Allah have mercy on them all!

The Reeve's Tale [1]

KNOW, O King, that last night I was at a party where they
made a perlection of the Koran and got together doctors
of law and religion skilled in recitation and intoning; and,
when the readers ended, the table was spread and amongst
other things they set before us was a marinated ragout
flavoured with cumin-seed. So we sat down, but one of our
number held back and refused to touch it. We conjured him
to eat of it but he swore he would not; and, when we again
pressed him, he said, "Be not instant with me; sufficeth me
that which hath already befallen me through eating it"; and
he began reciting:

> Shoulder thy tray and go straight to thy goal;
> And, if suit thee this Kohl why,—use this Kohl! [2]

---

[1] This, together with the "Barber's Tale of his Second Brother" (page 39) are, in
the original, stories within a story; they are told to the Sultan of China. (P.H.N.)
[2] *I.e.* let each man do as he seems fit.

When he ended his verse we said to him, "Allah upon thee, tell us thy reason for refusing to eat of the cumin-ragout?"

"If so it be," he replied, "and needs must I eat of it, I will not do so except I wash my hands forty times with soap, forty times with potash and forty times with galangale,[1] the total being one hundred and twenty washings." Thereupon the hospitable host bade his slaves bring water and whatso he required; and the young man washed his hand as afore mentioned. Then he sat down, as if disgusted and frightened withal and, dipping his hand in the ragout, began eating and at the same time showing signs of anger. And we wondered at him with extreme wonderment, for his hand trembled and the morsel in it shook and we saw that his thumb had been cut off and he ate with his four fingers only. So we said to him, "Allah upon thee, what happened to thy thumb? Is thy hand thus by the creation of God or hath some accident befallen it?" "O my brothers," he answered, "it is not only thus with this thumb, but also with my other thumb and with both my great toes, as you shall see." So saying, he uncovered his left hand and his feet, and we saw that the left hand was even as the right and in like manner that each of his feet lacked its great toe. When we saw him after this fashion, our amazement waxed still greater and we said to him, "We have hardly patience enough to await thy history and to hear the manner of the cutting off of thy thumbs, and the reason of thy washing both hands one hundred and twenty times."

Know then, said he, that my father was chief of the merchants and the wealthiest of them all in Baghdad city during the reign of Caliph Harun al-Rashid; and he was much given to wine-drinking and listening to the lute and the other instruments of pleasaunce; so that when he died he left nothing. I buried him and had perlections of the Koran made for him, and mourned for him days and nights: then I opened his shop and found that he had left in it few goods, while his debts were many. However, I compounded with his creditors for time to settle their demands and betook myself to buying and selling, paying them something from week to week on account; and I gave not over doing this till I had cleared off his obligations in full and began adding to my principal.

One day, as I sat in my shop, suddenly and unexpectedly there appeared before me a young lady, than whom I never

---

1 Arab. "Su'úd," an Alpinia with pungent rhizome like ginger: here used as a counter-odour.

saw a fairer, wearing the richest raiment and ornaments and riding a she-mule, with one negro slave walking before her and another behind her. She drew rein at the head of the exchange-bazar and entered followed by an eunuch who said to her, "O my lady come out and away without telling any-one, lest thou light a fire which will burn us all up." Moreover, he stood before her guarding her from view whilst she looked at the merchants' shops. She found none open but mine; so she came up with the eunuch behind her and, sitting down in my shop, saluted me; never heard I aught fairer than her speech or sweeter than her voice. Then she unveiled her face, and I saw that she was like the moon and I stole a glance at her whose sight caused me a thousand sighs, and my heart was captivated with love of her.

She asked me, "O youth, hast thou any fair stuffs by thee?"; and I answered, "O my lady, thy slave is poor; but have patience till the merchants open their shops, and I will suit thee with what thou wilt." Then we sat talking, I and she (and I was drowned in the sea of her love, dazed in the desert of my passion for her), till the merchants opened their shops; when I rose and fetched her all she sought to the tune of five thousand dirhams. She gave the stuff to the eunuch and, going forth by the door of the Exchange, she mounted mule and went away, without telling me whence she came, and I was ashamed to speak of such trifle. When the merchants dunned me for the price, I made myself answerable for five thousand dirhams and went home, drunken with the love of her. They set supper before me and I ate a mouthful, thinking only of her beauty and loveliness, and sought to sleep, but sleep came not to me.

And such was my condition for a whole week, when the merchants required their monies of me, but I persuaded them to have patience for another week, at the end of which time she again appeared mounted on a she-mule and attended by her eunuch and two slaves. She saluted me and said, "O my master, we have been long in bringing thee the price of the stuffs; but now fetch the Shroff and take thy monies." So I sent for the money-changer and the eunuch counted out the coin before him and made it over to me. Then we sat talking, I and she, till the market opened, when she said to me, "Get me this and that." So I got her from the merchants whatso she wanted, and she took it and went away without saying a word to me about the price. As soon as she was out of sight, I repented me of what I had done; for the worth of the stuffs bought for her amounted to a thousand dinars, and I said in my soul, "What manner of love is this? She hath brought me five thousand dirhams, and hath taken goods for a thousand dinars.[1] I feared lest I should be beggared through having to pay the merchants their money, and I said, "They know none other but me; this lovely lady is naught but a cheat and a swindler, who hath diddled me with her beauty and grace; for she saw that I was a mere youth and laughed at me for not asking her address." I ceased not to be troubled by these doubts and fears, as she was absent more than a month, till the merchants pestered me for their money and were so hard upon me that I put my property up for sale and stood on the very brink of ruin.

However, as I was sitting in my shop one day, drowned in melancholy musings, she suddenly rode up and, dismounting at the bazar gate, came straight towards me. When I saw her all my cares fell from me and I forgot every trouble. She came close up to me and greeted me with her sweet voice and pleasant speech and presently said, "Fetch me the Shroff and weigh thy money."[2] So she gave me the price of what goods I had gotten for her and more, and fell to talking freely with me, till I was like to die of joy and delight. Presently she asked me, "Hast thou a wife?"; and I answered, "No, indeed: I have never known woman"; and began to shed tears. Quoth she, "Why weepest thou?" Quoth I, "It is nothing!" Then giving the eunuch some of the gold pieces, I begged him to be go-between[3] in the matter; but he laughed and said, "She is more in love with thee than thou with her; she hath no occasion for the stuffs she hath bought of thee and did all this only for the love of thee; so ask of her what thou wilt and she will deny thee nothing." When she saw me giving the dinars to the eunuch, she returned and sat down again; and I said to her, "Be charitable to thy slave and pardon him what he is about to say." Then I told her what was in my mind and she assented and said to the eunuch, "Thou shalt carry my message to him," adding to me, "And do thou whatso the eunuch biddeth thee." Then she got up and went away, and I paid the merchants their monies and they all profited; but as for me, regret at the breaking off of our intercourse was all my gain and I slept not the whole of that night.

---

[1] *I.e.* £125 and £500.
[2] A large sum was weighed by a professional hand instead of being counted, the reason being that the coin is mostly old and worn.
[3] The eunuch is the best possible go-between on account of his almost unlimited power over the harim.

However, before many days passed her eunuch came to me, and I entreated him honourably and asked him after his mistress. "Truly she is sick with love of thee," he replied and I rejoined, "Tell me who and what she is." Quoth he, "The Lady Zubaydah, Queen-consort of Harun al-Rashid, brought her up as a rearling and hath advanced her to be stewardess of the Harim, and gave her the right of going in and out of her own sweet will. She spoke to her lady of thee and begged her to marry her to thee; but she said: 'I will not do this, till I see the young man; and, if he be worthy of thee, I will marry thee to him.' So now we look for the moment to smuggle thee into the palace and if you succeed in entering privily thou wilt win thy wish to wed her; but if the affair get wind, the Lady Zubaydah will strike off thy head. What sayest thou to this?"

I answered, "I will go with thee and abide the risk whereof thou speakest." Then said he, "As soon as it is night, go to the mosque built by the Lady Zubaydah on the Tigris and pray the night-prayers and sleep there." "With love and gladness," cried I. So at nightfall I repaired to the mosque, where I prayed and passed the night. With earliest dawn, behold, came sundry eunuchs in a skiff with a number of empty chests which they deposited in the mosque, then all of them went their ways but one, and looking curiously at him, I saw he was our go-between. Presently in came the handmaiden, my mistress, walking straight up to us; and I rose to her and embraced her while she kissed me and shed tears.[1] We talked awhile; after which she made me get into one of the chests which she locked upon me. Presently the other eunuchs came back with a quantity of packages and she fell to stowing them in the chests, which she locked down, one by one, till all were shut. When all was done the eunuchs embarked the chests in the boat and made for the Lady Zubaydah's palace. With this, thought began to beset me and I said to myself, "Verily thy lust and wantonness will be the death of thee; and the question is after all shalt thou win to thy wish or not?" And I began to weep, boxed up as I was in the box and suffering from cramp; and I prayed Allah that He deliver me from the dangerous strait I was in, whilst the boat gave not over going on till it reached the palace gate where they lifted out the chests and amongst them that in which I was. Then they carried them in, passing through a troop of eunuchs, guardians of the harim and of the ladies behind the curtain, till they came to the post of

_____

[1] These tears are shed over past separation.

the Eunuch-in-Chief[1] who started up from his slumbers and shouted to the damsel, "What is in those chests?"

"They are full of wares for the Lady Zubaydah!" "Open them, one by one, that I may see what is in them." "And wherefore wouldst thou open them?" "Give me no words and exceed not in talk! These chests must and shall be opened." So saying, he sprang to his feet, and the first which they brought to him to open was that wherein I was; and when I felt his hands upon it, my senses failed me and I bepissed myself in my funk, the water running out of the box. Then said she to the Eunuch-in-Chief, "O Steward! thou wilt cause me to be killed and thyself too, for thou hast damaged goods worth ten thousand dinars. This chest contains coloured dresses, and four gallon flasks of Zemzem water;[2] and now one of them hath got unstoppered and the water is running out over the clothes and it will spoil their colours." The eunuch answered, "Take up thy boxes and get thee gone to the curse of God!"

So the slaves carried off all the chests, including mine; and hastened on with them till suddenly I heard the voice of one saying, "Alack, and alack! the Caliph! the Caliph!" When that cry struck mine ears I died in my skin and said a saying which never yet shamed the sayer, "There is no Majesty and there is no Might save in Allah, the Glorious, the Great! I and only I have brought this calamity upon myself." Presently I heard the Caliph say to my mistress, "A plague upon thee, what is in those boxes?"; and she answered, "Dresses for the Lady Zubaydah"; whereupon he, "Open them before me!" When I heard this I died my death outright and said to myself, "By Allah, to-day is the very last of my days in this world: if I come safe out of this I am to marry her and no more words, but detection stares me in the face and my head is as good as stricken off." Then I repeated the profession of Faith, saying, "There is no god but *the* God, and Mohammed is the Apostle of God!"

Now when I testified, "I bear witness that there is no god

---

[1] A most important Jack in office whom one can see with his smooth chin and blubber lips starting up from his lazy snooze in the shade and delivering his orders more peremptorily than any Dogberry. These epicenes are as curious and exceptional in character as in external formation. Disconnected, after a fashion, with humanity they are brave, fierce and capable of any villainy or barbarity (as Agha Mohammed Khan in Persia 1795-98). The frame is unnaturally long and lean, especially the arms and legs; with high, flat, thin shoulders; big protruding joints and a face by contrast extraordinarily large, a veritable mask; the Castrato is expert in the use of weapons and sits his horse admirably, riding well "home" in the saddle for the best of reasons; and his hoarse thick voice, which apparently does not break, as in the European "Cappone," invests him with all the circumstance of command.

[2] From the Meccan well, used by Moslems much like Eau de Lourdes by Christians.

save *the* God, I heard my mistress the handmaid declare to the Caliph, "These chests, O Commander of the Faithful, have been committed to my charge by the Lady Zubaydah, and she doth not wish their contents to be seen by anyone." "No matter!" quoth the Caliph, "needs must they be opened, I *will* see what is in them"; and he cried aloud to the eunuchs, "Bring the chests here before me." At this I made sure of death (without benefit of a doubt) and swooned away. Then the eunuchs brought the chests up to him one after another and he fell to inspecting the contents, but he saw in them only ottars and stuffs and fine dresses; and they ceased not opening the chests and he ceased not looking to see what was in them, finding only clothes and such matters, till none remained unopened but the box in which I was boxed. They put forth their hands to open it, but my mistress the handmaid made haste and said to the Caliph, "This one thou shalt see only in the presence of the Lady Zubaydah, for that which is in it is her secret." When he heard this he gave orders to carry in the chests; so they took up that wherein I was and bore it with the rest into the harim and set it down in the midst of the saloon; and indeed my spittle was dried up for very fear.

Then my mistress opened the box and took me out, saying, "Fear not: no harm shall betide thee now nor dread; but broaden thy breast and strengthen thy heart and sit thee down till the Lady Zubaydah come, and surely thou shalt win thy wish of me." So I sat down and, after a while, in came ten handmaidens, virgins like moons, and ranged themselves in two rows, five facing five; and after them twenty other damsels, high-bosomed virginity, surrounding the Lady Zubaydah who could hardly walk for the weight of her raiment and ornaments. As she drew near, the slave-girls dispersed from around her, and I advanced and kissed the ground between her hands. She signed to me to sit and, when I sat down before her chair, she began questioning me of my forbears and family and condition, to which I made such answers that pleased her, and she said to my mistress, "Our nurturing of thee, O damsel, hath not disappointed us." Then she said to me, "Know that this handmaiden is to us even as our own child and she is a trust committed to thee by Allah." I again kissed the ground before her, well pleased that I should marry my mistress, and she bade me abide ten days in the palace. So I abode there ten days, during which time I saw not my mistress nor anybody save one of the concubines, who brought me the morning and evening meals.

After this the Lady Zubaydah took counsel with the Caliph on the marriage of her favourite handmaid, and he gave leave and assigned to her a wedding portion of ten thousand gold pieces. So the Lady Zubaydah sent for the Kazi and witnesses who wrote our marriage contract, after which the women made ready sweetmeats and rich viands and distributed them among all the Odahs of the harim. Thus they did other ten days, at the end of which time my mistress went to the baths.[1] Meanwhile, they set before me a tray of food whereon were various meats and among those dishes, which were enough to daze the wits, was a bowl of cumin-ragout containing chickens'-breasts, fricandoed and flavoured with sugar, pistachios, musk and rose-water. Then, by Allah, fair sirs, I did not long hesitate; but took my seat before the ragout and fell to and ate of it till I could no more. After this I wiped my hands, but forgot to wash them; and sat till it grew dark, when the wax candles were lighted and the singing women came in with their tambourines and proceeded to display the bride in various dresses and to carry her in procession from room to room all round the palace, getting their palms crossed with gold. Then they brought her to me and I disrobed her. When I found myself alone with her on the bed I embraced her, hardly believing in our union; but she smelt the strong odours of the ragout upon my hands and forthwith cried out with an exceeding loud cry, at which the slave-girls came running to her from all sides.

I trembled with alarm, unknowing what was the matter, and the girls asked her, "What aileth thee, O our sister?" She answered them, "Take this madman away from me: I had thought he was a man of sense!" Quoth I to her, "What makes thee think me mad?" Quoth she, "Thou madman! what made thee eat of cumin-ragout and forget to wash thy hand? By Allah, I will requite thee for thy misconduct. Shall the like of thee come to bed with the like of me with unclean hands?"[2] Then she took from her side a plaited scourge and came down with it on my back and the place where I sit, till her forearms were benumbed and I fainted away from the much beating; when she said to the handmaids, "Take him and carry him to the Chief of Police, that he may strike off the hand wherewith he ate of the cumin-ragout, and which he did not wash." When I heard this I said, "There is no Majesty and there is no Might save in Allah! Wilt

---

[1] Showing that her monthly ailment was over.
[2] The insolence and license of these palace girls was unlimited; especially when, as in the present case, they have to deal with a "softy."

thou cut off my hand, because I ate of the cumin-ragout and did not wash?" The handmaidens also interceded with her and kissed her hand, saying, "O our sister, this man is a simpleton, punish him not for what he hath done this nonce"; but she answered, "By Allah, there is no help but that I dock him of somewhat, especially the offending member." Then she went away and I saw no more of her for ten days, during which time she sent me meat and drink by a slave-girl who told me that she had fallen sick from the smell of the cumin-ragout.

After that time she came to me and said, "O black of face![1] I will teach thee how to eat cumin-ragout without washing thy hands!" Then she cried out to the handmaids, who pinioned me; and she took a sharp razor and cut off my thumbs and great toes; even as you see, O fair assembly! Thereupon I swooned away, and she sprinkled some powder of healing herbs upon the stumps and when the blood was staunched, I said, "Never again will I eat of cumin-ragout without washing my hands forty times with potash and forty times with galangale and forty times with soap!" And she took of me an oath and bound me by a covenant to that effect. When, therefore, you brought me the cumin-ragout[2] my colour changed and I said to myself, "It was this very dish that caused the cutting off of my thumbs and great toes"; and, when you forced me, I said, "Needs must I fulfil the oath I have sworn."

---

1 *I.e.* by the fires of Jehannam.
2 Meat dressed with vinegar, cumin-seed and hot spices.

Ma'aruf the Cobbler and His Wife Fatimah

THERE dwelt once upon a time in the God-guarded city of Cairo a cobbler who lived by patching old shoes. His name was Ma'aruf and he had a wife called Fatimah, whom the folk had nicknamed "The Dung"; for that she was a whorish, worthless wretch, scanty of shame and mickle of mischief. She ruled her spouse and used to abuse him and curse him a thousand times a day; and he feared her malice and dreaded her misdoings; for that he was a sensible man and careful of his repute, but poor-conditioned. When he earned much, he spent it on her, and when he gained little, she revenged herself on his body that night, leaving him no peace and making his night black as her look. Amongst other afflictions which befell him from her one day she said to him, "O Ma'aruf, I wish thee to bring me this night a vermicelli-cake dressed with bees' honey." He replied, "So Allah Almighty aid me to its price, I will bring it thee. By Allah, I have no dirhams to-day, but our Lord will make things easy."[1] Rejoined she, "I wot naught of these words; whether He aid thee or aid thee not, look thou come not to me save with the vermicelli and bees' honey; and if thou come without it I will make thy night black as thy fortune whenas thou marriedst me and fellest into my hand."

Quoth he, "Allah is bountiful!" and going out with grief scattering itself from his body, prayed the dawn-prayer and opened his shop, saying, "I beseech thee, O Lord, to

---

[1] *I.e.* will send us Aid. The shrew's rejoinder is highly impious in Moslem opinion.

vouchsafe me the price of the Kunafah and ward off from me the mischief of yonder wicked woman this night!" After which he sat in the shop till noon, but no work came to him and his fear of his wife redoubled. Then he arose and locking his shop, went out perplexed as to how he should do in the matter of the vermicelli-cake, seeing he had not even the wherewithal to buy bread. Presently he came to the shop of the Kunafah-seller and stood before it distraught, whilst his eyes brimmed with tears. The pastry-cook glanced at him and said, "O Master Ma'aruf, why dost thou weep? Tell me what hath befallen thee." So he acquainted him with his case, saying, "My wife is a shrew, a virago who would have me bring her a Kunafah; but I have sat in my shop till past mid-day and have not gained even the price of bread; wherefore I am in fear of her." The cook laughed and said, "No harm shall come to thee. How many pounds wilt thou have?" "Five pounds," answered Ma'aruf. So the man weighed him out five pounds of vermicelli-cake and said to him, "I have clarified butter, but no bees' honey. Here is drip-honey, however, which is better than bees' honey; and what harm will there be, if it be with drip-honey?"

Ma'aruf was ashamed to object, because the pastry-cook was to have patience with him for the price, and said, "Give it me with drip-honey." So he fried a vermicelli-cake for him with butter and drenched it with drip-honey, till it was fit to present to Kings. Then he asked him, "Dost thou want bread and cheese?"; and Ma'aruf answered, "Yes." So he gave him four half-dirhams' worth of bread and one of cheese, and the vermicelli was ten nusfs. Then said he, "Know, O Ma'aruf, that thou owest me fifteen nusfs; so go to thy wife and make merry and take this nusf for the Hammam, and thou shalt have credit for a day or two or three till Allah provide thee with thy daily bread. And straiten not thy wife, for I will have patience with thee till such time as thou shalt have dirhams to spare." So Ma'aruf took the vermicelli-cake and bread and cheese and went away, with a heart at ease, blessing the pastry-cook and saying, "extolled be Thy perfection, O my Lord! How bountiful art Thou!"

When he came home, his wife inquired of him, "Hast thou brought the vermicelli-cake?"; and, replying "Yes," he set it before her. She looked at it and seeing that it was dressed with cane-honey, said to him, "Did I not bid thee bring it with bees' honey? Wilt thou contrary my wish and have it dressed with cane-honey?" He excused himself to her, saying, "I bought it not save on credit"; but said she, "This talk is idle; I will not eat Kunafah save with bees' honey." And she was wroth with it and threw it in his face, saying, "Begone, thou pimp, and bring me other than this!" Then she dealt him a buffet on the cheek and knocked out one of his teeth. The blood ran down upon his breast and for stress of anger he smote her on the head a single blow and a slight; whereupon she clutched his beard and fell to shouting out and saying, "Help, O Moslems!" So the neighbours came in and freed his beard from her grip; then they reproved and reproached her, saying, "We are all content to eat Kunafah with cane-honey. Why, then, wilt thou oppress this poor man thus? Verily, this is disgraceful in thee!" And they went on to soothe her till they made peace between her and him.

But, when the folk were gone, she sware that she would not eat of the vermicelli, and Ma'aruf, burning with hunger, said in himself, "She sweareth that she will not eat; so I will e'en eat." Then he ate, and when she saw him eating, she said, "Inshallah, may the eating of it be poison to destroy the fat one's body." Quoth he, "It shall not be at thy bidding," and went on eating, laughing and saying, "Thou swarest that thou wouldst not eat of this; but Allah is bountiful, and to-morrow night, an the Lord decree, I will bring thee Kunafah dressed with bees' honey, and thou shalt eat it alone." And he applied himself to appeasing her, whilst she called down curses upon him; and she ceased not to rail at him and revile him with gross abuse till the morning, when she bared her forearm to beat him. Quoth he, "Give me time and I will bring thee other vermicelli-cake." Then he went out to the mosque and prayed, after which he betook himself to his shop and opening it, sat down; but hardly had he done this when up came two runners from the Kazi's court and said to him, "Up with thee, speak with the Kazi, for thy wife hath complained of thee to him and her favour is thus and thus." He recognised her by their description; and saying, "May Allah Almighty torment her!" walked with them till he came to the Kazi's presence, where he found Fatimah standing with her arm bound up and her face-veil besmeared with blood; and she was weeping and wiping away her tears.

Quoth the Kazi, "Ho man, hast thou no fear of Allah the Most High? Why hast thou beaten this good woman and broken her forearm and knocked out her tooth and entreated her thus?" And quoth Ma'aruf, "If I beat her or put out her tooth, sentence me to what thou wilt; but in truth the case was thus and thus and the neighbours made peace between me and her." And he told him the story from first to last.

Now this Kazi was a benevolent man; so he brought out to him a quarter-dinar, saying, "O man, take this and get her Kunafah with bees' honey and do ye make peace, thou and she." Quoth Ma'aruf, "Give it to her." So she took it and the Kazi made peace between them, saying, "O wife, obey thy husband; and thou, O man, deal kindly with her." Then they left the court, reconciled at the Kazi's hands, and the woman went one way, whilst her husband returned by another way to his shop and sat there, when, behold, the runners came up to him and said, "Give us our fee." Quoth he, "The Kazi took not of me aught; on the contrary, he gave me a quarter-dinar." But quoth they, "'Tis no concern of ours whether the Kazi took of thee or gave to thee, and if thou give us not our fee, we will exact it in despite of thee." And they fell to dragging him about the market; so he sold his tools and gave them half a dinar, whereupon they let him go and went away, whilst he put his hand to his cheek and sat sorrowful, for that he had no tools wherewith to work.

Presently, up came two ill-favoured fellows and said to him, "Come, O man, and speak with the Kazi; for thy wife hath complained of thee to him." Said he, "He made peace between us just now." But said they, "We come from another Kazi, and thy wife hath complained of thee to our Kazi." So he arose and went with them to their Kazi, calling on Allah for aid against her; and when he saw her, he said to her, "Did we not make peace, good woman?" Whereupon she cried, "There abideth no peace between me and thee." According he came forward and told the Kazi his story, adding, "And indeed the Kazi Such-an-one made peace between us this very hour." Whereupon the Kazi said to her, "O strumpet, since ye two have made peace each with other, why comest thou to me complaining?" Quoth she, "He beat me after that"; but quoth the Kazi, "Make peace each with other, and beat her not again, and she will cross thee no more." So they made peace and the Kazi said to Ma'aruf, "Give the runners their fee." So he gave them their fee and going back to his shop, opened it and sat down, as he were a drunken man for excess of the chagrin which befell him. Presently, while he was still sitting, behold, a man came up to him and said, "O Ma'aruf, rise and hide thyself, for thy wife hath complained of thee to the High Court and Abu Tabak is after thee." So he shut his shop and fled towards the Gate of Victory. He had five nusfs of silver left of the price of the lasts and gear; and therewith he bought four worth of bread and one of cheese, as he fled from her.

Now it was the winter season and the hour of mid-afternoon prayer; so, when he came out among the rubbish-mounds the rain descended upon him, like water from the mouths of waterskins, and his clothes were drenched. He therefore entered the 'Adiliyah, where he saw a ruined place and therein a deserted cell without a door; and in it he took refuge and found shelter from the rain. The tears streamed from his eyelids, and he fell to complaining of what had betided him and saying, "Whither shall I flee from this whore? I beseech Thee, O Lord, to vouchsafe me one who shall conduct me to a far country, where she shall not know the way to me!" Now while he sat weeping, behold, the wall clave and there came forth to him therefrom one of tall stature, whose aspect caused his body-pile to bristle and his flesh to creep, and said to him, "O man, what aileth thee that thou disturbest me this night? These two hundred years have I dwelt here and have never seen any enter this place and do as thou dost. Tell me what thou wishest and I will accomplish thy need, as ruth for thee hath got hold upon my heart." Quoth Ma'aruf, "Who and what art thou?"; and quoth he, "I am the Haunter of this place." So Ma'aruf told him all that had befallen him with his wife and he said, "Wilt thou have me convey thee to a country where thy wife shall know no way to thee?" "Yes," said Ma'aruf; and the other, "Then mount my back."

So he mounted on his back and he flew with him from after supper-tide till daybreak, when he set him down on the top of a high mountain and said to him, "O mortal, descend this mountain and thou wilt see the gate of a city. Enter it, for therein thy wife cannot come at thee." He then left him and went his way, whilst Ma'aruf abode in amazement and perplexity till the sun rose, when he said to himself, "I will up with me and go down into the city: indeed there is no profit in my abiding upon this highland." So he descended to the mountain-foot and saw a city girt by towering walls, full of lofty palaces and gold-adorned buildings which was a delight to beholders. He entered in at the gate and found it a place such as lightened the grieving heart; but, as he walked through the streets the townsfolk stared at him as a curiosity and gathered about him, marvelling at his dress, for it was unlike theirs. Presently, one of them said to him, "O man, art thou a stranger?" "Yes." "What countryman art thou?" "I am from the city of Cairo the Auspicious." "And when didst thou leave Cairo?" "I left it yesterday, at the hour of afternoon-prayer." Whereupon the man laughed at him and cried out, saying, "Come look, O folk, at this man and hear what he saith!" Quoth they, "What doth he say?"; and quoth the townsman, "He pretendeth that he cometh from Cairo and left it yesterday at the hour of afternoon-prayer!"

At this they all laughed and gathering round Ma'aruf, said to him, "O man, art thou mad to talk thus? How canst thou pretend that thou leftest Cairo at mid-afternoon yesterday and foundest thyself this morning here, when the truth is that between our city and Cairo lieth a full year's journey?" Quoth he, "None is mad but you. As for me, I speak sooth, for here is bread which I brought with me from Cairo, and see, 'tis yet new." Then he showed them the bread and they stared at it, for it was unlike their country bread. So the crowd increased about him and they said to one another, "This is Cairo bread: look at it"; and he became a gazing-stock in the city and some believed him, whilst others gave him the lie and made mock of him. Whilst this was going on, behold, up came a merchant riding on a she-mule and followed by two black slaves, and brake a way through the people, saying, "O folk, are ye not ashamed to mob this stranger and make mock of him and scoff at him?" And he went on to rate them till he drave them away from Ma'aruf, and none could make him any answer. Then he said to the stranger, "Come, O my brother, no harm shall betide thee from these folk. Verily they have no shame."

So he took him and carrying him to a spacious and richly adorned house, seated him in a speak-room fit for a King, whilst he gave an order to his slaves, who opened a chest and brought out to him a dress such as might be worn by a merchant worth a thousand. He clad him therewith and Ma'aruf, being a seemly man, became as he were Consul of the Merchants. Then his host called for food and they set before him a tray of all manner exquisite viands. The twain ate and drank and the merchant said to Ma'aruf, "O my brother, what is thy name?" "My name is Ma'aruf and I am a cobbler by trade and patch old shoes." "What countryman art thou?" "I am from Cairo." "What quarter?" "Dost thou know Cairo?" "I am of its children. I come from the Red Street." "And whom dost thou know in the Red Street?" "I know such an one and such an one," answered Ma'aruf and named several people to him. Quoth the other, "Knowest thou Shaykh Ahmad the druggist?" "He was my next neighbour, wall to wall." "Is he well?" "Yes." "How many sons hath he?" "Three, Mustafa, Mohammed and Ali." "And what hath Allah done with them?" "As for Mustafa, he is well and he is a learned man, and professor. Mohammed is a druggist and opened him a shop beside that of his father, after he had married, and his wife hath borne him a son named Hasan." "Allah gladden thee with good news!" said the merchant; and Ma'aruf continued, "As for Ali, he was my friend, when we were boys, and we always played together, I and he. We used to go in the guise of the children of the Nazarenes and enter the church and steal the books of the Christians and sell them and buy food with the price. It chanced once that the Nazarenes caught us with a book; whereupon they complained of us to our folk and said to Ali's father, 'An thou hinder not thy son from troubling us, we will complain of thee to the King.' So he appeased them and gave Ali a thrashing; wherefore he ran away none knew whither and he hath now been absent twenty years and no man hath brought news of him."

Quoth the host, "I am that very Ali, son of Shaykh Ahmad the druggist, and thou art my playmate Ma'aruf."[1] So they saluted each other and after the salam Ali said, "Tell me why, O Ma'aruf, thou camest from Cairo to this city." Then he told him all that had befallen him of ill-doing with his wife Fatimah the Dung and said, "So, when her annoy waxed on me, I fled from her towards the Gate of Victory and went forth the city. Presently, the rain fell heavy on me; so I entered a ruined cell in the 'Adiliyah and sat there, weeping; whereupon there came forth to me the Haunter of the place, which was an Ifrit of the Jinn, and questioned me. I acquainted him with my case and he took me on his back and flew with me all night between heaven and earth, till he set me down on yonder mountain and gave me to know of this city. So I came down from the mountain and entered the city, when the people crowded about me and questioned me. I told them that I had left Cairo yesterday, but they believed me not, and presently thou camest up and driving the folk away from me, carriedst me to this house. Such, then, is the cause of my quitting Cairo; and thou, what object brought thee hither?"

Quoth Ali, "The giddiness of folly turned my head when I was seven years old, from which time I wandered from land to land and city to city, till I came to this city, the name whereof is Ikhtiyan al-Khatan. I found its people an hospitable folk and a kindly, compassionate for the poor man and selling to him on credit and believing all he said. So quoth I to them, 'I am a merchant and have preceded my packs and I need a place wherein to bestow my baggage.' And they believed me and assigned me a lodging. Then quoth

---

[1] This thoroughly dramatic scene is told with a charming naïveté. No wonder that *The Nights* has been made the basis of a national theatre amongst the Turks.

I to them, 'Is there any of you will lend me a thousand dinars, till my loads arrive, when I will repay it to him; for I am in want of certain things before my goods come?' They gave me what I asked and I went to the merchants' bazar, where, seeing goods, I bought them and sold them next day at a profit of fifty gold pieces and bought others. And I consorted with the folk and entreated them liberally, so that they loved me, and I continued to sell and buy, till I grew rich. Know, O my brother, that the proverb saith, 'The world is show and trickery: and the land where none wotteth thee, there do whatso liketh thee.' Thou too, an thou say to all who ask thee, I'm a cobbler by trade and poor withal, and I fled from my wife and left Cairo yesterday, they will not believe thee and thou wilt be a laughing-stock among them as long as thou abidest in the city; whilst, an thou tell them, an Ifrit brought me hither, they will take fright at thee and none will come near thee; for they will say, 'This man is possessed of an Ifrit and harm will betide whoso approacheth him.' And such public report will be dishonouring both to thee and to me, because they ken I come from Cairo."

Ma'aruf asked, "How then shall I do?"; and Ali answered, "I will tell thee how thou shalt do, Inshallah! To-morrow I will give thee a thousand dinars and a she-mule to ride and a black slave, who shall walk before thee and guide thee to the gate of the merchants' bazar; and do thou go into them. I will be there sitting amongst them, and when I see thee, I will rise to thee and salute thee with the salam and kiss thy hand and make a great man of thee. Whenever I ask thee of any kind of stuff, saying, 'Hast thou brought with thee aught of such a kind?' do thou answer, 'Plenty.' And if they question me of thee, I will praise thee and magnify thee in their eyes and say to them, 'Get him a storehouse and a shop.' I also will give thee out for a man of great wealth and generosity; and if a beggar come to thee, bestow upon him what thou mayst; so will they put faith in what I say and believe in thy greatness and generosity and love thee. Then will I invite thee to my house and invite all the merchants on thy account and bring together thee and them, so that all may know thee and thou know them, whereby thou shalt sell and buy and take and give with them; nor will it be long ere thou become a man of money."

Accordingly, on the morrow, he gave him a thousand dinars and a suit of clothes and a black slave and, mounting him on a she-mule, said to him, "Allah give thee quittance of responsibility for all this,[1] inasmuch as thou art my friend and it behoveth me to deal generously with thee. Have no care; but put away from thee the thought of thy wife's misways and name her not to any." "Allah requite thee with good!" replied Ma'aruf, and rode on, preceded by his blackamoor till the slave brought him to the gate of the merchants' bazar, where they were all seated, and amongst them Ali, who, when he saw him, rose and threw himself upon him, crying, "A blessed day, O Merchant Ma'aruf, O man of good works and kindness!" And he kissed his hand before the merchants and said to them, "Our brothers, ye are honoured by knowing the merchant Ma'aruf." So they saluted him, and Ali signed to them to make much of him, wherefore he was magnified in their eyes. Then Ali helped him to dismount from his she-mule and saluted him with the salam; after which he took the merchants apart, one after other, and vaunted Ma'aruf to them. They asked, "Is this man a merchant?"; and he answered, "Yes; and indeed he is the chiefest of merchants, there liveth not a wealthier than he; for his wealth and the riches of his father and forefathers are famous among the merchants of Cairo. He hath partners in Hind and Sind and Al-Yaman and is high in repute for generosity. So know ye his rank and exalt ye his degree and do him service, and wot also that his coming to your city is not for the sake of traffic, and none other save to divert himself with the sight of folk's countries; indeed, he hath no need of strangerhood for the sake of gain and profit, having wealth that fires cannot consume, and I am one of his servants." And he ceased not to extol him, till they set him above their heads and began to tell one another of his qualities.

Then they gathered round him and offered him junkets and sherbets, and even the Consul of the Merchants came to him and saluted him; whilst Ali proceeded to ask him, in the presence of the traders, "O my lord, haply thou hast brought with thee somewhat of such and such a stuff?"; and Ma'aruf answered, "Plenty." Now Ali had that day shown him various kinds of costly clothes and had taught him the names of the different stuffs, dear and cheap. Then said one of the merchants, "O my lord, hast thou brought with thee yellow broad cloth?"; and Ma'aruf said, "Plenty!" Quoth another, "And gazelles' blood red?"; and quoth the cobbler, "Plenty"; and as often as he asked him of aught, he made the same answer. So the other said, "O Merchant Ali, had thy countryman a mind to transport a thousand loads of

---

[1] *I.e.* "May the Lord soon make thee able to repay me, but meanwhile I give to thee for thy own free use."

costly stuffs, he could do so"; and Ali said, "He would take them from a single one of his storehouses, and miss naught thereof."

Now, whilst they were sitting, behold, up came a beggar and went the round of the merchants. One gave him a half-dirham and another a copper, but most of them gave him nothing, till he came to Ma'aruf who pulled out a handful of gold and gave it to him, whereupon he blessed him and went his ways. The merchants marvelled at this and said, "Verily, this is a King's bestowal, for he gave the beggar gold without count, and were he not a man of vast wealth and money without end, he had not given a beggar a handful of gold." After a while, there came to him a poor woman and he gave her a handful of gold; whereupon she went away, blessing him, and told other beggars, who came to him, one after other, and he gave them each a handful of gold, till he disbursed the thousand dinars. Then he struck hand upon hand and said, "Allah is our sufficient aid and excellent is the Agent!" Quoth the Consul, "What aileth thee, O Merchant Ma'aruf?"; and quoth he, "It seemeth that the most part of the people of this city are poor and needy; had I known their misery I would have brought with me a large sum of money in my saddle-bags and given largesse thereof to the poor. I fear me I may be long abroad and 'tis not in my nature to baulk a beggar; and I have no gold left; so, if a pauper come to me, what shall I say to him?" Quoth the Consul, "Say, Allah will send thee thy daily bread!";[1] but Ma'aruf replied, "That is not my practice and I am care-ridden because of this. Would I had other thousand dinars, wherewith to give alms till my baggage come!" "Have no care for that," quoth the Consul, and sending one of his dependents for a thousand dinars handed them to Ma'aruf, who went on giving them to every beggar who passed the call to noon-prayer. Then they entered the cathedral-mosque and prayed the noon-prayers, and what was left him of the thousand gold pieces he scattered on the heads of the worshippers.

This drew the people's attention to him and they blessed him, whilst the merchants marvelled at the abundance of his generosity and openhandedness. Then he turned to another trader, and borrowing of him other thousand ducats gave these also away, while Merchant Ali looked on at what he did, but could not speak. He ceased not to do this till the call to mid-afternoon prayer, when he entered the mosque and prayed and distributed the rest of the money. On this wise,

---

1 One of the many formulas of polite refusal.

by the time they locked the doors of the bazar,[1] he had borrowed five thousand sequins and given them away, saying to everyone of whom he took aught, "Wait till my baggage come when, if thou desire gold I will give thee gold, and if thou desire stuffs, thou shalt have stuffs; for I have no end of them." At eventide Merchant Ali invited Ma'aruf and the rest of the traders to an entertainment and seated him in the upper end, the place of honour, where he talked of nothing but cloths and jewels, and whenever they made mention to him of aught, he said, "I have plenty of it." Next day, he again repaired to the market-street where he showed a friendly bias towards the merchants and borrowed of them more money, which he distributed to the poor; nor did he leave doing thus twenty days, till he had borrowed threescore thousand dinars and still there came no baggage, no, nor a burning plague.

At last folk began to clamour for their money and say, "The merchant Ma'aruf's baggage cometh not. How long will he take people's monies and give them to the poor?" And quoth one of them, "My rede is that we speak to Merchant Ali." So they went to him and said, "O Merchant Ali, Merchant Ma'aruf's baggage cometh not." Said he, "Have patience, it cannot fail to come soon." Then he took Ma'aruf aside and said to him, "O Ma'aruf, what fashion is this? Did I bid thee brown the bread or burn it? The merchants clamour for their coin and tell me that thou owest them sixty thousand dinars, which thou hast borrowed and given away to the poor. How wilt thou satisfy the folk, seeing that thou neither sellest nor buyest?" Said Ma'aruf, "What matters it, and what are threescore thousand dinars? When my baggage shall come, I will pay them in stuffs or in gold and silver, as they will." Quoth Merchant Ali, "Allah is Most Great! Hast thou then any baggage?"; and he said, "Plenty." Cried the other, "Allah and the Hallows requite thee thine impudence! Did I teach thee this saying, that thou shouldst repeat it to me? But I will acquaint the folk with thee." Ma'aruf rejoined, "Begone and prate no more! Am I a poor man? I have endless wealth in my baggage and as soon as it cometh, they shall have their money's worth, two for one. I have no need of them." At this Merchant Ali waxed wroth and said, "Unmannerly wight that thou art, I will teach thee to lie to me and be not ashamed!" Said Ma'aruf, "E'en work the worst thy hand can do! They must

---

[1] Each bazar, in a large city like Damascus, has its tall and heavy wooden doors which are locked every evening and opened in the morning by the Ghafir or guard. The "silver key," however, always lets one in.

wait till my baggage come, when they shall have their due and more."

So Ali left him and went away, saying in himself, "I praised him whilome and if I blame him now, I make myself out a liar and become of those of whom it is said, 'Whoso praiseth and then blameth lieth twice.'" And he knew not what to do. Presently, the traders came to him and said, "O Merchant Ali, hast thou spoken to him?" Said he, "O folk, I am ashamed and, though he owe me a thousand dinars, I cannot speak to him. When ye lent him your money ye consulted me not; so ye have no claim on me. Dun him yourselves, and if he pay you not, complain of him to the King of the city, saying, 'He is an imposter who hath imposed upon us.' And he will deliver you from the plague of him." Accordingly, they repaired to the King and told him what had passed, saying, "O King of the Age, we are perplexed anent this merchant, whose generosity is excessive; for he doeth thus and thus, and all he borroweth he giveth away to the poor by handfuls. Were he a man of naught, his sense would not suffer him to lavish gold on this wise; and were he a man of wealth, his good faith had been made manifest to us by the coming of his baggage; but we see none of his luggage, although he avoucheth that he hath a baggage-train and hath preceded it. Now some time hath passed, but there appeareth no sign of his baggage-train, and he oweth us sixty thousand gold pieces, all of which he hath given away in alms." And they went on to praise him and extol his generosity.

Now this King was a very covetous man, a more covetous than Ash'ab; and when he heard tell of Ma'aruf's generosity and openhandedness, greed of gain got the better of him and he said to his Wazir, "Were not this merchant a man of immense wealth, he had not shown all this munificence. His baggage-train will assuredly come, whereupon these merchants will flock to him and he will scatter amongst them riches galore. Now I have more right to this money than they; wherefore I have a mind to make friends with him and profess affection for him, so that, when his baggage cometh whatso the merchants would have had I shall get of him; and I will give him my daughter to wife and join his wealth to my wealth." Replied the Wazir, "O King of the Age, methinks he is naught but an imposter, and 'tis the imposter who ruineth the house of the covetous"; and the King said, "O Wazir, I will prove him and soon know if he be an imposter or a true man and whether he be a reading of Fortune or not." The Wazir asked, "And how wilt thou prove him?"; and the King answered, "I will send for him to the presence and entreat him with honour and give him a jewel which I have. An he know it and wot its price, he is a man of worth and wealth; but an he know it not, he is an imposter and an upstart and I will do him die by the foulest of deaths."

So he sent for Ma'aruf, who came and saluted him. The King returned his salam and, seating him beside himself, said to him, "Art thou the merchant Ma'aruf?"; and said he, "Yes." Quoth the King, "The merchants declare that thou owest them sixty thousand ducats. Is this true?" "Yes," quoth he. Asked the King, "Then why dost thou not give them their money?"; and he answered, "Let them wait till my baggage come and I will repay them twofold. An they wish for gold, they shall have gold; and should they wish for silver, they shall have silver; or an they prefer for merchandise, I will give them merchandise; and to whom I owe a thousand I will give two thousand in requital of that wherewith he hath veiled my face before the poor; for I have plenty." Then said the King, "O merchant, take this and look what is its kind and value." And he gave him a jewel the bigness of a hazel-nut, which he had bought for a thousand sequins and, not having its fellow, prized it highly. Ma'aruf took it and, pressing it between his thumb and forefinger, brake it, for it was brittle and would not brook the squeeze. Quoth the King, "Why hast thou broken the jewel?"; and Ma'aruf laughed and said, "O King of the Age, this is no jewel. This is but a bittock of mineral worth a thousand dinars; why dost thou style it a jewel? A jewel I call such as is worth threescore and ten thousand gold pieces and this is called but a piece of stone. A jewel that is not of the bigness of a walnut hath no worth in my eyes and I take no account thereof. How cometh it, then, that thou, who art King, stylest this thing a jewel, when 'tis but a bit of mineral worth a thousand dinars? But ye are excusable, for that ye are poor folk and have not in your possession things of price."

The King asked, "O merchant, hast thou jewels such as those whereof thou speakest?"; and he answered, "Plenty." Whereupon avarice overcame the King and he said, "Wilt thou give me real jewels?" Said Ma'aruf, "When my baggage-train shall come, I will give thee no end of jewels; and all that thou canst desire I have in plenty and will give thee, without price." At this the King rejoiced and said to the traders, "Wend your ways and have patience with him, till his baggage arrive, when do ye come to me and receive your monies from me." So they fared forth and the King turned to his Wazir and said to him, "Pay court to Merchant Ma'aruf and take and give with him in talk and bespeak him of my daughter, Princess Dunya, that he may wed her and so we gain these riches he hath." Said the Wazir, "O King of the Age, this man's fashion misliketh me and methinks he is an imposter and a liar: so leave this whereof thou speakest lest thou lose thy daughter for naught." Now this Minister had sued the King aforetime to give him his daughter to wife and he was willing to do so, but when she heard of it she consented not to marry him. Accordingly, the King said to him, "O traitor, thou desirest no good for me, because in past time thou soughtest my daughter in wedlock, but she would none of thee; so now thou wouldst cut off the way of her marriage and wouldst have the Princess lie fallow, that thou mayst take her; but hear from me one word. Thou hast no concern in this matter. How can he be an imposter and a liar, seeing that he knew the price of the jewel, even that for which I bought it, and brake it because it pleased him not? He hath jewels in plenty, and when he goeth in to my daughter and seeth her to be beautiful, she will captivate his reason and he will love her and give her jewels and things of price: but, as for thee, thou wouldst forbid my daughter and myself these good things." So the Minister was silent, for fear of the King's anger, and said to himself, "Set the curs on the cattle!"[1]

Then with show of friendly bias he betook himself to Ma'aruf and said to him, "His highness the King loveth thee and hath a daughter, a winsome lady and a lovesome, to whom he is minded to marry thee. What sayst thou?" Said he, "No harm in that; but let him wait till my baggage come, for marriage settlements on Kings' daughters are large and their rank demandeth that they be not endowed save with a dowry befitting their degree. At this present I have no money with me till the coming of my baggage, for I have wealth in plenty and needs must I make her marriage portion five thousand purses. Then I shall need a thousand purses to distribute among the poor and needy on my wedding night, and other thousand to give to those who walk in the bridal procession and yet other thousand wherewith to provide provaunt for the troops and others;[2] and I shall want an hundred jewels to give to the Princess on the wedding morning and other hundred gems to distribute among the slave-girls and eunuchs, for I must give each of them a jewel in honour of the bride; and I need wherewithal to clothe a

---

[1] *I.e.* "Show a miser money and hold him back, if you can."
[2] He wants £40,000 to begin with.

thousand naked paupers, and alms, too, needs must be given. All this cannot be done till my baggage come; but I have plenty and, once it is here, I shall make no account of all this outlay."

The Wazir returned to the King and told him what Ma'aruf said, whereupon quoth he, "Since this is his wish, how canst thou style him imposter and liar?" Replied the Minister, "And I cease not to say this." But the King chid him angrily and threatened him, saying, "By the life of my head, an thou cease not this talk, I will slay thee! Go back to him and fetch him to me and I will manage matters with him myself." So the Wazir returned to Ma'aruf and said to him, "Come and speak with the King." "I hear and I obey," said Ma'aruf and went in to the King, who said to him, "Thou shalt not put me off with these excuses, for my treasury is full; so take the keys and spend all thou needest and give what thou wilt and clothe the poor and do thy desire and have no care for the girl and the handmaids. When the baggage shall come, do what thou wilt with thy wife, by way of generosity, and we will have patience with thee anent the marriage portion till then, for there is no manner of difference betwixt me and thee; none at all." Then he sent for the Shaykh Al-Islam and bade him write out the marriage contract between his daughter and Merchant Ma'aruf, and he did so; after which the King gave the signal for beginning the wedding festivities and bade decorate the city.

The kettle-drums beat and the tables were spread with meats of all kinds and there came performers who paraded their tricks. Merchant Ma'aruf sat upon a throne in a parlour and the players and gymnasts and effeminates[1] and dancing-men of wondrous movements and posture-makers of marvellous cunning came before him, whilst he called out to the treasurer and said to him, "Bring gold and silver." So he brought gold and silver and Ma'aruf went round among the spectators and largessed each performer by the handful; and he gave alms to the poor and needy and clothes to the naked and it was a clamorous festival and a right merry. The treasurer could not bring money fast enough from the treasury, and the Wazir's heart was like to burst for rage; but he dared not say a word, whilst Merchant Ali marvelled at

---

[1] Arab. "Al-Jink" (from Turk.) are boys and youths, mostly Jews, Armenians, Greeks and Turks, who dress in woman's dress with long hair braided. Lane (M. E. chapters xix and xxv) gives same account of the customs of the "Gink" (as the Egyptians call them), but cannot enter into details concerning these catamites. Respectable Moslems often employ them to dance at festivals in preference to the Ghawazi-women, a freak of Mohammedan decorum. When they grow old they often preserve their costume, and a glance at them makes a European's blood run cold.

this waste of wealth and said to Merchant Ma'aruf, "Allah and the Hallows visit this upon thy headsides! Doth it not suffice thee to squander the traders' money, but thou must squander that of the King to boot?" Replied Ma'aruf, "'Tis none of thy concern: whenas my baggage shall come, I will requite the King manifold." And he went on lavishing money and saying in himself, "A burning plague! What will happen will happen and there is no flying from that which is fore-ordained."

The festivities ceased not for the space of forty days, and on the one-and-fortieth day, they made the bride's cortège and all the Emirs and troops walked before her. When they brought her in before Ma'aruf, he began scattering gold on the people's heads, and they made her a mighty fine procession, whilst Ma'aruf expended in her honour vast sums of money. Then they brought him in to Princess Dunya and he sat down on the high divan; after which they let fall the curtains and shut the doors and withdrew, leaving him alone with his bride; whereupon he smote hand upon hand and sat awhile sorrowful and saying, "There is no Majesty and there is no Might save in Allah, the Glorious, the Great!" Quoth the Princess, "O my lord, Allah preserve thee! What aileth thee that thou art troubled?" Quoth he, "And how should I be other than troubled, seeing that thy father hath embarrassed me and done with me a deed which is like the burning of green corn?" She asked, "And what hath my father done with thee? Tell me!"; and he answered, "He hath brought me in to thee before the coming of my baggage, and I want at very least an hundred jewels to distribute among thy handmaids, to each a jewel, so that she might rejoice therein and say, 'My lord gave me a jewel on the night of his going in to my lady.' This good deed would I have done in honour of thy station and for the increase of thy dignity; and I have no need to stint myself in lavishing jewels, for I have of them great plenty." Rejoined she, "Be not concerned for that. As for me, trouble not thyself about me, for I will have patience with thee till thy baggage shall come, and as for my women have no care for them. Rise, doff thy clothes and take thy pleasure; and when the baggage cometh we shall get the jewels and the rest."

So he arose and putting off his clothes sat down on the bed and sought love-liesse and they fell to toying with each other. He laid his hand on her knee and she sat down in his lap and thrust her lip like a tit-bit of meat into his mouth, and that hour was such as maketh a man to forget his father and his mother. So he clasped her in his arms and

strained her fast to his breast and sucked her lip, till the
honey-dew ran out into his mouth; and he laid his hand
under her left armpit, whereupon his vitals and her vitals
yearned for coition. Then he clapped her between the breast
and his hand slipped down between her thighs and she girded
him with her legs, whereupon he made of the two parts proof
amain and crying out, "O sire of the chin-veils twain!"
applied the priming and kindled the match and set it to

the touch-hole and gave fire and breached the citadel in its
four corners; so there befell the mystery concerning which
there is no inquiry; and she cried the cry that needs must be
cried. Merchant Ma'aruf abated her maidenhead and that
night was one not to be counted among lives for that which
it comprised of the enjoyment of the fair, clipping and dally-
ing *langue fourrée* and futtering till the dawn of day, when
he arose and entered the Hammam whence, after donning a
suit for sovrans suitable he betook himself to the King.

All who were there rose to him and received him with
honour and worship, giving him joy and invoking blessings
upon him; and he sat down by the King's side and asked,

"Where is the treasurer?" They answered, "Here he is, before thee," and he said to him, "Bring robes of honour for all the Wazirs and Emirs and dignitaries and clothe them therewith." The treasurer brought him all he sought and he sat giving to all who came to him and lavishing largesse upon every man according to his station. On this wise he abode twenty days, whilst no baggage appeared for him nor aught else, till the treasurer was straitened by him to the uttermost and going in to the King, as he sat alone with the Wazir in Ma'aruf's absence, kissed the ground between his hands and said, "O King of the Age, I must tell thee somewhat, lest haply thou blame me for not acquainting thee therewith. Know that the treasury is being exhausted; there is none but a little money left in it and in ten days more we shall shut it upon emptiness." Quoth the King, "O Wazir, verily my son-in-law's baggage-train tarrieth long and there appeareth no news thereof." The Minister laughed and said, "Allah be gracious to thee, O King of the Age! Thou art none other but heedless with respect to this imposter, this liar. As thy head liveth, there is no baggage for him, no, nor a burning plague to rid us of him! Nay, he hath but imposed on thee without surcease, so that he hath wasted thy treasures and married thy daughter for naught. How long therefore wilt thou be heedless of this liar?"

Then quoth the King, "O Wazir, how shall we do to learn the truth of his case?" and quoth the Wazir, "O King of the Age, none may come at a man's secret but his wife; so send for thy daughter and let her come behind the curtain, that I may question her of the truth of his estate, to the intent that she may make question of him and acquaint us with his case." Cried the King, "There is no harm in that; and as my head liveth, if it be proved that he is a liar and an imposter, I will verily do him die by the foulest of deaths!" Then he carried the Wazir into the sitting-chamber and sent for his daughter, who came behind the curtain, her husband being absent, and said, "What wouldst thou, O my father? Said he "Speak with the Wazir." So she asked, "Ho thou, the Wazir, what is thy will?"; and he answered, "O my lady, thou must know that thy husband hath squandered thy father's substance and married thee without a dower; and he ceaseth not to promise us and break his promises, nor cometh there any tidings of his baggage; in short we would have thee inform us concerning him." Quoth she, "Indeed his words be many, and he still cometh and promiseth me jewels and treasures and costly stuffs; but I see nothing." Quoth the Wazir, "O my lady, canst thou this night take and give with him in talk and whisper to him, 'Say me sooth and fear from me naught, for thou art become my husband and I will not transgress against thee. So tell me the truth of the matter and I will devise thee a device whereby thou shalt be set at rest.' And do thou play near and far[1] with him in words and profess love to him and win him to confess and after tell us the facts of his case." And she answered, "O my papa, I know how I will make proof of him."

Then she went away and after supper her husband came in to her, according to his wont, whereupon Princess Dunya rose to him and took him under the armpit and wheedled him with winsomest wheedling (and all-sufficient are women's wiles whenas she would aught of men); and she ceased not to caress him and beguile him with speech sweeter than the honey till she stole his reason; and when she saw that he altogether inclined to her, she said to him, "O my beloved, O coolth of my eyes and fruit of my vitals, Allah never desolate me by less of thee nor Time sunder us twain me and thee! Indeed, the love of thee hath homed in my heart and the fire of passion hath consumed my liver, nor will I ever forsake thee or transgress against thee. But I would have thee tell me the truth, for that the sleights of falsehood profit not, nor do they secure credit at all seasons. How long wilt thou impose upon my father and lie to him? I fear lest thine affair be discovered to him, ere we can devise some device and he lay violent hands upon thee? So acquaint me with the facts of the case for naught shall befall thee save that which shall begladden thee; and, when thou shalt have spoken sooth, fear not harm shall betide thee. How often wilt thou declare that thou art a merchant and a man of money and hast a luggage-train? This long while past thou sayest, 'My baggage! my baggage!' but there appeareth no sign of thy baggage, and visible in thy face is anxiety on this account. So an there be no worthy in thy words, tell me and I will contrive thee a contrivance whereby thou shalt come off safe, Inshallah!"

He replied, "I will tell thee the truth, and then do thou whatso thou wilt." Rejoined she, "Speak and look thou speak soothly; for sooth is the ark of safety, and beware of lying, for it dishonoureth the liar. He said, "Know, then, O my lady, that I am no merchant and have no baggage, no, nor a burning plague; nay, I was but a cobbler in my own country and had a wife called Fatimah the Dung, with whom there befell me this and that." And he told her his story from

---

[1] As we should say, "play fast and loose."

beginning to end; whereat she laughed and said, "Verily, thou art clever in the practice of lying and imposture!" Whereto he answered, "O my lady, may Allah Almighty preserve thee to veil sins and countervail chagrins!" Rejoined she, "Know, that thou imposedst upon my sire and deceivedst him by dint of thy deluding vaunts, so that of his greed for gain he married me to thee. Then thou squanderedst his wealth and the Wazir beareth thee a grudge for this. How many a time hath he spoken against thee to my father, saying, 'Indeed, he is an imposter, a liar!' But my sire hearkened not to his say, for that he had sought me in wedlock and I consented not that he be baron and I femme. However, the time grew longsome upon my sire and he became straitened and said to me, 'Make him confess.' So I have made thee confess and that which was covered is discovered. Now my father purposeth thee a mischief because of this; but thou art become my husband and I will never transgress against thee.

"An I told my father what I have learnt from thee, he would be certified of thy falsehood and imposture and that thou imposedst upon Kings' daughters and squanderest royal wealth: so would thine offence find with him no pardon and he would slay thee sans a doubt: wherefore it would be bruited among the folk that I married a man who was a liar, an imposter, and this would smirch mine honour. Furthermore an he kill thee, most like he will require me to wed another, and to such thing I will never consent; no, not though I die! So rise now and don a Mameluke's dress and take these fifty thousand dinars of my monies, and mount a swift steed and get thee to a land whither the rule of my father doth not reach. Then make thee a merchant and send me a letter by a courier who shall bring it privily to me, that I may know in what land thou art, so I may send thee all my hand can attain. Thus shall thy wealth wax great and if my father die, I will send for thee, and thou shalt return in respect and honour; and if we die, thou or I, and go to the mercy of God the Most Great, the Resurrection shall unite us. This, then, is the rede that is right: and while we both abide alive and well, I will not cease to send thee letters and monies. Arise ere the day wax bright and thou be in perplexed plight and perdition upon thy head alight!"

Quoth he, "O my lady, I beseech thee of thy favour to bid me farewell with thine embracement"; and quoth she, "No harm in that." So he embraced her and knew her carnally; after which he made the Ghusl-ablution; then, donning the dress of a white slave, he bade the syces saddle him a thoroughbred steed. Accordingly, they saddled him a courser and he mounted and farewelling his wife, rode forth the city at the last of the night, whilst all who saw him deemed him one of the Mamelukes of the Sultan going abroad on some business.

Next morning, the King and his Wazir repaired to the sitting-chamber and sent for Princess Dunya who came behind the curtain; and her father said to her, "O my daughter, what sayst thou?" Said she, "I say, Allah blacken thy Wazir's face, because he would have blackened my face in my husband's eyes!" Asked the King, "How so?" and she answered, "He came in to me yesterday, but before I could name the matter to him, behold, in walked Faraj the Chief Eunuch, letter in hand, and said, 'Ten white slaves stand under the palace window and have given me this letter, saying, "Kiss for us the hands of our lord, Merchant Ma'aruf, and give him this letter, for we are of his Mamelukes with the baggage, and it hath reached us that he hath wedded the King's daughter, so we are come to acquaint him with that which befell us by the way."' Accordingly, I took the letter and read as follows: 'From the five hundred Mamelukes to his highness our lord Merchant Ma'aruf. But further. We give thee to know that, after thou quittedst us, the Arabs came out upon us and attacked us. They were two thousand horse and we five hundred mounted slaves and there befell a mighty sore fight between us and them. They hindered us from the road thirty days doing battle with them and this is the cause of our tarrying from thee. They also took from us of the luggage two hundred loads of cloth and slew of us fifty Mamelukes.'

"When the news reached my husband he cried, "Allah disappoint them! What aileth them to wage war with the Arabs for the sake of two hundred loads of merchandise? What are two hundred loads? It behoved them not to tarry on that account, for verily the value of the two hundred loads is only some seven thousand dinars. But needs must I go to them and hasten them. As for that which the Arabs have taken, 'twill not be missed from the baggage, nor doth it weigh with me a whit, for I reckon it as if I had given it to them by way of alms.' Then he went down from me, laughing and taking no concern for the wastage of his wealth nor the slaughter of his slaves. As soon as he was gone, I looked out from the lattice and saw the ten Mamelukes who had brought him the letter, as they were moons, each clad in a suit of clothes worth two thousand dinars, there is not with my father a chattel to match one of them. He went forth with them to bring up his baggage and

171

hallowed be Allah who hindered me from saying to him aught of that thou badest me, for he would have made mock of me and thee, and haply he would have eyed me with the eye of disparagement and hated me. But the fault is all with thy Wazir, who speaketh against my husband words that befit him not."

Replied the King, "O my daughter, thy husband's wealth is indeed endless and he recketh not of it; for, from the day he entered our city, he hath done naught but give alms to the poor. Inshallah, he will speedily return with the baggage, and good in plenty shall betide us from him." And he went on to appease her and menace the Wazir, being duped by her device.

So fared it with the King; but as regards Merchant Ma'aruf he rode on into waste lands, perplexed and knowing not to what quarter he should betake him; and for the anguish of parting he lamented and in the pangs of passion and love-longing he wept with sore weeping, for indeed the ways were walled up before his face and death seemed to him better than dreeing life, and he walked on like a drunken man for stress of distraction, and stayed not till noontide, when he came to a little town and saw a plougher hard by, ploughing with a yoke of bulls. Now hunger was sore upon him; and he went up to the ploughman and said to him, "Peace be with thee!"; and he returned his salam and said to him, "Welcome, O my lord! Art thou one of the Sultan's Mamelukes?" Quoth Ma'aruf, "Yes"; and the other said, "Alight with me for a guest-meal." Whereupon Ma'aruf knew him to be of the liberal and said to him, "O my brother, I see with thee naught with which thou mayst feed me: how is it, then, that thou invitest me?" Answered the husbandman, "O my lord, weal is well nigh. Dismount thee here: the town is near hand and I will go and fetch thee dinner and fodder for thy stallion." Rejoined Ma'aruf, "Since the town is near at hand, I can go thither as quickly as thou canst and buy me what I have a mind to in the bazar and eat." The peasant replied, "O my lord, the place is but a little village and there is no bazar there, neither selling nor buying. So I conjure thee by Allah, alight here with me and hearten my heart, and I will run thither and return to thee in haste."

Accordingly, he dismounted and the Fellah left him and went off to the village, to fetch dinner for him whilst Ma'aruf sat awaiting him. Presently he said in himself, "I have taken this poor man away from his work; but I will arise and plough in his stead, till he come back, to make up for having hindered him from his work." Then he took the plough and starting the bulls, ploughed a little, till the share

172

struck against something and the beasts stopped. He goaded them on, but they could not move the plough; so he looked at the share and finding it caught in a ring of gold, cleared away the soil and saw that it was set centre-most a slab of alabaster, the size of the nether millstone. He strave at the stone till he pulled it from its place, when there appeared beneath it a souterrain with a stair. Presently he descended the flight of steps and came to a place like a Hammam, with four daises, the first full of gold, from floor to roof, the second full of emeralds and pearls and coral also from ground to ceiling; the third of jacinths and rubies and turquoises and the fourth of diamonds and all manner other preciousest stones. At the upper end of the place stood a coffer of clearest crystal, full of union-gems each the size of a walnut, and upon the coffer lay a casket of gold, the bigness of a lemon. When he saw this, he marvelled and rejoiced with joy exceeding and said to himself, "I wonder what is in this casket?"

So he opened it and found therein a seal-ring of gold, whereon were graven names and talismans, as they were the tracks of creeping ants. He rubbed the ring and behold a voice said, "Adsum! Here am I, at thy service, O my lord! Ask and it shall be given unto thee. Wilt thou raise a city or ruin a capital or kill a king or dig a river-channel or aught of the kind? Whatso thou seekest, it shall come to pass, by leave of the King of Allmight, Creator of day and night." Ma'afur asked, "O creature of my lord, who and what art thou?"; and the other answered, "I am the slave of this seal-ring standing in the service of him who possesseth it. Whatsoever he seeketh, that I accomplish for him, and I have no excuse in neglecting that he biddeth me do; because I am Sultan over two-and-seventy tribes of the Jinn, each two-and-seventy thousand in number every one of which thousand ruleth over a thousand Marids, each Marid over a thousand Ifrits, each Ifrit over a thousand Satans and each Satan over a thousand Jinn: and they are all under command of me and may not gainsay me. As for me, I am spelled to this seal-ring and may not thwart whoso holdeth it. Lo! thou hast gotten hold of it and I am become thy slave; so ask what thou wilt, for I hearken to thy word and obey thy bidding; and if thou have need of me at any time, by land or by sea, rub the signet-ring and thou wilt find me with thee. But beware of rubbing it twice in succession, or thou wilt consume me with the fire of the names graven thereon; and thus wouldst thou lose me and after regret me. Now I have acquainted thee with my case and—the Peace!"

Ma'aruf asked him, "What is thy name?" and the Jinni

answered, "My name is Abu al-Sa'adat." Quoth Ma'aruf, "O Abu al-Sa'adat what is this place and who enchanted thee in this casket?"; and quoth he, "O my lord, this is a treasure called the Hoard of Shaddad son of Ad, him who the base of 'Many-columned Iram laid, the like of which in the lands was never made.' I was his slave in his lifetime and this is his seal-ring, which he laid up in his treasure; but it hath fallen to thy lot." Ma'aruf inquired, "Canst thou transport that which is in this hoard to the surface of the earth?"; and the Jinni replied, "Yes! Nothing were easier." Said Ma'aruf, "Bring it forth and leave naught." So the Jinni signed with his hand to the ground, which clave asunder, and he sank and was absent a little while. Presently, there came forth young boys full of grace, and fair of face bearing golden baskets filled with gold which they emptied out and going away, returned with more; nor did they cease to transport the gold and jewels, till ere an hour had sped they said, "Naught is left in the hoard." Thereupon out came Abu al-Sa'adat and said to Ma'aruf, "O my lord, thou seest that we have brought forth all that was in the hoard." Ma'aruf asked, "Who be these beautiful boys?" and the Jinni answered, "They are my sons. This matter merited not that I should muster for it the Marids, wherefore my sons have done thy desire and are honoured by such service. So ask what thou wilt beside this."

Quoth Ma'aruf, "Canst thou bring me he-mules and chests and fill the chests with the treasure and load them on the mules?" Quoth Abu al-Sa'adat, "Nothing easier," and cried a great cry; whereupon his sons presented themselves before him, to the number of eight hundred, and he said to them, "Let some of you take the semblance of he-mules and others of muleteers and handsome Mamelukes, the like of the least of whom is not found with any of the Kings; and others of you be transmewed to muleteers, and the rest to menials." So seven hundred of them changed themselves into bât-mules and other hundred took the shape of slaves. Then Abu al-Sa'adat called upon his Marids, who presented themselves between his hands and he commanded some of them to assume the aspect of horses saddled with saddles of gold crusted with jewels. And when Ma'aruf saw them do as he bade he cried, "Where be the chests?" They brought them before him and he said, "Pack the gold and the stones, each sort by itself." So they packed them and loaded three hundred he-mules with them. Then asked Ma'aruf, "O Abu al-Sa'adat, canst thou bring me some loads of costly stuffs?"; and the Jinni answered, "Wilt thou have Egyptian stuffs or

Syrian or Persian or Greek?" Ma'aruf said, "Bring me an hundred loads of each kind, on five hundred mules"; and Abu al-Sa'adat, "O my lord accord me delay that I may dispose my Marids for this and send a company of them to each country to fetch an hundred loads of its stuffs and then take the form of he-mules and return, carrying the stuffs." Ma'aruf inquired, "What time dost thou want?"; and Abu al-Sa'adat replied, "The time of the blackness of the night, and day shall not dawn ere thou have all thou desirest." Said Ma'aruf, "I grant thee this time," and bade them pitch him a pavilion.

So they pitched it and he sat down therein and they brought him a table of food. Then said Abu al-'Sa'adat to him, "O my lord, tarry thou in this tent and these my sons shall guard thee: so fear thou nothing; for I go to muster my Marids and despatch them to do thy desire." So saying, he departed, leaving Ma'aruf seated in the pavilion with the table before him and the Jinni's sons attending upon him, in the guise of slaves and servants and suite. And while he sat in this state behold, up came the husbandman, with a great porringer of lentils and a nosebag full of barley and seeing the pavilion pitched and the Mamelukes standing, hands upon breasts, thought that the Sultan was come and had halted on that stead. So he stood open-mouthed and said in himself, "Would I had killed a couple of chickens and fried them red with clarified cow-butter for the Sultan!" And he would have turned back to kill the chickens as a regale for the Sultan; but Ma'aruf saw him and cried out to him and said to the Mamelukes, "Bring him hither." So they brought him and his porringer of lentils before Ma'aruf, who said to him, "What is this?" Said the peasant, "This is thy dinner and thy horse's fodder! Excuse me, for I thought not that the Sultan would come hither; and, had I known that, I would have killed a couple of chickens and entertained him in goodly guise." Quoth Ma'aruf, "The Sultan is not come. I am his son-in-law and I was vexed with him. However, he hath sent his officers to make his peace with me, and now I am minded to return to the city. But thou hast made me this guest-meal without knowing me, and I accept it from thee, lentils though it be, and will not eat save of thy cheer."

Accordingly he bade him set the porringer amiddlemost the table and ate of it his sufficiency, whilst the Fellāh filled his belly with those rich meats. Then Ma'aruf washed his hands and gave the Mamelukes leave to eat; so they fell upon the remains of the meal and ate; and, when the porringer was empty, he filled it with gold and gave it to the peasant, saying, "Carry this to thy dwelling and come to me in the city, and

I will entreat thee with honour." Thereupon the peasant took the porringer full of gold and returned to the village, driving the bulls before him and deeming himself akin to the King. Meanwhile, they brought Ma'aruf girls of the Brides of the Treasure, who smote on instruments of music and danced before him, and he passed that night in joyance and delight, a night not to be reckoned among lives. Hardly had dawned the day when there arose a great cloud of dust, which presently lifting discovered seven hundred mules laden with stuffs and attended by muleteers and baggage-tenders and cresset-bearers. With them came Abu al-Sa'adat, riding on a she-mule, in the guise of a caravan-leader, and before him was a travelling-litter, with four corner-terminals of glittering red gold, set with gems. When Abu al-Sa'adat came up to the tent, he dismounted and, kissing the earth, said to Ma'aruf, "O my lord, thy desire hath been done to the uttermost and in the litter is a treasure-suit which hath not its match among Kings' raiment; so don it and mount the litter and bid us do what thou wilt." Quoth Ma'aruf, "O Abu al-Sa'adat, I wish thee to go to the city of Ikhtiyan al-Khatan and present thyself to my father-in-law the King; and go thou not in to him but in the guise of a mortal courier"; and quoth he, "To hear is to obey."

So Ma'aruf wrote a letter to the Sultan and sealed it and Abu al-Sa'adat took it and set out with it; and when he arrived, he found the King saying, "O Wazir, indeed my heart is concerned for my son-in-law and I fear lest the Arabs slay him. Would Heaven I wot whither he was bound, that I might have followed him with the troops! Would he had told me his destination!" Said the Wazir, "Allah be merciful to thee for this thy heedlessness! As thy head liveth, the wight saw that we were awake to him and feared dishonour and fled, for he is nothing but an imposter—a liar." And behold, at this moment in came the courier and, kissing the ground before the King, wished him permanent glory and prosperity and length of life. Asked the King, "Who art thou and what is thy business?" "I am a courier," answered the Jinni, "and thy son-in-law, who is come with the baggage, sendeth me to thee with a letter, and here it is!" So he took the letter and read therein these words, "After salutations galore to our uncle[1] the glorious King! Know that I am at hand with the baggage-train; so come thou forth to meet me with the troops." Cried the King, "Allah blacken thy brow,

[1] Arab. "Amm" = father's brother, courteously used for "father-in-law," which suggests having slept with his daughter and which is indecent in writing. Thus, by a pleasant fiction, the husband represents himself as having married his first cousin.

O Wazir! How often wilt thou defame my son-in-law's name and call him liar and imposter? Behold, he is come with the baggage-train and thou art naught but a traitor." The Minister hung his head groundwards in shame and confusion and replied, "O King of the Age, I said not this save because of the long delay of the baggage and because I feared the loss of the wealth he had wasted." The King exclaimed, "O traitor, what are my riches! Now that his baggage is come he will give me plenty in their stead." Then he bade decorate the city, and going in to his daughter said to her, "Good news for thee! Thy husband will be here anon with his baggage; for he hath sent me a letter to that effect and here am I now going forth to meet him."

The Princess Dunya marvelled at this and said in herself, "This is a wondrous thing! Was he laughing at me and making mock of me, or had he a mind to try me, when he told me that he was a pauper? But Alhamdolillah, Glory to God, for that I failed not of my duty to him!" On this wise fared it in the palace; but as regards Merchant Ali, the Cairene, when he saw the decoration of the city and asked the cause thereof, they said to him, "The baggage-train of Merchant Ma'aruf, the King's son-in-law, is come." Said he, "Allah is Almighty! What a calamity is this man! He came to me, fleeing from his wife, and he was a poor man. Whence then should he get a baggage-train? But haply this is a device which the Kings daughter hath contrived for him, fearing his disgrace, and Kings are not unable to do anything. May Allah the Most High veil his fame and not bring him to public shame!" And all the merchants rejoiced and were glad for that they would get their monies. Then the King assembled his troops and rode forth, whilst Abu al-Sa'adat returned to Ma'aruf and acquainted him with the delivering of the letter. Quoth Ma'aruf, "Bind on the loads"; and when they had done so, he donned the treasure-suit, and mounting the litter became a thousand times greater and more majestic than the King.

Then he set forward; but, when he had gone half-way, behold, the King met him with the troops, and seeing him riding in the Takhtrawan and clad in the dress aforesaid, threw himself upon him and saluted him, and giving him joy of his safety, greeted him with the greeting of peace. Then all the lords of the land saluted him and it was made manifest that he had spoken the truth and that in him there was no lie. Presently he entered the city in such state procession as would have caused the gall-bladder of the lion to burst for envy, and the traders pressed up to him and kissed his hands, whilst Merchant Ali said to him, "Thou hast played off this trick and it hath prospered to thy hand, O Shaykh of Imposters! But thou deservest it and may Allah the Most High increase thee of His bounty!"; whereupon Ma'aruf laughed. Then he entered the palace, and sitting down on the throne said, "Carry the loads of gold into the treasury of my uncle the King and bring me the bales of cloth." So they brought them to him and opened them before him, bale after bale, till they had unpacked the seven hundred loads, whereof he chose out the best and said, "Bear these to Princess Dunya that she may distribute them among her slave-girls; and carry her also this coffer of jewels, that she may divide them among her handmaids and eunuchs."

Then he proceeded to make over to the merchants in whose debt he was stuffs by way of payment for their arrears, giving him whose due was a thousand, stuffs worth two thousand or more; after which he fell to distributing to the poor and needy, whilst the King looked on with greedy eyes and could not hinder him; nor did he cease largesse till he had made an end of the seven hundred loads, when he turned to the troops and proceeded to apportion amongst them emeralds and rubies and pearls and coral and other jewels by handfuls, without count, till the King said to him, "Enough of this giving, O my son! There is but little left of the baggage." But he said, "I have plenty." Then indeed, his good faith was become manifest and none could give him the lie; and he had come to reck not of giving, for that the Slave of the Seal-ring brought him whatsoever he sought. Presently, the treasurer came in to the King and said, "O King of the Age, the treasury is full indeed and will not hold the rest of the loads. Where shall we lay that which is left of the gold and jewels?" And he assigned to him another place. As for the Princess Dunya, when she saw this, her joy redoubled and she marvelled and said in herself, "Would I wot how came he by all this wealth!" In like manner the traders rejoiced in that which he had given them and blessed him; whilst Merchant Ali marvelled and said to himself, "I wonder how he hath lied and swindled, that he hath gotten him all these treasures? Had they come from the King's daughter, he had not wasted them on this wise!"

So far concerning him; but as regards the King, he also marvelled with passing marvel at that which he saw of Ma'aruf's generosity and openhandedness in the largesse of wealth. Then the merchant went in to his wife, who met him, smiling and laughing-lipped, and kissed his hand, saying, "Didst thou mock me or hadst thou a mind to prove me with thy saying, 'I am a poor man and a fugitive from my wife?'

Praised be Allah for that I failed not of my duty to thee! For thou art my beloved and there is none dearer to me than thou, whether thou be rich or poor. But I would have thee tell me what didst thou design by these words." Said Ma'aruf, "I wished to prove thee and see whether thy love were sincere or for the sake of wealth and the greed of worldly good. But now 'tis become manifest to me that thine affection is sincere, and as thou art a true woman, so welcome to thee! I know thy worth." Then he went apart into a place by himself and rubbed the seal-ring, whereupon Abu al-Sa'adat presented himself and said to him, "Adsum, at thy service; Ask what thou wilt." Quoth Ma'aruf, "I want a treasure-suit and treasure-trinkets for my wife, including a necklace of forty unique jewels." Quoth the Jinni, "To hear is to obey," and brought him what he sought, whereupon Ma'aruf dismissed him, and carrying the dress and ornaments in to his wife, laid them before her and said, "Take these and put them on and welcome!" When she saw this, her wits fled for joy, and she found among the ornaments a pair of anklets of gold set with jewels of the handiwork of the magicians, and bracelets and ear-rings and a belt such as no money could buy. So she donned the dress and ornaments and said to Ma'aruf, "O my lord, I will treasure these up for holidays and festivals." But he answered, "Wear them always, for I have others in plenty." And when she put them on and her women beheld her, they rejoiced and bussed his hands.

Then he left them, and going apart by himself rubbed the seal-ring, whereupon its slave appeared and he said to him, "Bring me an hundred suits of apparel, with their ornaments of gold." "Hearing and obeying," answered Abu al Sa'adat and brought him the hundred suits, each with its ornaments wrapped up within it. Ma'aruf took them and called aloud to the slavegirls, who came to him and he gave them each a suit; so they donned them and became like the black-eyed girls of Paradise whilst the Princess Dunya shone amongst them as the moon among the stars. One of the handmaids told the King of this and he came in to his daughter and saw her and her women dazzling all who beheld them; whereat he wondered with passing wonderment. Then he went out, and calling his Wazir, said to him, "O Wazir, such and such things have happened; what sayst thou now of this affair?" Said he, "O King of the Age, this be no merchant's fashion; for a merchant keepeth a piece of linen by him for years and selleth it not but at a profit. How should a merchant have generosity such as this generosity, and whence should he get the like of these monies and jewels, of which but a slight matter is found with the Kings? So how should loads thereof be found with merchants? Needs must there be a cause for this; but, an thou wilt hearken to me, I will make the truth of the case manifest to thee." Answered the King, "O Wazir, I will do thy bidding," Rejoined the Minister, "Do thou foregather with thy son-in-law and make a show of affect to him and talk with him and say, 'O my son-in-law, I have a mind to go, I and thou and the Wazir, but no more, to a flower garden that we may take our pleasure there. When we come to the garden, we will set on the table wine, and I will ply him therewith and compel him to drink; for, when he shall have drunken, he will lose his reason and his judgment will forsake him. Then we will question him of the truth of his case and he will discover to us his secrets, for wine is a traitor. Then we shall ken his case and may deal with him as we will; because I fear for thee the consequences of this his present fashion; haply he will covet the kingship and win over the troops by generosity and lavishing money and so depose thee and take the kingdom from thee."

"Thou hast spoken sooth!" said the King, and they passed the night on this agreement. And when morning morrowed the King went forth and sat in the guest-chamber, when, lo and behold! the grooms and serving-men came in to him in dismay. Quoth he, "What hath befallen you?"; and quoth they, "O King of the Age, the Syces curried the horses and foddered them and the he-mules which brought the baggage; but, when we arose in the morning, we found that thy son-in-law's Mamelukes had stolen the horses and mules. We searched the stables, but found neither horse nor mule; so we entered the lodging of the Mamelukes and found none there, nor know we how they fled."

The King marvelled at this, unknowing that the horses and Mamelukes were all Ifrits, the subjects of the Slave of the Spell, and asked the grooms, "O accursed, how could a thousand beasts and five hundred slaves and servants flee without your knowledge?" Answered they, "We know not how it happened"; and he cried, "Go, and when your lord cometh forth of the harim, tell him the case." So they went out from before the King and sat down bewildered, till Ma'aruf came out and, seeing them chagrined, inquired of them, "What may be the matter?" They told him all that had happened and he said, "What is their worth that ye should be concerned for them? Wend your ways." And he sat laughing and was neither angry nor grieved concerning the case; whereupon the King looked in the Wazir's face and said to him, "What manner of man is this, with whom wealth is of no worth? Needs must there be a reason for this!"

Then they talked with him awhile and the King said to him, "O my son-in-law, I have a mind to go, I, thou and the Wazir, to a garden, where we may divert ourselves." "No harm in that," said Ma'aruf. So they went forth to a flower garden, wherein every sort of fruit was of kinds twain and its waters were flowing and its trees towering and its birds carolling. There they entered a pavilion, whose sight did away sorrow from the soul, and sat talking, whilst the Minister entertained them with rare tales and quoted merry quips and mirth-provoking sayings and Ma'aruf attentively listened, till the time of dinner came, when they set on a tray of meats and a flagon of wine. When they had eaten and washed hands, the Wazir filled the cup and gave it to the King, who drank it off; then he filled a second and handed it to Ma'aruf, saying, "Take the cup of the drink to which Reason boweth neck in reverence." Quoth Ma'aruf, "What is this, O Wazir?"; and quoth he, "This is the grizzled[1] virgin and the old maid long kept at home,[2] the giver of joy to hearts." And he ceased not to egg him on to the drink, naming to him such of the virtues of wine as he thought well, and reciting to him what occurred to him of poetry and pleasantries on the subject, till Ma'aruf addressed himself to sucking the cup-lips and cared no longer for aught else. The Wazir ceased not to fill for him and he to drink and enjoy himself and make merry, till his wits wandered and he could not distinguish right from wrong.

When the Minister saw that drunkenness had attained in him to utterest and the bounds transgressed, he said to him, "By Allah, O Merchant Ma'aruf, I admire whence thou gottest these jewels whose like the Kings of the Chosroës possess not! In all our lives never saw we a merchant that had heaped up riches like unto thine or more generous than thou, for thy doings are the doings of Kings and not merchants' doings. Wherefore, Allah upon thee, do thou acquaint me with this, that I may know thy rank and condition." And he went on to test him with questions and cajole him, till Ma'aruf, being reft of reason, said to him, "I'm neither merchant nor King," and told him his whole story from first to last. Then said the Wazir, "I conjure thee by Allah, O my lord Ma'aruf, show us the ring, that we may see its make." So, in his drunkenness, he pulled off the ring and said, "Take it and look upon it." The Minister took it and turning it over, said, "If I rub it, will

---

[1] Arab. "Shamta," one of the many names of wine, the "speckled" alluding to the bubbles which dance upon the freshly filled cup.

[2] *I.e.* in the cask. These "merry quips" strongly suggest the dismal toasts of our not remote ancestors.

its slave appear?" Replied Ma'aruf, "Yes. Rub it and he will appear to thee, and do thou divert thyself with the sight of him." Thereupon the Wazir rubbed the ring and behold forthright appeared the Jinni and said, "Adsum, at thy service, O my lord! Ask and it shall be given to thee. Wilt thou ruin a city or raise a capital or kill a king? Whatso thou seekest, I will do for thee, sans fail."

The Wazir pointed to Ma'aruf and said, "Take up yonder wretch and cast him down in the most desolate of desert lands, where he shall find nothing to eat nor drink, so he may die of hunger and perish miserably, and none know of him." Accordingly, the Jinni snatched him up and flew with him betwixt heaven and earth, which when Ma'aruf saw, he made sure of destruction and wept and said, "O Abu al-Sa'adat, whither goest thou with me?" Replied the Jinni, "I go to cast thee down in the Desert Quarter, O ill-bred wight of gross wits. Shall one have the like of this talisman and give it to the folk to gaze at? Verily, thou deservest that which hath befallen thee; and but that I fear Allah, I would let thee fall from a height of a thousand fathoms, nor shouldst thou reach the earth, till the winds had torn thee to threds." Ma'aruf was silent[1] and did not again bespeak him till he reached the Desert Quarter and casting him down there, went away and left him in that horrible place.

So much concerning him; but returning to the Wazir who was now in possession of the talisman, he said to the King, "How deemest thou now? Did I not tell thee that this fellow was a liar, an imposter, but thou wouldst not credit me?" Replied the King, "Thou wast in the right, O my Wazir, Allah grant thee weal! But give me the ring, that I may solace myself with the sight." The Minister looked at him angrily and spat in his face, saying, "O lack-wits, how shall I give it to thee and abide thy servant, after I am become thy master? But I will spare thee no more on life." Then he rubbed the seal-ring and said to the Slave, "Take up this ill-mannered churl and cast him down by his son-in-law the swindlerman." So the Jinni took him up and flew off with him, whereupon quoth the King to him, "O creature of my Lord, what is my crime?" Abu al-Sa'adat replied, "That wot I not, but my master hath commanded me and I cannot cross whoso hath compassed the enchanted ring." Then he flew on with him, till he came to the Desert Quarter and, casting him down where he had cast Ma'aruf, left him and returned. The King hearing Ma'aruf weeping, went up to him and acquainted him

---

1 This is the noble resignation of the Moslem. What a dialogue there would have been in a European book between man and devil!

with his case; and they sat weeping over that which had befallen them and found neither meat nor drink.

Meanwhile the Minister, after driving father-in-law and son-in-law from the country, went forth from the garden and summoning all the troops held a Divan, and told them what he had done with the King and Ma'aruf and acquainted them with the affair of the talisman, adding, "Unless ye make me Sultan over you, I will bid the Slave of the Seal-ring take you up one and all and cast you down in the Desert Quarter, where you shall die of hunger and thirst." They replied, "Do us no damage, for we accept thee as Sultan over us and will not anywise gainsay thy bidding." So they agreed, in their own despite, to his being Sultan over them, and he bestowed on them robes of honour, seeking all he had a mind to of Abu al-Sa'adat, who brought it to him forthwith. Then he sat down on the throne and the troops did homage to him; and he sent to Princess Dunya, the King's daughter, saying, "Make thee ready, for I mean to come in unto thee this night, because I long for thee with love." When she heard this, she wept, for the case of her husband and father was grievous to her, and sent to him saying, "Have patience with me till my period of widowhood[1] he ended: then draw up thy contract of marriage with me and go in to me according to law." But he sent back to say to her, "I know neither period of widowhood nor to delay have I a mood; and I need not a contract nor know I lawful from unlawful; but needs must I go in unto thee this night."

She answered him saying, "So be it, then, and welcome to thee!"; but this was a trick on her part. When the answer reached the Wazir, he rejoiced and his breast was broadened, for that he was passionately in love with her. He bade set food before all the folk, saying, "Eat; this is my bride-feast; for I purpose to go in to the Princess Dunya this night." Quoth the Shaykh al-Islam, "It is not lawful for thee to go in unto her till her days of widowhood be ended and thou have drawn up thy contract of marriage with her." But he answered, "I know neither days of widowhood nor other period; so multiply not words on me." The Shaykh Al-Islam was silent, fearing his mischief, and said to the troops, "Verily, this man is a Kafir, a Miscreant, and hath neither creed nor religious conduct." As soon as it was evenfall, he went in to her and found her robed in her richest raiment and

---

1 Arab. "Al-'iddah," the period of four months and ten days which must elapse before she could legally marry again. But this was a palpable wile: she was not sure of her husband's death and he had not divorced her: so that although a "grass widow," a "Strohwitwe" as the Germans say, she could not wed again either with or without interval.

decked with her goodliest adornments. When she saw him, she came to meet him, laughing and said, "A blessed night! But hadst thou slain my father and my husband, it had been more to my mind." And he said, "There is no help but I slay them."

Then she made him sit down and began to jest with him and make show of love, caressing him and smiling in his face so that his reason fled; but she cajoled him with her coaxing and cunning only that she might get possession of the ring and change his joy into calamity on the mother of his forehead. When he saw her caress him and smile upon him, desire surged up in him and he besought her of carnal knowledge; but, when he approached her, she drew away from him and burst into tears, saying, "O my lord, seest thou not the man looking at us? I conjure thee by Allah screen me from his eyes! How canst thou know me what while he looketh on us?" When he heard this, he was angry and asked, "Where is the man?"; and answered she, "There he is, in the bezel of the ring! putting out his head and staring at us." He thought that the Jinni was looking at them and said laughing, "Fear not; this is the Slave of the Seal-ring, and he is subject to me." Quoth she, "I am afraid of Ifrits; pull it off and throw it afar from me." So he plucked it off and laying it on the cushion, drew near to her, but she dealt him a kick, her foot striking him full in the stomach, and he fell over on his back senseless; whereupon she cried out to her attendants, who came to her in haste, and said to them, "Seize him!" So forty slave-girls laid hold on him, whilst she hurriedly snatched up the ring from the cushion and rubbed it; whereupon Abu al-Sa'adat presented himself, saying, "Adsum, at thy service O my mistress."

Cried she, "Take up yonder Infidel and clap him in jail and shackle him heavily." So he took him and throwing him into the Prison of Wrath[1] returned and reported, "I have laid him in limbo." Quoth she, "Whither wentest thou with my father and my husband?"; and quoth he, "I cast them down in the Desert Quarter." Then cried she, "I command thee to fetch them to me forthwith." He replied, "I hear and I obey," and taking flight at once, stayed not till he reached the Desert Quarter, where he lighted down upon them and found them sitting weeping and complaining each to other. Quoth he, "Fear not, for relief is come to you"; and, he told them what the Wazir had done, adding, "Indeed I imprisoned him with my own hands in obedience to her, and she hath bidden me

---

1 Arab. "Sijn al-Ghazab," the dungeons appropriated to the worst of criminals, where they suffer penalties far worse than hanging or guillotining.

bear you back." And they rejoiced in his news. Then he took them both up and flew home with them; nor was it more than an hour before he brought them in to Princess Dunya, who rose and saluted sire and spouse. Then she made them sit down and brought them food and sweetmeats, and they passed the rest of the night with her.

On the next day she clad them in rich clothing and said to the King, "O my papa, sit thou upon thy throne and be King as before and make my husband thy Wazir of the Right and tell thy troops that which hath happened. Then send for the Minister out of prison and do him die, and after burn him, for that he is a Miscreant, and would have gone in unto me in the way of lewdness, without the rites of wedlock and he hath testified against himself that he is an Infidel and believeth in no religion. And do tenderly by thy son-in-law, whom thou makest thy Wazir of the Right." He replied, "Hearing and obeying, O my daughter. But do thou give me the ring or give it to thy husband." Quoth she, "It behoveth not that either thou or he have the ring. I will keep the ring myself, and belike I shall be more careful of it than you. Whatso ye wish seek it of me and I will demand it for you of the Slave of the Seal-ring. So fear no harm so long as I live and after my death, do what ye twain will with the ring." Quoth the King, "This is the right rede, O my daughter," and taking his son-in-law went forth to the Divan. Now the troops had passed the night in sore chagrin for Princess Dunya and that which the Wazir had done with her, in going in to her after the way of lewdness, without marriage-rites, and for his ill-usage of the King and Ma'aruf, and they feared lest the law of Al-Islam be dishonoured, because it was manifest to them that he was a Kafir. So they assembled in the Divan and fell to reproaching the Shaykh Al-Islam, saying, "Why didst thou not forbid him from going in to the Princess in the way of lewdness?" Said he, "O folk, the man is a Miscreant and hath gotten possession of the ring and I and you may not prevail against him. But Almighty Allah will requite him his deed, and be ye silent, lest he slay you."

And as the host was thus engaged in talk, behold the King and Ma'aruf entered the Divan. Then the King bade decorate the city and sent to fetch the Wazir from the place of duresse. So they brought him, and as he passed by the troops, they cursed him and abused him and menaced him, till he came to the King, who commanded to do him dead by the vilest of deaths. Accordingly, they slew him and after burned his body, and he went to Hell after the foulest of plights. The King made Ma'aruf his Wazir of the Right and the times were pleasant to them and their joys were untroubled.

They abode thus five years till, in the sixth year, the King died and Princess Dunya made Ma'aruf Sultan in her father's stead, but she gave him not the seal-ring. During this time she had conceived by him and borne him a boy of passing loveliness, excelling in beauty and perfection, who ceased not to be reared in the laps of nurses till he reached the age of five, when his mother fell sick of a deadly sickness and calling her husband to her, said to him, "I am ill." Quoth he, "Allah preserve thee, O dearling of my heart!" But quoth she, "Haply I shall die and thou needest not that I commend to thy care thy son: wherefore I charge thee but be careful of the ring, for thine own sake and for the sake of this thy boy." And he answered, "No harm shall befall him whom Allah preserveth!" Then she pulled off the ring and gave it to him, and on the morrow she was admitted to the mercy of Allah the Most High, whilst Ma'aruf abode in possession of the Kingship and applied himself to the business of governing.

Now it chanced that one day, as he shook the handkerchief and the troops withdrew to their places that he betook himself to the sitting-chamber, where he sat till the day departed and the night advanced with murks bedight. Then came in to him his cup-companions of the notables according to their custom, and sat with him by way of solace and diversion, till midnight, when they craved permission to withdraw. He gave them leave and they retired to their houses; after which there came in to him a slave-girl affected to the service of his bed, who spread him the mattress and doffing his apparel, clad him in his sleeping-gown. Then he lay down and she kneaded his feet, till sleep overpowered him; whereupon she withdrew to her own chamber and slept. But suddenly he felt something beside him in the bed and awaking started up in alarm and cried, "I seek refuge with Allah from Satan the stoned!" Then he opened his eyes and seeing by his side a woman foul of favour, said to her, "Who art thou?" Said she, "Fear not, I am thy wife Fatimah al-Urrah." Whereupon he looked in her face and knew her by her loathly form and the length of her dog-teeth: so he asked her, "Whence camest thou in to me and who brought thee to this country?" "In what country art thou at this present?" "In the city of Ikhtiyan al-Khatan. But thou, when didst thou leave Cairo?" "But now." "How can that be?"

"Know," said she, "that, when I fell out with thee and Satan prompted me to do thee a damage, I complained of thee to the magistrates, who sought for thee and the Kazis inquired of thee, but found thee not. When two days were past, repentance gat hold upon me and I knew that the fault was with me; but penitence availed me not, and I abode for some days weeping for thy loss, till what was in my hand failed and I was obliged to beg my bread. So I fell to begging of all, from the courted rich to the contemned poor, and since thou leftest me, I have eaten of the bitterness of beggary and have been in the sorriest of conditions. Every night I sat beweeping our separation and that which I suffered, since thy departure, of humiliation and ignominy, of abjection and misery." And she went on to tell him what had befallen her, whilst he stared at her in amazement, till she said, "Yesterday, I went about begging all day but none gave me aught; and as often as I accosted anyone and craved of him a crust of bread, he reviled me and gave me naught. When night came, I went to bed supperless, and hunger burned me and sore on me was that which I suffered: and I sat weeping when, behold, one appeared to me and said, 'O woman why weepest thou?' Said I, 'Erst I had a husband who used to provide for me and fulfil my wishes; but he is lost to me and I know not whither he went and have been in sore straits since he left me.' Asked he, 'What is thy husband's name?' and I answered, 'His name is Ma'aruf.' Quoth he, 'I ken him. Know that thy husband is now Sultan in a certain city, and if thou wilt, I will carry thee to him.' Cried I, 'I am under thy protection: of thy bounty bring me to him!' So he took me up and flew with me between heaven and earth, till he brought me to this pavilion and said to me, 'Enter yonder chamber, and thou shalt see thy husband asleep on the couch.' Accordingly I entered and found thee in this state of lordship. Indeed I had not thought thou wouldst forsake me, who am thy mate, and praised be Allah who hath united thee with me!"

Quoth Ma'aruf, "Did I forsake thee or thou me? Thou complainedst of me from Kazi to Kazi and endedst by denouncing me to the High Court and bringing down on me Abu Tabak from the Citadel: so I fled in mine own despite." And he went on to tell her all that had befallen him and how he was become Sultan and had married the King's daughter and how his beloved Dunya had died, leaving him a son who was then seven years old. She rejoined, "That which happened was fore-ordained of Allah; but I repent me and I place myself under thy protection beseeching thee not to abandon me, but suffer me eat bread, with thee by way of an alms." And she ceased not to humble herself to him and to supplicate him till his heart relented towards her and he said, "Repent from mischief and abide with me, and naught shall betide thee save what shall pleasure thee: but, and thou work any wickedness,

I will slay thee nor fear anyone. And fancy not that thou canst complain of me to the High Court and that Abu Tabak will come down on me from the Citadel; for I am become Sultan and the folk dread me: but I fear none save Allah Almighty, because I have a talismanic ring which when I rub, the Slave of the Signet appeareth to me. His name is Abu al-Sa'adat, and whatsoever I demand of him he bringeth to me. So, an thou desire to return to thine own country, I will give thee what shall suffice thee all thy life long and will send thee thither speedily; but, an thou desire to abide with me, I will clear for thee a palace and furnish it with the choicest of silks and appoint thee twenty slave-girls to serve thee and provide thee with dainty dishes and sumptuous suits, and thou shalt be a Queen and live in all delight till thou die or I die. What sayest thou of this?" "I wish to abide with thee," she answered and kissed his hand and vowed repentance from frowardness.

Accordingly he set apart a palace for her sole use and gave her slave-girls and eunuchs, and she became a Queen. The young Prince used to visit her as he visited his sire; but she hated him for that he was not her son; and when the boy saw that she looked on him with the eye of aversion and anger, he shunned her and took a dislike to her. As for Ma'aruf, he occupied himself with the love of fair hand-maidens and bethought him not of his wife Fatimah the Dung, for that she was grown a grizzled old fright, foul-favoured to the sight, a bald-headed blight, loathlier than the snake speckled black and white; the more that she had beyond measure evil entreated him aforetime; and as said the adage, "Ill-usage the root of desire disparts and sows hate in the soil of hearts." And indeed Ma'aruf had not given her shelter by reason of any praiseworthy quality in her, but he dealt with her thus generously only of desire for the approval of Allah Almighty.

Now when she saw that he held aloof from her bed and occupied himself with other women, she hated him and jealousy gat the mastery of her and Iblis prompted her to take the seal-ring from him and slay him and make herself Queen in his stead. So she went forth one night from her pavilion, intending for that in which was her husband King Ma'aruf; and it chanced by decree of the Decreer and His written destiny, that Ma'aruf lay that night with one of his concubines; a damsel endowed with beauty and loveliness, symmetry and a stature all grace. And it was his wont, of the excellence of his piety, that, when he was minded to have to lie with a woman, he would doff the enchanted seal-ring from his finger, in reverence to the Holy Names graven thereon, and lay it on the pillow, nor would he don it again till he had purified himself by the Ghusl-ablution. Moreover, when he had lain with a woman, he was used to order her go forth from him before daybreak, of his fear for the seal-ring; and when he went to the Hammam he locked the door of the pavilion till his return, when he put on the ring, and after this, all were free to enter according to custom. His wife Fatimah the Dung knew of all this and went not forth from her place till she had certified herself of the case. So she sallied out, when the night was dark, purposing to go in to him, whilst he was drowned in sleep, and steal the ring, unseen of him.

Now it chanced at this time that the King's son had gone out, without light, to the Chapel of Ease for an occasion, and sat down over the marble slab of the jakes in the dark, leaving the door open. Presently, he saw Fatimah come forth of her pavilion and make stealthily for that of his father and said in himself, "What aileth this witch to leave her lodging in the dead of night and make for my father's pavilion? Needs must there be some reason for this": so he went out after her and followed in her steps unseen of her. Now he had a short sword of watered steel, which he held so dear that he went not to his father's Divan, except he were girt therewith; and his father used to laugh at him and exclaim, 'Mahallah! This is a mighty fine sword of thine, O my son! But thou hast not gone down with it to battle nor cut off a head therewith." Whereupon the boy would reply, "I will not fail to cut off with it some head which deserveth cutting." And Ma'aruf would laugh at his words. Now when treading in her track, he drew the sword from its sheath and he followed her till she came to his father's pavilion and entered, whilst he stood and watched her from the door. He saw her searching about and heard her say to herself, "Where hath he laid the seal-ring?"; whereby he knew that she was looking for the ring and he waited till she found it and said, "Here it is." Then she picked it up and turned to go out; but he hid behind the door. As she came forth, she looked at the ring and turned it about in her grasp. But when she was about to rub it, he raised his hand with the sword and smote her on the neck; and she cried a single cry and fell down dead.

With this Ma'aruf awoke and seeing his wife strown on the ground, with her blood flowing, and his son standing with the drawn sword in his hand, said to him, "What is this, O my son?" He replied, "O my father, how often hast thou said to me, 'Thou hast a mighty fine sword; but thou hast not gone down with it to battle nor cut off a head'? And I have answered thee, saying, 'I will not fail to cut off with it a head which deserveth cutting.' And now, behold, I have therewith cut off for thee a head well worth the cutting!" And he told him what had passed. Ma'aruf sought for the seal-ring, but found it not; so he searched the dead woman's body till he saw her hand closed upon it; whereupon he took it from her grasp and said to the boy, "Thou art indeed my very son, without doubt or dispute; Allah ease thee in this world and the next, even as thou hast eased me of this vile woman! Her attempt led only to her own destruction."

Then King Ma'aruf called aloud to some of his attendants, who came in haste, and he told them what his wife Fatimah the Dung had done and bade them to take her and lay her in a place till the morning. They did his bidding, and next day he gave her in charge to a number of eunuchs, who washed her and shrouded her and made her a tomb and buried her. Thus her coming from Cairo was but to her grave. After this, King Ma'aruf sent for the husbandman, whose guest he had been when he was a fugitive, and made him his Wazir of the Right and his Chief Counsellor. Then, learning that he had a daughter of passing beauty and loveliness, of qualities nature-ennobled at birth and exalted of worth, he took her to wife; and in due time he married his son. So they abode awhile in all solace of life and its delight and their days were serene and their joys untroubled, till there came to them the Destroyer of Delights and the Sunderer of Societies, the Depopulator of Populous Places and the Orphaner of Sons and Daughters. And glory be to the Living who dieth not and in whose hand are the Keys of the Seen and the Unseen!

THE END

FAMOUS AUTHORS IN PANTHER BOOKS

JOHN O'HARA ISAAC ASIMOV

JAMES JONES ALFRED BESTER

CHARLES MERGENDAHL ROBERT A. HEINLEIN

NICHOLAS MONSARRAT JAMES T. FARRELL

HOWARD FAST JEAN-PAUL SARTRE

H. E. BATES JAMES HADLEY CHASE

JAMES M. CAIN SAX ROHMER

EDMUND WILSON

ALAN PATON

BUDD SCHULBERG

JOHN LODWICK

ALAN MOOREHEAD

ERIC LINKLATER

PETER FLEMING

LOUIS GOLDING

NORMAN MAILER

BERNARD V. DRYER

PANTHER
BOOKS
the finest
value in
Paperbacks

MIKA WALTARI SINCLAIR LEWIS

FRANK G. SLAUGHTER DONALD HAMILTON

KATHLEEN WINSOR HENRY BELLAMANN

ALAN LE MAY A. A. FAIR

GEORGES SIMENON HEINRICH MANN

MICHAEL SADLEIR FRANCIS BRETT YOUNG

KATE O'BRIEN FRANK O'ROURKE

Is Your Name On Our Mailing List?

READ THE SENSATIONAL NOVEL THAT HAS ALREADY SOLD MORE THAN 2,000,000 COPIES!

A big, humane, earthy novel, "The Bramble Bush" is centred on the affairs and dilemmas of Guy Montford, a doctor in a small New England town. The terrible problem facing him is that of the morality of euthenasia. His best friend, Larry McFie, is dying a slow and painful death, and the temptation to 'mercy-killing' is unbearably increased by the presence of McFie's wife. This powerful, uninhibited novel will shock many with its frankness, but its immense readability puts the author in the front rank of contemporary writers.

THE Bramble BUSH

BY CHARLES MERGENDAHL

"Makes PEYTON PLACE read like a book of hymns!"
—*Walter Winchell*

3/6